Why Birches Are White

Why Birches Are White
Elena S. Smith

***

Text copyright © 2006 by Elena S. Smith
Any similarity to real persons in this fictional story is purely coincidental.

***

Cover art by Pavel Egorov and Larisa Dubova

***

www.booksurge.com
Real Books…Real Fast…Worldwide

***

ISBN: 1-4196-2751-1
ISBN-13: 978-1419627514
Library of Congress Control Number: 2007904812

Printed in North Charleston, South Carolina
U.S.A.

Visit www.booksurge.com to order additional copies.

Why Birches Are White

Elena S. Smith

www.booksurge.com
Real Books...Real Fast...Worldwide
2006

Why Birches Are White

Special thanks to Birgitta Ingemanson and Tiffany Scripter for their help and encouragement.

Many times in my life I would ask myself why most trees have such rough dark brown or green bark while birches have this amazingly delicate white-silky-misty mantel. I finally found the answer. . .

Do you believe in angels?
I do.
A friend of mine thinks angels don't exist and instead some wicked, evil creatures rule the world.
My other friend truly believes in the presence of Heavenly Angels—the ones we can find in Titian's paintings.
For me angels are not elusive shining beings with wings. They are human, here, among us, constantly at work, acting as guides and guards, friends and loved ones.
I dedicate this book to My Angels.

CHAPTER ONE

The Playful Cupids
May 11, 1987, Leningrad, Russia

It was an amazingly warm and bright morning after a week of cold rain and piercing Baltic wind so common in Leningrad. The sky looked thoroughly washed, almost translucent blue.

The air was filled with wonderful spring scents of fresh blooming Persian lilacs and Dutch tulips that always cover the city in May. I felt like I was right inside of an impressionists' paintings, say my favorite Claude Monet's landscapes, but it was even better as it was all real and natural.

I had to teach at the university at eleven, but I left home early in order not to be in a hurry. I wanted to walk along Nevsky Prospect and enjoy the late arrival of spring in Leningrad. As usual, I was waiting for the bus, and as usual, it would not come.

It was getting hot in the sun. I moved to stand in the shade of a huge birch tree. Its leaves had just started to come out of tight buds. Their color was a soft-tender-emerald green, and they exuded a thrilling and soul-soothing scent. No perfume could produce such fragrance of an early spring day.

I leaned over the cool trunk and felt its smoothness. I even touched it with my cheek. How soft and white was this bark. Why do birches have such unusual white and tender bark?

I enjoyed my meditation about birches—the beautiful companions of young lovers for centuries—so much that when the bus finally arrived, I felt sad to leave.

The few passengers in the bus were quiet and looked unusually cheery—apparently the spring air influenced them too. At this time of the morning, the main mass of people was already gone, and the bus ride was almost pleasant; nobody was pushing, squeezing, screaming, or cursing—the routine of rush hours. I was still thinking about the birches when I found myself on the Fontanka Embankment, the place where I usually changed buses. I had plenty of time, so I decided to stop by the House of Friendship to have a cup of coffee and a little chat with my good friend Nadya, who worked there.

When I approached the building, this elaborate work of architecture of the 18th century, the former residence of the Shuvalovs—one of Russia's richest and most noble families of that time, I could not help stopping, as I always did, to admire the exquisite iron railings of the balcony on the second floor above the polished mahogany entrance door. I noticed the moldings over the door in the shape of two cupids with plump faces squinting at me with playful smiles. What made the whole thing strange was that although I had visited the House of Friendship for years, I could not remember ever having seen them before. Too bad they were so high above my head or I would have reached up to touch them to see if they were real. I hesitated for another moment before I opened the door and entered the building. But as I was walking up the wide marble stairs, I could not help wondering why I had not noticed them before. Perhaps they were a testimony to my bad memory, or simply a recent architectural addition, a tribute to love with all of its surprises.

Nadya met me as usual with a pleasant smile on her beautiful face. At the age of forty-five she was a very attractive slim woman with a long neck set on the shoulders of a prima ballerina. The dignified posture developed in her at an early age when she attended the famous Vaganov Ballet School remained forever. Each time I looked at her, I had a feeling that she had just finished the 'pas de pas' in Tchaikovsky's *Swan Lake* and had frozen in a triumphant pose at the orchestra's final chord.

Unfortunately, Nadya never had a chance to become a famous ballerina. Her father had been killed in the war with the Nazis, and her mother, Lydia, struggled to raise a daughter without a husband. Lydia had deprived herself of ample food, sleep, and the simple joys of life. She worked three or four jobs at a time trying to provide for her little girl. She managed to help Nadya go through the ballet school, and she was incredibly proud when her daughter became a ballerina at the prestigious Kirov Opera and Ballet Theater. However, her joy did not last long because she fell ill and could no longer work. Nadya's salary at the theater was too small to support two people, and she had to quit dancing and find a better-paying job.

The promising career of a ballerina of course could never be compared with a position of an administrative secretary, but Nadya made the most of her new job—as assistant to the vice-president of the House of Friendship. In the late 1970's, early 1980's friendship and peace were hot topics and it was fashionable to be part of the peace movement. Famous actors, artists, scientists, teachers and doctors often participated in the peace activities held in the Friendship House. Nadya had a great opportunity to meet interesting and influential people. Her job also required her to travel abroad. Consequently, she knew more about the world than most Russians who did not enjoy such a privilege. This woman was like an encyclopedia; if she did not know the answer to a question, she knew whom to call and ask.

When I entered her office that May morning, she seemed more excited than usual. Her first words were, "Elena, dear, I have great news for you! Do you want to walk from Leningrad to Moscow?"

"Nadya, you don't mean 'walk', do you? As far as I know it's about seven hundred kilometers from here to Moscow," I was genuinely surprised.

"Yes, I do! I mean exactly 'walk'! I didn't tell you earlier because it wasn't clear if the Moscow bosses would give their consent. But they did. Yesterday." She was beaming.

"Wait a minute, I don't get it. Am I supposed to get permission from Moscow to walk? Can I breathe without their consent? What are you talking about? Is this unusually warm weather doing something to your mind?" I was totally confused.

Nadya's eyes sparkled with excitement. It was always like this. If there was something really extraordinary happening, she was like a lightning rod attracting the energy of the moment. Oh, my Nadya, my dearest friend. Though she was fifteen years older than me, I never felt it. Nadya was an adventurous soul, who was always open to new escapades that life might offer. She was also generous, kindhearted, extremely bright and funny. She had numerous friends and a job that she loved. There were so many wonderful things in her life except one—she had never married nor had any children. She probably decided to sacrifice her private life for the sake of her elderly mother's piece of mind. But Nadya never complained. We usually did not talk about it.

Pouring coffee into small pretty white-and-blue porcelain cups she said, "Listen, Elena, I am not crazy, and I am talking about a joint American-Soviet Peace Walk from Leningrad to Moscow. Two hundred and sixty-five Americans are coming. The American peace activists from California had a long and painful process of negotiations with the Moscow Peace Committee, and they finally agreed to support this American initiative. I like Gorbachev; what a smart man."

I could hardly track what she was saying—she was talking so fast. "The ice is breaking, it really is. This is Glasnost and Perestroika at work. Oh, I am so happy. Can you imagine Americans walking through old villages scattered between Leningrad and Moscow, forgotten by God and people, and never visited by anybody? Very few foreigners have stepped on that soil since the Communist Revolution in 1917. As far as I know this territory has been since forbidden for foreigners and especially for Americans. I can't believe it; what a great change; don't you think?"

This woman was never indifferent about good or bad—both made her equally passionate. And those around her could not help catching the same mood, getting as inspired as she was.

I did not understand why, but I, too, felt happy for those two hundred and sixty five unknown Americans who would come to Russia and walk hundreds of kilometers.

We were sipping hot coffee, laughing and praising Gorbachev, his Perestroika and the warm beautiful morning.

And suddenly, "You should join the walk," Nadya stared at me.

"Nadya, don't be silly. Maybe tough Americans can walk all those kilometers—don't they use miles? will that be like four hundred miles?—but I can't. I am a weak Russian woman struck by socialism and hard work on my Ph.D. I like to ride in buses, subway and cars. I usually go to Moscow by the night express, the *Red Arrow*. I can't even think about *walking* to Moscow. I'm not *that* crazy!" I hoped I sounded convincing.

"Yes, you are! You are crazy if you refuse such a great opportunity in your life. It'll be a historic action. They'll show us on TV; our pictures will be in the newspapers. And you'll get to know two hundred and sixty five Americans. Isn't it great?"

"No, it's not great at all. I don't want to know two hundred and sixty five Americans, not even one. I am too busy with my own life, and there's no place for Americans, Germans, Italians or any other people of the world in it." I thought I made my point. "Do you mean you are going?" I asked.

"Sure, I am. And you, too. I won't let you miss such a chance. And don't be so exact, we won't walk all four hundred miles; it'll be only about 15-20 miles a day, and there'll be some bus rides, too," she smiled cunningly.

"Do you mean that 15-20 miles a day is nothing?"

"Well, it's not nothing, but you can do it. I don't want to hear "no" from you."

"But…" I was still trying to protest.

"No "buts". You'll have a wonderful time. You'll remember it forever!"

"Well, you might be right and probably I wouldn't forget something like that, but I can't go on this "walk"—we really have different opinions as far as what a "walk" means." I decided to explain my reasons. "First, I plan to work on my dissertation all summer; I've been terribly behind schedule. Second, if I go on this "walk", who will take care of my son? And third, my husband—he'll never let me go. You know Vadim; he'll say, 'Walk? Why can't you walk around here?' He doesn't believe in 'peace and friendship'. He's always been sarcastic about my membership with the Peace Committee."

"Nonsense!" Nadya would not give up. "The walk will be in the end of June and will last only for three weeks. You'll be pretty much done with your teaching by this time, and you'll need a break anyway. We'll find a baby sitter for Alexei. As for your husband, I'll talk to him and convince him that we need you on the Walk. It'll be fine and please don't worry so much." Everything Nadya said sounded very simple, but I knew it would not be so easy in real life.

"How can I not worry? But…if only I could take my boy with me?" I was surprised I said that, but I did.

"I'm not sure about that," all of a sudden Nadya started whispering. "They mentioned in Moscow that there should be no kids."

"But why?" I exclaimed rather loudly, "On the contrary, we should teach our kids to build new relations with Americans, to live in peace and be against war. I don't get it."

"Elena, please calm down. I agree with you. The bosses don't," she kept talking in a soft voice, "they are afraid of everything—possible diseases, kidnappings, terrorist acts. The fact that they have allowed the Peace Walk is already a miracle. Don't you understand? Sorry, no kids."

"If we don't even trust the peacemakers, what is the purpose of this Walk? I don't want to participate in such a false venture. It doesn't make sense. It's all wrong!" I got angry.

There was a minute of unpleasant silence.

"Please don't say "no". Think it over, please." Nadya looked disappointed.

"If you really want me to go, try to accept the fact that I'll take Alexei so that he can experience an honest and open attitude to the world," I insisted.

"Listen, I'll write down your name in the list of participants from Leningrad, but I can't put down Alexei's name. He's only eight—too young for such an adventure."

"He loves adventures." I protested, "Also, it'll be a wonderful practice in English for him; he's just started it in school. You know what? I'll pretend I didn't know about the stupid rule, and when we're actually with the group, nobody will dare make us leave in the presence of the Americans."

"There might be a scandal, and I may lose my job," Nadya made one more attempt to make me change my mind.

"Come on! You won't lose your job. And as for the scandal, maybe we need one." I looked at my watch, "Nadya, I've got to run, or I'll be late for my classes. I am so excited, Nadya. It's less than a month left; there is a lot to do. What have you done to me? I lived such a quiet life and now...yes, we'll walk to Moscow for PEACE!"

"I am glad you have decided to go. Keep in touch; call for more information. Bye." Nadya saw me to the door.

I was about to leave but hesitated for a moment, "Nadya, have you seen those cupids over the main entrance?"

"What cupids? I don't think so. Why?"

"Never mind. Forget about it. Bye."

CHAPTER TWO

The Potato Teacher
June 14, 1987, Leningrad

It promised to be a difficult day.

I had to proctor a two-hour final exam at 10:00 A.M., and then at 2 P.M. the last faculty meeting was scheduled. It was mandatory for all department professors to attend that meeting. And that same day, at 1:00 P.M. the American participants of the Peace Walk were arriving in Leningrad. It was clear to me I would not be able to make it to the airport to welcome the Americans and then get back to the university on time for the meeting. Nadya was extremely upset about it, and she gave me a long speech over the phone—a mixture of pleadings and threats. She was worried that few Russians would come to meet the American delegation, and our famous Russian hospitality would fail to be recognized. I dreaded the idea of turning into the "one stone" that would have "to kill a whole flock of birds," but that would be easier than to continue arguing with Nadya. If the airplane with the Americans arrived on time, it would give me at least thirty minutes to hang out at the airport, to welcome the Americans, to have Nadya see me there, and I would still have enough time to get back to work by a taxi.

The morning started really well. All the students came on time and the exam finished by noon. Right after it, I took a cab and went to the airport. The weather was beautiful, and I felt pretty in my new silver-grey suit with a mother-of-pearl string of beads around my neck. I was in a great mood and bought a grotesquely big red carnation in a miniature flower booth in the airport lobby. Pan Am's arrival had just been announced. Everything was going well. It looked as if I could make it back to the meeting on time after all.

In the far corner of the lobby, I saw some friends, members of the Peace Committee, who had also managed to sneak away from work to meet the Americans, their future 'co-walkers'. They were standing in a circle talking excitedly. In the center of that circle was Nadya giving instructions and handing out the booklets with the schedule of the Leningrad tours. When I came up to the group, Nadya nodded at me and said, "Elena, go to the arrival gate and greet the first Americans coming out. We'll join you in a minute."

I did what she asked. It was past 1 o'clock, but I saw no Americans. I began to worry about being late for the meeting. I cursed the Soviet Customs—what else could keep them from appearing at the arrival gate? Finally, the first person came out. I rushed up to him to give him the carnation, a smile and a few words of greetings. I hoped he would say "thank you"; I would say "welcome" and then I would be free. My mission would be accomplished, and I would be able to catch a taxi and get back to work on time.

"Hello, welcome to Russia!" I exclaimed maybe a little too enthusiastically and smiled as sweetly as I could so that he would not notice my impatience.

The man to whom I handed the carnation was rather tall with a light brown beard. He was in his early forties. A heavy camera bag hung over his right shoulder. He was wearing gray shorts and a vest with probably a hundred pockets. Yes, he was wearing shorts in Leningrad, the city where people dress up even when they go out to walk a dog. His shorts really 'impressed' me. "Oh, these Americans with their free manners," I thought, "they probably think it's hot in Leningrad in June (ha! not really!), and it doesn't occur to them that in Russia it is appropriate to wear shorts only at the beach and only when there are no mosquitoes around. Well, we'll see how many of them will be wearing shorts after they live here for a couple of days."

"Oh, Hi," the guy smiled happily, "Thank you very much. It's a pretty flower. I am Stan Banks."

"Pleased to meet you. I am Elena Snezhkova."

"Are you a native of Leningrad?" He asked.

"Yes, I am," I anxiously looked at my watch and was about to say 'bye', but Stan continued, "I see. And I come from Moscow. But my little Moscow is not like your big Moscow. It's in Idaho. They grow potatoes and wheat there, but I'm not a farmer. I am a high school teacher. I'm so excited about this trip. I think it's important to do something about Peace today, when..."

He went on and on and on. I looked at the big clock over the entrance to the airport. It was 1:50. I was desperate imagining my boss announcing that Elena Snezhkova had not found the time to be present at the last meeting this school year, and instead, she of course had had 'some more important things to do.' I knew he would not embarrass me like that, but I was still 'hearing' him say all of those nasty things and my colleagues whispering, "Why must we be here when the weather is so nice, and Lady Snezhkova is free to enjoy her life?"

The teacher from Idaho was still talking. Now I knew that he was married. He had three children, a boy and two girls. His parents and two brothers lived in Boise, the capital of Idaho. He was a Unitarian Universalist (oh, boy, what did that mean?); he had never tried Russian food; he had read *War and Peace* and *Crime and Punishment* (ha—what an accomplishment.) He liked fishing and hunting. Idaho was exceptionally beautiful with lots of wildlife, white tail deer and coyotes. In fact, the coyotes had recently eaten one of his cats even though he lived in town. "Could that be true?" I thought, "I saw those animals only in the Zoo." Northern Idaho was famous for growing wonderful wheat because of a very unusual soil that kept moisture like a sponge without any irrigation all through the dry summer season. The Idaho State flower was syringa and its bird was…. This man was not a teacher; he was a talking encyclopedia.

It was 2:00 P.M. I was forcing a smile and continued to nod pretending I was very interested, but all my thoughts were concentrated on how I could escape from this chatterbox without being too rude. I was afraid there would be a scandal even before I showed up with my son. "Poor Nadya; she'll really lose her job because of me." I thought.

More and more Americans were coming into the hall and were immediately surrounded by Russian greeters. They shook hands, but you could tell both sides were a little tense. The only person who seemed to be completely relaxed and confident was my Idaho teacher. He was still talking, but I could neither hear nor understand what he was saying. In my mind, I was creating a plan how to get away. I was trying to catch a moment when he would pause to take a breath, and finally I got it. I exclaimed, "All this is so interesting! Will you tell me more later? I am awfully sorry, but I have to leave now."

"Are you walking to Moscow?"

"Yes, I am. But we're not taking off until Saturday, and it's only

Wednesday. You'll have tours and visits in Leningrad. Here's the schedule for you," I handed him the booklet, "believe me, there is a lot to see. I'll have to work for two more days, but I'll join the group on Saturday. Thank you for coming. Bye."

I did not hear what he was saying behind my back, and he did say something! I was probably acting rude, but I really did not care at that point. I did not care if I would ever see this guy again. No, that was not true—I definitely did not want to see him again.

I jumped in a bus that could take me to the nearest metro station as there was no taxi around. What a talkative man. Were all the rest of the two hundred and sixty four American walkers for peace like that one? Well, I decided that in the future, during the Walk, I would try to keep away from this 'potato teacher.'

"And where is this Idaho? I've never even heard of such a state. I need to study the map of the U.S."

CHAPTER THREE

Don't Judge a Book by Its Cover
June 16, 1987, Repino

I had arrived at Repino, a small country place on the picturesque shore of the Gulf of Finland, the night before the Peace Walk was to start. My son came with me. One of my friends, Olga, also decided to walk with her twelve-year-old son, Andrey, without a special permission from Moscow. The boys knew each other and played happily on the beach that warm June evening. Olga and I did not discuss what could happen the next day if the boys were not allowed to join the walk. As a Russian saying reads: "morning is wiser than evening."

That night was full of events. It was the farewell to Leningrad.

During the past four days, Americans had had a unique chance to see the most fascinating places of the city known in the world as the Venice of the North. This is perhaps the best name for this enchanting romantic jewel located on one hundred and one islands.

This City has been known by many names since it was first founded in 1703 by Peter the Great. It was named after Russia's patron-saint—Peter at a time when German was the fashionable language of Russia's royalty. Later, in 1914, during World War I with Germany that name was changed from the enemy's language to Russian and it became Petrograd. In 1924 it received a new strange name, Leningrad, after the death of Vladimir Lenin, the leader of the communist revolution. Oddly, this was not even his real name; it was his pseudonym. Fortunately, the City finally got its original name back in 1991, but in June of 1987 the Americans were still touring Leningrad.

They went to the St. Peter and Paul Fortress where they were amazed to see Russians bringing flowers to Peter the Great's tomb in the cathedral of the Fortress. They had thought that everything connected with the royal dynasties in old Russia had been exterminated by the communists, and it was a discovery to see how precious the history of the country was to these people. The cathedral was the burial place of all the Russian czars, czarinas and the children of the Romanov dynasty except for the last czar, Nicholas II.

Eleven years later, on July 17th, 1998, the remains of Nicholas II, his wife and children were finally found in the Urals not far from Yekaterinburg, and it was decided by the Russian Parliament to bury them in the St. Peter and Paul Fortress. The authenticity of the remains had been proven scientifically, but even today, there are still people abroad claiming that they are buried somewhere in Switzerland. We will probably never find out the complete truth about this crime. Many of the unanswered questions were buried along with the bones of the royal family.

A large group of Americans also went on a tour of St.Isaac's Cathedral, the third highest dome in the world after St. Paul's in London and St. Peter's in Rome. The magnificence of the interior decorations astounded the American walkers for peace, but even more impressive was the story of the guide about Russian serfs who were forced by the nobility to build the Cathedral. Thousands died during the forty-year period between 1818 and 1858. Like a swarm of drones building a hive the serfs moved forward over these forty years in spite of tremendous hardships and dangers. Their ribs like the beams of the dome stood out from hunger but unlike the dome's frame were never covered. They labored day and night in all types of weather using only the most primitive technology with little thought being given to their safety. They were exposed to mercury poisoning while applying the gold leaf to the dome. As a result, thousands of them died at the site and were buried right there under the foundation of the stairs. This magnificent Cathedral literally stands on the bones and blood of Russian peasants.

There, during the tour, for a lot of American participants on the Peace Walk it was an astonishing discovery that serfdom was abolished in Russia in 1861—the same year that Abraham Lincoln issued the Emancipation Proclamation. It was quite fascinating that Americans and Russians had a lot in common in their history; both went through slavery or serfdom and civil wars; both fought twice against Germany in the 20th century; both had a multinational population and lived on vast territories.

Unfortunately, the truth about our similarities as people had been hidden by two opposing political systems. The leaders of the West and East had each conspired to make us enemies from 1917 till recent times.

As pioneers for peace, that June of 1987, Soviet and American Walkers committed themselves to build windows of understanding to replace the old walls of suspicion, hatred, and ignorance.

The importance of each step of our trek from Leningrad to Moscow was much more than just sharing a place together on the map. The chance to get to know each other as human beings allowed us individually and collectively to know about one another's birth date, parents, children and siblings, education, occupations, hopes, fears, and concerns. Our knowledge and understanding about these important personal landmarks helped us appreciate more fully our shared humanity…while bringing into sharper focus the insanity of an arms race that threatened our existence.

After the visit to St. Isaac's Cathedral, many Americans went to have lunch at the famous Astoria Hotel. There they heard the story about World War II when Adolph Hitler conceived a plan to occupy St. Petersburg. Hitler dreamed to celebrate his victory at the Astoria, famous at that time for its delicious and exquisitely served meals. Hitler was so sure of his success that he ordered banquet invitations for the high ranking officers in the Nazi Army. But not a single invitation was ever used. In spite of the fact that Leningrad was under siege for 900 days, the proud City was never occupied. Over one million people sacrificed their lives to protect Leningrad from the enemy but did not let the Nazis step on the soil of this beautiful City, and ONE MILLION Leningrad patriots were buried in the Piskariovskoye Memorial Cemetery in mass graves without names.

When I read in the tour schedule for Americans about their lunch at Astoria, I thought of what that place meant to me. The Astoria restaurant had an exceptional meaning to me and occupied a special corner in my heart. It was the place where my mother and father used to have dinner once a year on the anniversary of their wedding day, October 6th. After my mother died, my dad would invite my brother, me, and our spouses to this gorgeous restaurant each year, on October 6th. During those dinners my father would tell us wonderful stories from his life with our mom, his beloved wife, whom he always called Rayichka.

What amazed me was that each time there were more new stories as if their life together had been centuries long. And once it struck me that those stories were mostly about the friends and relatives who surrounded my parents, and how important all those people had been for them. I think they were my mom and dad's angels. They helped them to overcome difficulties, to solve problems, and to share fun and happiness; they guided their lives and protected them.

One story stands out above the rest. Long before my appearance in this world, my mother and father had been separated by the war for four long years. In the small town in the Ural Mountains where my mother was evacuated with her baby-son, there lived a woman who would visit my mother a couple times a month to tell her fortune with Tarot cards. Each time she would place the cards in mysterious configurations on the wide wooden table, look at the pictures for a long time, and finally tell my mother that her husband was still alive. My mother needed nothing else. Those words kept her alive and gave her hope that one day her husband would find her and their son. And he did find them after the War was over. My dad thought that the woman in the small Ural town was an angel who had given my mom strength and faith.

After three days of sightseeing and meeting with lots of Russian people, the Americans felt more relaxed, their fear and caution somewhat dissipated, and they were in a good mood, ready to begin their mission for Peace.

The night before the Walk all the official participants, about five hundred people, got together to know one another a little better at a fare-well party. The party was scheduled after dinner. There was to be a dance and games in the ballroom in one of the many pavilions scattered along the shore in Repino.

When it was time for dinner, Alexei and I entered the huge entrance hall of the restaurant. Many people were standing in-groups, talking, Americans and Russians together. This was the first time that all the Peace Walk participants finally met. A few kids were playing hide-and-seek in the hall, and I saw a woman holding a baby in her arms.

"Well," I thought, "here are some Americans with children; this is a good sign. I wonder in what spirit the Moscow officials will now try to exclude Russians with kids from the Walk."

I was looking for Nadya or anybody I knew when a man in a light gray suit and a dark red tie came up to me smiling, stretching out his hand to greet me. I was sure I did not know him and that it was a mistake. But he said, "You are Elena, and you are Alexei, right?"

"Excuse me? Do I know you?" I was trying to remember who he was.

"Let me introduce myself. Ivan Maximovich Sviridov, I am from the

Moscow Peace Committee. Nadya told me about you. And you are the one who has decided to walk to Moscow with a child, aren't you?"

My heart started to race. Here was that moment when he would tell me that I should leave. No, I could not let him get rid of me so easily. I noticed a man with a video camera filming some Americans in one of the corners of the huge hall. I was about to go straight up to him when the man in the gray suit said, "We really appreciate your decision. On behalf of the Moscow and Leningrad Peace Committees, thank you so much. And good luck!"

He disappeared as quickly as he had appeared. What was this? Why did Moscow all of a sudden have such a different opinion? Well, at least it sounded as if I had official permission for Alexei to participate in the Walk. It seemed strange, but it gave me a lot of relief. Usually if Moscow said "no", it was "no".

Finally, I noticed Nadya waving at me, and Alexei and I came up to her.

"Hi, Elena, Alexei! I am glad you are here. I was worried you had changed your mind and would not come. Was that Ivan Maximovich?"

"Do you know him? He said 'thank you and good luck!' Isn't it strange?"

"Nothing strange. Listen to the whole story." Nadya told us how she had called Ivan Maximovich in Moscow and said there would be a Russian woman with a child on the Peace Walk. He yelled that it was out of the question. She decided not to tell me anything then but to wait and see. Later, two more Russian activists were considering taking their sons on the Peace Walk, and Nadya secretly hoped that Moscow authorities would have to give in. And then she received the list of American participants. There were thirteen children on that list, and the youngest one was only seven months old. An hour after the list arrived, Nadya got a phone call from Moscow; it was Ivan Maximovich, "Please don't forget to include all the children—the Peace Walk participants—in the list." It sounded as if he were just reminding Nadya about something that had been confirmed long ago—the usual hypocrisy of bureaucrats.

"I'm happy all's okay, and we can relax now. Shall we go and have dinner? I am hungry," I said.

"Sure. Go to the dining hall and take any place you like. The only request is, please spend more time with the Americans, and mix with them.

We need to get to know one another and be like one big family. After all, don't forget that we'll have to be together for more than three weeks," Nadya said.

"Well, we'll show the World that it's not impossible to live in peace, right Alexei? Did you hear what Nadya said? You should be making friends with the Americans. Here, look, there are two girls of your age over there. Do you want me to introduce you to them?" I asked my eight-year-old son.

"Mom, I can introduce myself, I am not a baby," Alexei said proudly.

He bravely walked up to where two pretty girls were playing. I watched him slow down when he got closer and then stop in hesitation. The girls noticed him and stopped playing. I heard them say 'hi'. Alexei responded. The ice was broken. A minute later they were playing together. "That was easy," I thought and went into the dining hall to 'mix with the Americans.'

At the entrance I stopped for a second to look around. The dining hall was still pretty empty; there were only early birds there. I noticed someone waving at me. He was at a table in a cozy corner by the window with a fantastic sun set view over the Gulf of Finland. Only when I came up closer did I recognize the person. To my horror it was that Idaho 'potato teacher' I had met at the airport. He was smiling and inviting me to join him at the table.

"Hi, how are you?" I said forcing a smile.

"Hi, Ealaina, am I pronouncing your name right? Is it Ealaina?"

"Not really, but it's okay. I feel that you pronounce my name as if it has a very different spelling. In fact it's simple—E-l-e-n-a," I said.

"Eleena?" Repeated the teacher. This time it sounded much better.

"Yes, it's close. Don't worry about it. So, how do you like it here? What do you think of Leningrad?" I asked him politely avoiding his name because I couldn't recall what it was.

"It's a beautiful city. But I'm not very knowledgeable about art and architecture. I've always been more interested in people. I'm an anthropologist and a psychologist. I enjoy observing people."

"What have you learned about Russian people so far? Are they different from Americans?" I asked frantically trying to recall his name, but just couldn't.

"Yes and no. The culture is different, but people…they are Homo sapiens everywhere."

"I think I know what you mean. Oh, by the way, do you see that little boy over there by the door? It's Alexei, my son. He'll be walking to Moscow too," I said pointing at the kids at the door waiting to be seated to have dinner.

"Oh, that's nice. I'll be happy to meet Alexei," the Idaho teacher said. I noticed that he was not wearing shorts this time. He was not that terribly talkative either.

People began to fill up the restaurant. Two Americans joined us at the table.

"Hi, Stan, we saw your picture in the newspaper today. That's great!"

"Of course his name is Stan." I sighed in relief.

"Oh, did you?" Stan did not look surprised, but I did not know what they were talking about.

"Your picture…in the newspaper? Why is that so? What did you do?" I asked.

"Believe me, if I had only known they would have taken a picture of me, I would have done it somewhere in the bushes where nobody could see me," Stan said.

"What were you doing that was better done in the bushes?" I was more than surprised; what could it be? I felt embarrassed.

"I…I don't know how to explain. It's better if you look at the picture."

Stan took the front page of the newspaper out of his pocket and unfolded it. There was a picture of him standing on his knees in front of the Eternal Flame in the center of the Piskariovskoye Memorial Cemetery where one million victims of the siege of Leningrad had been buried. Stan's head was bent forward, and his eyes were closed, his hands put together in a prayer position. He was praying. His posture was solemn and full of sorrow and gratitude. It was a very powerful picture that filled my heart with inexplicable warmth and tenderness. There was something interesting about this person; he was definitely not like the others.

At dinner we had a pleasant conversation, and I no longer thought that Stan was a chatterbox. The famous proverb crossed my mind: Don't judge a book by its cover. The funny shorts that Stan was wearing at the airport had nothing to do with what he had in his soul.

CHAPTER FOUR

The Christening
June 16, 1987, Repino

That same evening I experienced the power of a human soul—the messenger of God's spirit and love—twice.

Stan's simple and sincere expression of compassion and respect for the unknown victims of the most devastating war in the twentieth century strongly captured my heart that night. Sitting at that dinner table, I was thinking how shallow my soul must have been when a month ago I had stupidly told Nadya that I did not want to know one American let alone two hundred and sixty five of them. Now that "one American" was in front of me. On his knees he had humbly paid tribute to the million who had died in Leningrad. Stan's picture on the front page of one of the major newspapers in Russia had dramatically changed my first impression about this "primitive, provincial school teacher." Now I saw him in a different light. He actually was a person with sympathy and compassion for others, which made him special.

But that was not the only magic surprise awaiting me that night of metamorphoses.

A few hours later the same evening, I met an American couple who would influence my life and help me out in a very difficult situation several years later. But that warm summer night we just got acquainted.

Audrey and John Palmer came to Russia to participate in the Peace Walk together with their four children. The oldest, Andria, was 12, Tracy was 10, Aaron was 4, and Billy was fourteen months old. John recorded on video a short interview with me for his future home-made movie about the Walk, and after that we simply talked about Russia and America. Audrey told me that they belonged to the Methodist church where they had been very active. Both John and Audrey taught Sunday school classes for young people and adults. They were extremely religious, and they were bringing up their children with Christian values. After they told me about their church life, they asked which church I belonged to. That very moment, to my shame I did not know what to say as I was not religious; at least I thought I was not. However, I suddenly felt inspired and I knew exactly what to say.

I told them that I had been christened when I was four. John and Audrey seemed very interested and asked me to describe what I remembered about that day. I was happy they wanted to hear about it—amazingly, I felt comfortable sharing that intimate childhood experience with these two strangers. Another puzzling thing was that I usually could not remember anything from my childhood before the age of five or six, but John and Audrey asked me about something that had always been one of the most powerful and clear pictures of my childhood recollections—the day of my christening.

I remembered the weather that day and the happy face of my grandmother and the beautiful holiday scarf with a flowery design she had put over her silver hair before we entered the church.

I remembered the light blue 'Volga' car in which my future godmother and godfather had taken me to that church. We drove up and down the hills of Stavropol where I spent the summer with my grandmother that year. For quite a long time we drove along a highway. Then we stopped and parked the car and walked across a field covered with a carpet of colorful wild flowers and shiny green grasses.

I remembered the heat of the southern morning sun, the huge clear blue sky everywhere above us, the sound of grasshoppers and dragon flies and the onion-shaped golden dome of a small church that was proudly set right in the center of the field in the shade of a few tall graceful white birch trees.

I remembered my pink lace dress, the silk white and rosy bow in my hair, and the little white lacquer shoes with tiny heels, just like my mom's black dress shoes. I was holding a small gray, soft leather purse in which I was carrying a miniature icon with the Virgin Mary and baby Jesus—a gift from one of my aunts.

I remembered the tender melody of the choir singing in the church, the coolness of the air inside, the beautiful colors of the decorations: mostly white, golden and light blue, and the huge ancient round silver bowl on a tripod—three lion paws—in the center of the hall.

I remembered the priest in a velvet and silk purple garment richly embroidered with gold, and that he was wearing a huge diamond cross on a massive golden chain on his chest. He had a strange hat, like a crown, on the top of his head. He was holding a thick book in his left hand and something else, I could not tell what, in his right hand. His eyes were dark brown, very quiet and kind. I was not afraid of him.

I remembered the chilly water running over my chest and back when I was standing in the silver bowl, the soft baritone of the priest's voice, and the warmth of his palm on my forehead, and an unusual sensation that radiated all over my little body.

I remembered the smiling faces of my granny and my godparents when the priest put a thin elegant golden chain with an elongated cross around my neck, and I remembered that wonderful feeling of being blessed and loved, protected and cherished—the proud feeling that overwhelmed me at that moment. I had a strong belief that from that moment on God's angels would protect me from any harm in this world. I felt special and I was happy.

I remembered that later that day there were lots of people, mostly the neighbors, in my granny's cozy house, and that everybody touched my head and the cross on my neck and said something sweet to me. I enjoyed being the center of everybody's attention. I could remember the taste of the cream puffs, cookies and the cool cranberry drink—compote from that day so long ago.

I remembered that I was a little sad that my mom and dad had not been there to celebrate such a great event in my life. Only much later did I understand that although they approved of the christening, they had specially left a day before the ceremony to visit my mom's friend in a different city, pretending they had no idea about my granny's plans. My father had been a high ranking naval officer, a member of the Communist Party, and he could not jeopardize his career by openly allowing his daughter to be baptized.

I remembered all those wonderful things that had happened to me then, and yet after that day, there had hardly been anything significant in my life connected with religion. I had always liked to go to churches in different towns when my parents and I traveled. We had visited lots of cathedrals in Moscow and in other parts of the Soviet Union. My parents had taken me to many places in Russia, Estonia, Latvia and Ukraine. In the churches and cathedrals I would always admire the beauty of the icons and enjoy looking into Virgin Mary's or Christ's eyes. They were so expressive and soul penetrating. In my thoughts I would often say something like, "God, please save and protect me and give mercy." I did not know where it had come from; perhaps I had heard my grandmother saying those words when praying in front of her traditional orthodox icon in the corner of her bedroom.

So, I remembered all of it, and yet I really did not know what to tell Audrey and John about my church. Did I have a church?

Then John asked me, "Do you ever pray or meditate?"

"Pray or meditate? What do you mean?"

"I mean, do you ever spend time just with your own thoughts and God in your mind, heart and soul; do you privately speak with God?" He explained gently.

"No, I don't think so..." I hesitated.

"Are you sure? Have you ever experienced the need to do so?" He insisted.

"I can't tell you; I have never thought about it."

John looked at me with obvious pity. Though he tried hard not to show it, I felt it anyway. I wished my new friends good night and left a little hurt. Yet to this day I am thankful to John for his pity. Later, many times in my life, I would recall that look and that talk, and each time I would feel more and more a need to communicate with God, but I discovered that I simply did not know how to begin until finally, one day I just began to talk with God while sitting on a bench in a park and...yes...exactly...I did feel the connection with God in my thoughts. I felt the same sensation of happiness I had experienced during my baptism.

Since that very moment on the park bench, meditating and even praying started being a practice for me. Over the years I have found that prayer has also helped me in my work and given me the inner strength and wisdom to improve my relationships with people. The cumulative effect of meditation has harmonized my connection with the universe, with God and myself.

CHAPTER FIVE

Love like Salt
July 4, 1987, Moscow, Russia

It was hard to believe we had walked all that long way to Moscow and finally reached the 'Heart of Russia.' In four days everybody would go home to the usual routine of their lives. Among the peaceniks (a casual name for peace walkers) there was an atmosphere of joy about our important accomplishment tempered by our knowledge that very soon we would be separated from our new, dear friends forever.

Nadya, as always, was right. We will never forget these three weeks of sharing precious moments of life: having simple meals in schools, tents and even fields; walking in the summer sun and showers; and working in a human chain with no link identified by nationality but bound nevertheless by a joyous commitment to accomplish the mundane task of packing and unpacking our belongings at the start and end of each day. All of these moments were seasoned with the spices of lively, honest, sometimes passionate exchanges about life, politics, religion, culture, and love. Over these few weeks we discovered that in spite of some real differences our similarities as human beings were far more numerous. Our children were a powerful reminder of why we were walking and that we all desired a better world for every one. We had been members of the human family before the walk, but the day to day experience of living and working together became a powerful affirmation of our shared humanity—we were Family. It was hard to accept that part of our family was soon going to leave forever. So much occurred during this historical mission that a separate book should be written about the American-Russian walkers and the thousands of Soviet citizens who greeted us along the way from Leningrad to Moscow. Maybe one day someone will describe all of the miraculous and poignant moments that happened during the walk, but this narration is not about them.

The day of the departure of the American delegation was approaching—the 8th of July, and I was packing my suit case in the hotel room thinking how sorry I was that the Walk finally was coming to an end. Even if I had not changed the world for the better, at least I made many wonderful friends, and Stan was one of them. The Walk was worth it. I thought of those rare moments when Stan and I had a chance to sit and talk, just the two of us.

Once he had shown me an album with pictures of his family, his second wife, Carol, and two daughters, Megan and Ashley. The girls were Carol's daughters from her first marriage, but Stan raised them since they were seven and two. He loved them as dearly as if they were his own.

He also showed me a picture of his biological son from his first marriage. Michael was sixteen years old, a handsome but a difficult teenager who had not yet realized what to do with his life. He had been an object of Stan's constant worry. Stan loved the boy very much but unfortunately had not had a chance to see him as often as he would want to. Linda, the boy's mother, had made any visits so difficult that Stan for a time had left decisions about visitations up to him. Weeks and months had passed by without much contact, but Stan was still hopeful that the two would be reunited again. He told me that a very wise counselor had asked him one question, "What do you want this to look like in the end?" Stan used that comment as a compass to guide him to act in ways that would help his son and at the same time give him cause to hope for more normal relations at some future point.

I could not understand why there was so much hostility between him and his first wife because Stan seemed to be such an intelligent, kind and calm person. It seemed to me that he could only be a good influence on the boy. When Stan was showing those pictures to me, there was a lot of pain in his eyes.

Another time we spent together was when Stan was chosen as the hero of a short documentary featuring an American visiting a Russian artist's studio in Moscow. I was asked to be his interpreter. While waiting for the camera settings to be done, we had a short talk.

Stan asked me about my personal life, and I told him it was all right and there was nothing really special to describe. I had decided not to tell Stan that my marriage was not very successful because of the hostility between my husband and my parents. I still hoped to find a way to improve that relationship, so there was no need to discuss the temporary problems in my private life with someone I had just met and realistically would never see again. Actually, even if I wanted to talk about those problems at that point, we had no time left, as the cameramen were ready for the shooting.

And now we only had a few days to spend in Moscow, and Stan was going to disappear from my life as if he had never been there before. I knew that the Fourth of July was a very special day for every American—Independence Day. As Stan was the first American I greeted three weeks ago at the airport in Leningrad, I thought it would be right to do something nice for him at the end of his stay in my country. It would be in the tradition of good manners if I gave Stan a little special attention before his departure. Probably, I should be the person who would take him to the core of the 'Heart of Russia'—Red Square. For him as a history teacher it could be of importance. That is why right after dinner, I decided to find Stan and invite him to take a short trip to Red Square.

While in Moscow, all the participants of the Walk were staying at different hotels situated close to each other. I did not know where Stan was staying, so I was on my way to the information desk when I heard someone calling my name with this terrible pronunciation 'Ealaina'. I turned around and there was Stan. He had never learned to pronounce my name correctly.

"Hi, Stan, glad to see you. I was just about to try to find you. It's good luck I have run into you."

"Hi, Ealaina, I haven't seen you for several days and thought that probably you had left earlier."

"Oh, do you think I could leave without saying good bye to you, the first American whom I had greeted with such an expensive carnation?" I teased Stan.

"I wasn't sure, but I hoped you wouldn't. Why were you looking for me?" Stan smiled.

"I was wondering if you would like to go to Red Square. The evening is so warm. Alexei has been invited to a party to watch *Star Wars*. I was planning to visit my cousins, but they both are at their dachas, you know, their summer homes. It's too far for me to go to any of these places. So I was thinking about going to my favorite sites in Moscow, and one of them is Red Square. Would you like to join me?"

"I'd love to. The only problem is that I promised my roommate to spend this evening with him; I need to talk with Al before I leave," Stan seemed very pleased with my invitation.

"You can invite your roommate to join us," I suggested.

"Okay. Let me go and talk to him. Will you please wait for us here? It won't be very long," Stan was definitely excited.

"Sure, I'll wait, but only if it's not too long. I hate waiting."

We laughed, and Stan left. He came back really soon.

"Where's your friend?" I asked but for some reason I was glad Stan was alone.

"He wasn't there. I found a note on the table. He and his new Russian friends have gone to a steam bath house—do you call it 'parilka?' We both tried it in Tver last week and loved it. This is one of the things about Russia we'll miss in America."

"Is that the only thing you'll be missing? What about your new friends? Will you miss them?" I wondered if he would mention me.

"Oh, my new friends are not things. They are all very precious to me. I'll surely miss them a lot," Stan looked straight in my eyes. I felt a little awkward.

"Have you made many friends?" I asked quickly.

"I think I have. I've got at least one notebook full of names and addresses," Stan said proudly.

"Great! Well, shall we go? We can discuss all your new friends on our way," but at the same time I thought, "hmm...he hasn't asked me to give him my address. I wonder why?"

"Okay. Are we walking?" Stan was so used to walking anymore.

"Walking to Red Square from the Cosmos hotel? It'll take us another three weeks, Stan," I laughed, "No, we'll go by subway. It'll take only 30 minutes."

"Sounds good to me," Stan nodded.

"Now you'll have to wait for me, I've got to leave a note for Alexei so that he shouldn't worry about his mama when he comes to the room after the movie."

In my hotel room I changed quickly into my favorite light blue blouse and a long white skirt with diagonal ruffles that were fashionable at that time. I wrote a short note to Alexei and wrapped a little gift for Stan. I might not be able to see him before his departure, but I wanted him to have some typical Russian souvenir to remember Alexei and me, his Russian friends.

We walked to the nearest subway station. As usual, there were many people in the Moscow Metro. Stan was very surprised to see such a long escalator, and he was really scared when he stepped on it; it was too fast for him. I laughed because it did not seem fast to me; moreover, I liked to walk down the stairs while the escalator was moving to get downstairs even faster. Many people were walking up and down the moving stairs. Stan was shocked. He was holding tightly onto the slowly moving banister. He whispered, "Now I know..." Then he was muttering something I couldn't understand.

"What do you know? I'm sorry but I can't get it when you're mumbling. Can you repeat clearly?"

"I know this is how I will die. Now I realize what my mother-in-law meant when she told me, 'Stan, please don't go to Russia. It will be the end of you.' I didn't understand what she meant then. But now I get it. This is it. The Moscow Metro!" His eyes were wide open and fixed on his feet; his body was tense, and his legs were bent a little at the knees. He was prepared to jump if necessary. He seemed to be genuinely scared.

It was unkind but I couldn't help laughing. "Don't be silly. It won't be the end of you. It's only the beginning of an interesting trip," I giggled.

Stan produced a weak resemblance of a smile. I tapped him on his shoulder. He began to feel better by the time we got safely underground, and he saw a beautifully decorated station with crystal chandeliers, bronze statues, and white and blue Carrara marble floor. There were people selling newspapers, magazines, books, and flowers standing or sitting along the long walls. Stan was amazed to find another town under the huge city of Moscow. This place did not feel scary to him anymore.

We entered a train and were lucky to find seats. Only when we sat down did Stan notice a wrapped package in my hands and asked what it was.

"Oh, actually it's for you," I said handling him the gift.

"For me? What is it?"

"You can look; it's yours. It's just a small gift from Alexei and me—a Russian tradition is to give gifts to friends."

"It's very unexpected. Thank you." Stan unwrapped the gift. He found a wooden round box with a lid on it. It was carved in a traditional Russian design, and there was something written in Russian on it.

"What is it, Ealaina?" Apparently, Stan had no clue what it was.

"Well, it's a container for salt," I said.

"For salt?" Now Stan was really surprised.

"Yes, for salt. Why are you so surprised? Do you know the story about King Mathesh, his three daughters and salt?"

"No, I don't think so. Does it explain why you have given me a salt container? Can you tell me the story?"

"Sure I can."

I started telling the story that I had heard from my grandmother when I was probably five or six years old:

"Once upon a time there was a king. His wife died, leaving him with three little daughters. When the oldest daughter was eighteen, the middle one—seventeen, and the youngest one—sixteen, the king called all three daughters to the throne hall and said, "I feel I am getting old and weak, and it's time for me to write a will, but I don't know how I should divide my property among three of you."

The wise man of the court stepped forward and said, "Your Majesty, there is a simple solution to this problem. Ask your daughters to tell you how much they love you, and the one who loves you more, will get more, and the one who loves you less, will get less."

"I like the idea," the king said. "Now you, my oldest daughter, tell me how you love me."

"Oh, my father," the oldest daughter answered, "I love you like sugar."

The king nodded with approval and looked at his middle daughter, "Now, what will you tell me, my girl?"

"I love you like honey, my dear father," the second daughter answered.

The king seemed to be even happier. Next, he turned to his youngest daughter and asked, "What will you tell me, my dearest?"

"I love you like salt, my father."

The king was astounded. Could it be that his favorite little one did not love him; moreover, she was mocking him! Was he dreaming? Was this real life?

"Please think it over again very carefully and tell me how you really love me," he insisted.

"Your Majesty, I don't need to think it over. I know how I love you. I love you like salt," the girl repeated.

The two older daughters started giggling and whispering something to each other. The king grew pale and shouted, "You…you…you are a disgrace to the family! How dare you say such stupid things to your father! I don't even want to see you anymore. You are an ungrateful, spoiled girl! Get away from me! Get out of the palace!" The King's men took Mary to the northern most boundary of the kingdom and left her in a forest.

The king's anger had no limits. He loved his three daughters very much, but he had always felt a special bond with the youngest one; that was why her answer made him so mad. He decided to divide his kingdom between his two oldest daughters.

Now Mary found herself alone, cold, and scared in the world. She did not know where to go or what to do. She was wandering in the forest till it became dark. Finally, she sat on the grass under a big pine tree and began to cry. At this moment, a forester was passing by and heard strange noises. He moved in the direction of those sounds and practically bumped into the girl. She screamed and fainted. When she came to, she found herself on a bed in a large well lit room with a cold wet cloth on her forehead.

She whispered, "Where am I?"

"You are in a safe place, please don't worry. You were very sick for a week, but now I think you will be all right."

The woman who was speaking had a kind soft face. She was wearing a round cook's hat and a starched snow-white apron. She stroked the girl's hair tenderly. She said, "There was a time when we were very worried about you. You had lost your consciousness and were constantly saying 'daddy, daddy'. Where is your father? Where do you live? What is your name?"

"I am…Mary. My father…he died. I have nowhere to go. Please let me stay here. I will do any work you need in the house. I…"

The girl began to cry.

"Please don't worry so much. We won't send you away. This is the palace of King Theo. He is a kind man. I think I can persuade him that you are a good cook. We need a hand in the kitchen. Sure you know how to cook, don't you?"

"Well, not really. My father used to…cook our meals," the girl said. Then she added quickly, "But I can clean in the kitchen."

"Okay. You will be cleaning in the kitchen, and later you will learn how to cook."

The woman seemed very pleased.

The girl stayed in the palace. She worked hard. Soon everybody in the kitchen and other servants of the palace loved her because she was a friendly, smiling, good-humored girl. Days, months, and even a whole year passed. The girl gradually learned to cook and became the right hand of the chef. She felt happy, but at times she grew sad and when asked what it was about she would say, "I miss my poor father."

One day King Theo decided that it was time for his only son to get married and take over the kingdom. He knew that his neighbor, King Mathesh, had three daughters. So he invited the king and his daughters to a feast with the hope that his son would choose a bride.

On the day of the feast all the cooks of the kitchen were very busy. Mary seemed to be a little nervous and excited. She cooked several dishes especially for King Mathesh.

When the guests arrived, she was peeking through a little window in the kitchen and saw her beloved daddy and sisters. Her father looked much older; she could hardly recognize him. Tears were streaming down her cheeks.

When the feast began, she asked the chef to have the honor to serve the visiting king. She put on a broad brim hat to hide her face and brought the first dish to the king. While serving she heard him saying to King Theo, "Yes, you are right, I did have three daughters, but my youngest daughter, she…died." King Mathesh's voice trembled. King Theo apologized, "Oh, I did not know that. I am sorry. What happened?"

"Please don't ask me; it's very painful for me. I wasn't a good father. When I think about what I have done, I think she died because of me."

"I am really sorry," King Theo repeated. He did not like what he had heard, and in general he thought King Mathesh seemed strange. Maybe it was not a very good idea to invite him after all.

Meanwhile, the feast was in full swing, noisy and merry. The people enjoyed their food and praised the chef. The only unhappy person was King Mathesh. All the dishes served to him tasted terribly sweet. He tried the salad; it was sweet. He tried a piece of duck; it was disgustingly sweet. He could not take another piece into his mouth. Even the salmon had a strong honey flavor. Finally, he stole a little piece from the plate of King Theo, and that piece was delicious! King Mathesh grew very angry. He exclaimed, "King Theo, what is it? Why is everybody here enjoying the meal, and I am the only one served this terrible inedible food! Are you trying to humiliate me?"

"Oh no, Your Majesty, of course not. Please let me find out what is happening." The chef was called in and asked who was cooking for King Mathesh. The chef knew it was Mary, but he could not believe she had cooked something that was not tasty. He loved this kind, timid girl and did not want her to get into trouble. That is why he said, "Your Majesty, I was the cook."

"You? How dare you cook such trash for my most honored guest? You are fired immediately!" The king was enraged.

At this moment Mary stepped forward and took off her hat. There was dead silence in the big dining hall. Everybody was looking at the king and this young girl who came up to King Mathesh, knelt in front of him and whispered, "Don't you recognize me, my dear father?"

King Mathesh stared at the girl. It was his daughter Mary, the daughter whom he had sent away. He thought she was dead. Oh, he had loved her so much. But why on earth hadn't she loved him?

"Tell me why you said such a terrible thing to me, that you loved me like salt. You made me very sad," hot tears were streaming down King Mathesh's wrinkled cheeks.

"Dearest father, I put sugar and honey instead of salt into all your dishes. You couldn't eat them. I hope you understand now what salt means for a human being. People simply cannot live without salt. That's why I said I loved you like salt."

The king started sobbing, "Can you forgive me, my daughter?"

The guests gasped. This girl-cook was the king's daughter!

"Oh, yes, my father. I love you!"

"I love you too. I nearly died of grief when you left. I'm so happy I've found you. Only now do I understand that you are the one who loves me the most. You are right, people can live without sugar or honey, but they can't live without salt. What a fool I was! But I'm proud that you, my dearest daughter, are so smart."

Here the prince came up to them and said, "Dear Mary, I have been in love with you for many months, but I was afraid to tell you or my father because you were just a girl working in the kitchen. Today, when I have to choose a bride, I was about to announce to all the people present here that I have chosen a simple girl, a cook from our kitchen. But you turned out to be a princess, and I do not know about your feelings for me."

"I won't conceal from you that I have been in love with you from the first moment I saw you," Mary said shyly.

Everybody in the banquet room began to smile, embrace, and kiss and...Well, that's the end of the story."

Stan fell silent.

Then he uttered, "I love this story. I've never heard it before. It's true; salt is more important than sugar. I'm very flattered to get such a gift from you. I'll keep salt in this pretty wooden jar and remember the story."

I suddenly realized that he might have understood me wrong. I did not mean *I loved* him like salt—it was just a tale. I said quickly, "I hope you'll remember that Alexei and I are your good friends, and that Russians are not all communist monsters, but they are just people like you."

"There's no need to tell me that. I've never thought Russians were monsters. But you're right; there are still stereotypes that really mess up people's outlook and perception of the world."

Months after Stan had gone home, I was reading a magazine and came across his interview with a Russian journalist about the same topic, stereotypes. One passage caught my eye in which Stan said, "...One evil in our life is using stereotypes when thinking about those who are "different". I'm sure we live in the century of stereotypes. But still the worst evil is the evil of an undeveloped, unaccomplished and faded human life..."

When I was reading it, I was thinking about my life: was it accomplished? Did I feel like it was undeveloped? I had a wonderful loving family, a solid education, an inspiring job, and truly devoted friends. I lived in one of the most beautiful cities in the world. I could not think of my life as faded. But was it complete?

CHAPTER SIX

A Pair of Jeans for Mikhail Gorbachev
July 4, 1987, Moscow, Red Square

My story about love like salt was over exactly when the train stopped at Sverdlov Square. On our way up the escalator, Stan felt a little less dizzy than when he was underground and much more confident anticipating that firm soil was about to be under his feet again.

Sverdlov Square is very close to Red Square, but instead of going straight there, I decided to turn right, make a circle and come to it from a different side. Thus we could have a nice stroll in the Alexandrovski Park around the Kremlin. The evening was magical. The sky was dark violet blue with bright stars and planets smiling at us. The park smelled of roses and freshly mown grass. There were many parents with children, elderly people, and young lovers walking or sitting on benches. Several dogs were playing on the grass. The whole atmosphere was peaceful and relaxing. We did not talk for a while but just enjoyed the night.

Moscow is not my favorite Russian city. Its style of life 'to be always on the run,' its eclectic architecture, its high potential for crime, coupled with an attitude of rudeness and a general feeling of superiority by Moscow's residents—all of these features never appealed to me. I am a great patriot of St. Petersburg, of its noble calm beauty, exquisite architecture, and inexplicable atmosphere of special manners, polite behavior, and classy taste. But Alexandrovski Park and Red Square—these special places in Moscow—have always caused a strange feeling of gratitude and pride deep in my "mysterious Russian" soul.

"This is amazing. When I look at this quiet happy life around me and think that people can be so terribly selfish and stupid as to wage wars, kill each other and to destroy all that is so beautiful about the world, I'm convinced I did the right thing to sacrifice my summer holiday, time with my family, work on my doctorate, and to come here to walk for peace. It's the most important thing today—peace on the planet Earth," Stan said.

"Well, to tell you the truth I've never thought that I, as one single little Elena, can make any difference in the world. And I still think that I can't. But together with hundreds of people and thousands of those who supported us during the Walk I think I can make a difference. *We* can make a difference."

"Absolutely! That's what makes the difference—the unity, the togetherness, and the motivation. I am happy I have come here. I've learned a lot about life."

"Do you feel sorry that it's the end of the Walk, and you're leaving for home soon?" I asked.

For a moment Stan was silent. Then he said, "Yes and no. I do feel sorry because I'll leave so many new and wonderful friends here like you; on the other hand, I do miss my wife and children, and, honestly, I miss American food—hamburgers, donuts, and especially the apple pie that my wife makes, the best in the world."

"What is a hamburger, a donut and what can be so extraordinary in an apple pie?" American food was not popular in Russia yet in those days.

"A hamburger is a very tasty meat patty in a bun with melted cheese, onions, and other vegetables. Actually, it's probably not that tasty but seems tasty now to me when I haven't had one for about a month. And donuts are sweet and very fattening, but I like them anyway. My wife's apple pie has that special soft but crispy crust; only she can make it that way."

"Do you mean you don't like Russian food?" I was a little offended as I had always assumed that food was excellent in my country.

"It's not bad, but it's very bland. It's meat and potatoes with no spices most of the time. We had a funny story last night with my roommate, Al. We decided to go to a Chinese restaurant to have Chinese food because we were really tired of beef and potatoes. The taxi driver took us to the restaurant Peking in the center of Moscow. What restaurant could be more Chinese than the one with a name like that? We got the menu which, of course, was in Russian, and that's okay because it wouldn't make any difference if it had been in Chinese. We couldn't read it, so we simply showed the waiter that we were hungry. Any Chinese food would be different from mashed potatoes. What a surprise it was when the waiter brought beef and potatoes to us. Again!"

"I know. Russia is a funny place. The name Peking does not mean you'll have Chinese food there. It's only a name," I said laughing.

"Yes, Russia is indeed a funny place. I don't understand why the restaurant would have a Chinese name if it doesn't serve Chinese food."

"I have lots of examples of the same inexplicable phenomena. For instance, in Leningrad I once saw a huge sign above a beer pub 'Beer' and a small one on the entrance that said 'No Beer'."

"It just doesn't make sense, does it?"

"Maybe it's to show that we are friendly with China or simply to confuse people, otherwise if everything is very logical, it's boring," I teased Stan.

"I see. Believe me, Russia for me is anything but boring."

"Really? What are some other interesting things here that are so different from America?"

"Sorry to say it, but the public bathrooms and the roads here are incredibly different." Stan paused, "and…disgusting." Stan was trying to find a better word to avoid hurting my feelings, but obviously his disgust was an honest first impulse.

"I agree with you about that. I never thought it could be different until I went to Finland several years ago. It was such an amazing contrast right after we crossed the border; I couldn't believe my eyes. I don't understand this phenomenon in full. Partly the problem is that people who work in public bathrooms are paid very little and have no desire to try their best. The roads belong to the state, and because Russian people have small salaries and pay low taxes, the infrastructure is in poor shape. I suppose Americans pay high taxes and the government can afford to maintain bathrooms and roads in good condition. As far as meat and potatoes, I hope you understand that it's just an impression of a tourist, but people here do eat a lot of different kinds of food products, not only potatoes. Now tell me if there is anything that you like about Russia." I wanted to change the subject.

"I like the people. Everybody I have met without exception was very kind, friendly, and generous. I have so many gifts to take home: books, pins, souvenirs, tapes, slides, pictures, posters and even a salt container." Stan winked at me smiling. Then his face became serious, "But the greatest gift I'll take back will be the memories of all these wonderful people. By the way, Elaina, I need your advice. I have brought a gift for Mikhail Gorbachev, but I don't know how I can give it to him. Can you help me?"

"What? Are you kidding? A gift for Gorbachev? What is it?" I was shocked.

ELENA S. SMITH

"It's a pair of Levi's jeans. I thought he might like something very American to remind him of our Walk," Stan said simply.

"Are you serious?"

"Absolutely. What's so strange about it?" Stan could not understand why I was so surprised.

"Well, I don't think I can help you because I've never given gifts to Gorbachev. I have no idea how to get in touch with him. I'm sure he's unreachable for common people."

"Can't we simply send the package to the Kremlin?" Stan insisted.

"I guess you can, but it doesn't mean that Gorbachev will ever get it."

"What do you mean?" Stan was sincerely puzzled.

"I mean, one of his guards will successfully wear your jeans, say, for security reasons," I laughed. I actually did not know what to say; it never occurred to me to send gifts to the Soviet leaders because they always seemed to have more than I did. I asked, "Do you send things to your president?"

"Well, I haven't yet, but I don't see why I couldn't. Actually, it's probably illegal to send gifts to the President. It could be considered a bribe. I do send letters to him."

"Does he personally reply or does his secretary do it for him?"

"Probably one of the hundreds of people who work for the executive branch does, but the most important letters can be personally answered by Mr. President. So, what do you think about sending the jeans?"

"I don't think anything good about it. I don't see anything bad about it either. Why don't you talk to people from the Peace Committee; they'll give you advice."

"Okay, I will do that."

We were coming up to the bridge across the Moskva River. I said, "Here is the famous bridge."

"Why is it famous?"

"Have you heard of the German pilot who landed on this bridge right in the center of Moscow? It was a big scandal a couple months ago. Lots of military heads were chopped off."

"Really? Were they executed?" Stan was horrified.

"No, no, I meant figuratively; a few generals had to retire."

"Uh, a big relief. I'm glad the heads were not really chopped off. But

36

I can imagine the scale of the scandal. It's incredible to land right here, practically in front of the Kremlin."

"Yes, it's incredible and also stupid. Now the guy is serving time in a Russian prison—not exactly a resort. But people make choices; that was his choice. I'm sure he knew what he was doing," I said.

We were approaching Red Square. The ruby stars on the Towers of the Kremlin Wall looked like celebrities—glamorous, proud, and high above the whole city, above Russia. We stepped on the cobble stones of the square. There was no asphalt there. Stan and I paused for a moment to look up at the Kremlin "celebrities", and it was at that moment I could hear the footsteps of people as they passed by. The rhythm of their strides was absorbed by the stones to join the chorus of sounds captured by these hard score sheets for the past eight centuries. This square has recorded the full human history of Mother Russia and if that symphony of wisdom and stupidity, happiness and tragedy, beauty and ugliness could be ever played back in full, it would still not be enough to explain the mysterious Russian soul.

Stan asked, "What are these beautiful domes?"

"This is St. Basil's cathedral. There are nine churches adjacent to each other in one building. That's why there are so many domes. Its unique style makes it the most well known cathedral in Russia. Its beauty stands in stark contrast to the dark stories regarding its construction. Legend has it that the architects, Postnik and Barma, were blinded by order of Ivan the Terrible so they could never create anything so spectacular for anyone else. What do you think about that?"

"It's very Russian. You'll never find anything like this in the U.S."

"Wow," I thought, "not only Russian food did he hate but Russian architecture as well." All I could say to that was, "I would never expect to see anything like that in the U.S. I assume we have something you don't have there, and you have something we don't have here—the universal equilibrium."

"That's right. So, are we on Red Square now?"

"Yes, we are. I love this place. Isn't it unusual—golden domes and spires, precious ruby stars, heavy terracotta brick walls—what a combina-tion?"

"Sure, it is. It's especially unusual for me to be on Red Square where every year so many tanks and missiles are shown to the world during your big Revolutionary holidays. It's pretty horrifying."

"Don't try to make me think that the U.S. doesn't have terrible weapons."

"Unfortunately, we have the same and maybe even more," Stan said sadly.

"Didn't we walk over four hundred miles to put an end to this madness?" I could feel that both of us had been victims of propaganda. In the United States people had been told that the Soviet Union was enemy number one while in Russia people had always supported their government's armament initiatives in order to be safely protected from our main enemy—the U.S.

"Yes, we did," Stan agreed, "We'll hope for the best. So far all the peaceniks including you and me have achieved a lot—the attention of mass media and the support of hundreds of thousands of people in the Soviet Union and Europe. All this is no small matter. I hope that our leaders will stop and think what to do next—to escalate the arms race or to disarm. Actually, there are a lot of things that I hope for."

"I've already got the feeling that you're one of those 'hope-full' guys," I teased Stan, "What else do you hope for?"

"I hope…" he paused as if he was putting all his hopes together creating a hope-full necklace.

Then he began slowly and thoughtfully:

"I hope that there will be a day when we will redefine intelligence as the capacity to love another.

"I hope there will be a day when we will redefine success as the conscious, consistent action by men and women to care for the human family near and far.

"I hope there will be a day when people will make their pilgrimages to the cottages of the humble and kind rather than to the castles of the rich and the famous. And when they arrive I hope they will hear and see with their ears and eyes and hearts and minds and leave filled with the knowledge and wonder of how to make the 'broken world' we live in whole once more.

"I hope that there will be a day when all humanity will listen to the voices of the earth's creatures and will be so moved that they will put down their weapons, step out of their cars, and shut down their computers to hear life's song and understand that we have been entrusted with its care. Only by being wise care takers of the earth can we sustain the song. Beyond the symphony is dreadful silence.

"I hope there will be a day when men and women will once again find the magic and mystery of a night's sky…a day to celebrate star light before human blackness becomes the night and to wonder about our rightful place and responsibility in creation.

"I hope there will be a day when all these discoveries will enrich us with the ideals, knowledge, and wisdom to restore Eden. I hope there will be a day…"

Stan stopped and looked into my eyes. I could not hide the tears that had been flowing down my cheeks. I was overwhelmed with a strong feeling of gratitude. I felt very thankful that my destiny had allowed me to meet such a wonderful man who could feel as I did, but who by contrast could also express what he felt in beautiful words. Those words convinced me then that our walk for peace had not been in vain. I was sure it would prove to be the foundation for realizing our mutual human hopes in a bright happy future.

"Stan, thank you for making my life more hopeful. Usually, my immediate instinct is to be pessimistic. When Nadya encouraged me to participate in the Peace Walk, I was very skeptical about its meaning. But now I feel different; I am more hopeful than I've ever been before: the Walk and your words have inspired me. I think you should write them down if only you could ever repeat what you have just said."

"You know, I did write them down. A few days before the Walk I wrote this short list of my hopes. When I was writing, my feelings were so powerful that I remembered every word. I'm not surprised that I could repeat them to you word for word. I'm sorry, though, that I made you cry."

I wiped my tears away. They were happy tears of hope, so they disappeared easily. "Don't worry about my tears; you touched my heart. I think I have a great idea. Maybe one day you'll write a book. Please include your 'hope list' in it so that other people can hope together with you. I, for example, will be less pessimistic from now on. If only what you hope for could come true, our lives would be so much more fulfilling."

"I agree, and I'm happy that my 'hope list' has made you less pessimistic," Stan smiled.

"Yes, it has indeed. Let's look at the light of the stars on top of the towers. They are made of genuine rubies. You can see them glowing from afar. Aren't they magnificent?"

"They are beautiful," Stan nodded.

We continued walking. I did not notice how it had happened that Stan was holding my hand. Maybe he took my hand when he saw my tears. His palm was wide, soft and warm. I felt very confident and secure with this true friend by my side. The feeling—a sort of *Déjà vu*—was like the one I already had. It was similar to the sensation I had when I touched the birch tree the day I learned about the Peace Walk—a feeling so strong in both cases that it was almost mystical.

The clock on Spasskaya Tower struck three times. It was 9:45 P.M. In fifteen minutes there would be the performance of the changing of the guards at the doors of the mausoleum where the remains of Lenin had been secured for over sixty years.

"Do you want to see the changing of the guards at the mausoleum?" I asked.

"I guess..." It sounded as if Stan was scared of the ghost that could appear during the performance. I felt a little uneasy myself.

The idea of a mausoleum had always seemed ridiculous to me. I could not understand why that poor individual had been granted such terrible disgrace as to be exposed to the world in his dead state, instead of being buried according to the good old Russian Orthodox traditions. Eventually, I decided that because Lenin had committed so many sins and perhaps was the greatest villain the world had known, it was a form of justice delayed to put his grotesque corpse on display as a reminder of a monster who was even uglier in life. I remembered the long lines of people standing for hours to get into the mausoleum to see the dead Lenin. I could never understand why people would like to see something so gross.

In 1987 there was no long line to this place anymore. With the coming of new fresh inspirations of democracy people lost interest in Lenin's communist-utopian-ideas, and since his ideas were dead, the dead body did not impress anyone either. With Glasnost everybody had learned that it was stuffed with straw, and in the skull under the stretched skin there was a softly gleaming bulb that produced an illusion of pink cheeks. This mummified corpse was as empty and false as communist ideology was fruitless.

There has been a lot of discussion in the press about burying Lenin, but even today, in the 21st century, the dreadful remains are still there in the mausoleum. The lines of people wanting to see the unburied ghost are mysteriously becoming longer again. What is this power that does not

allow people to act reasonably? Unfortunately, the existence of the mausoleum and the dead body of Lenin in it are not the only ridiculous things
happening in my mysterious Motherland—even I, her daughter, cannot
understand many of them.

"Why do they still have the remains of Lenin in the mausoleum?"
Stan asked.

"It's exactly what I'm thinking about right now, and I can't tell you; I
don't know."

"Do you think Lenin's body will ever be buried?"

"I wish it were."

The Spasskaya Tower chimes started playing a beautiful melody. Two
guards, like the little tin solders in Anderson's tale, appeared from under
the huge gate; they were marching very solemnly towards the entrance
of the mausoleum visually becoming bigger and bigger with every step.
There gathered a group of people of different nationalities including some
women from India in long saris, a few Japanese, a German couple, a group
speaking French, and some Russians.

The changing of the guards is always a fascinating procedure whether
it takes place in front of the Buckingham Palace, the Royal palace in Copenhagen, the Vatican, or the Kremlin. Everywhere the changing of the
guards is a performance where the participants wear unusual uniforms and
make robot-like movements with their legs, arms, and heads. The show
on Red Square was spectacular. It was carried out meticulously without a
single flaw, and when the clock struck ten, two new guards were standing
on both sides of the heavy bronze door leading to one of the most unat-
tractive Russian mysteries.

At that very moment I did not care about that mystery; I felt calm
and happy as if there were no questions or problems in my life. Everything
was clear and right. And I knew why. It was because Stan was still holding
my hand. I knew it, and yet I asked him, "Stan, why are you holding my
hand?"

"Oh, sorry, did I make you feel uncomfortable? I didn't mean to. I was
just trying to protect you when more people began to gather around us."

"I was simply surprised to find my hand in yours. Thank you for trying to protect me, but for me even hundreds of people around me are not
a problem. I've grown up in a city of five million."

He slowly let my hand go. I was free, and what can be better than freedom? But I lost that strange and wonderful feeling of absolute calmness and security.

It was getting late, and we had to return to the hotel. Tomorrow, very early in the morning, the American-Soviet walkers were going to Zagorsk, one of Russia's foremost religious centers with many beautiful, ancient churches and a monastery.

After that there would be briefings and press conferences held in Moscow for two days. The concluding document calling for peace and disarmament between the U.S.A. and the U.S.S.R. would be signed by all the participants and then…the Americans would go home.

CHAPTER SEVEN

Why Birches Are White
July 7, 1987, Moscow, Russia

I was on my way to the lounge of the hotel where the Moscow and Leningrad media crews that had been filming the Peace Walk for the past three weeks were having a farewell party. I was invited to it because I had helped the photographers and directors of both film companies with some translations when they were doing interviews or filming short documentary pieces about the walkers. There were professional interpreters on the Walk, but the need for translations always exceeded the availability of professionals, so many of those who were not interpreters but could speak English were also popular, and I was among them.

I pushed the button for the elevator and waited for a long time. Cosmos was a huge and busy hotel. I was about to give up and walk downstairs on foot, when the door of the elevator finally opened. Stan was in it and exclaimed happily, "Elaina, it's good luck. I've been trying to find you for at least an hour. Many people had seen you here and there, but nobody knew exactly where you were. Are you busy now?"

"Well, I'm going to a party. Is there anything I can do for you?"

"Yes, I need your help; I've written something that needs to be translated into Russian."

"Is it long?" I was a little disappointed that instead of partying I would work.

"It's only a couple of sentences; it won't take long. But if you are busy and can't do it now, I can wait."

Stan sounded so polite that I could not refuse, "I have an idea; why don't we go to the party together. I'm already an hour late and if I start working on the translation, it'll be probably useless to go there at all. Let's first go to the party, stay there for a little while, and after that I'll help you."

"Sounds good to me," Stan was obviously quite satisfied.

When we got to the lounge, the director of the Moscow film group, Galina, a dark-haired beauty in her late forties, greeted us with a pleasant smile on her face,

"Elena, how wonderful that you have brought Stan with you, what a girl!"

"Is it okay? I wasn't sure I did the right thing. Maybe the Russians wanted to party without Americans among them."

"No, no, it's great. In this mess of so many people in this monster-hotel we couldn't find him to invite to the party. But he's been one of the main characters of the Walk, and the film about him is practically finished; though I am afraid it won't be ready by tomorrow, when everybody is leaving. Can you apologize for me and tell Stan that as soon as the film is done, we'll send him a copy?"

"Sure I can." I translated her words to Stan.

"Thank you, I am flattered. Why is there a special film about me?" Stan seemed a little bashful but thrilled.

"You are very special, believe me. First, you came from your little Moscow in Idaho all the way to our big Moscow—do you see the underlying connection there? But second, and more important, you've captured the hearts of many Russians showing your deep feelings of compassion and understanding for others. No wonder you became the celebrity of our little film production." Galina hugged Stan and then moved an extra chair up to the long table.

"Thank you for saying these kind words about me, but I don't think I am special. The walk simply reinforced my basic belief that all people in the universe are precious. I also understand no one is safe from tragedy. We can all minimize the risk by proper conduct, but chance and miracles also play an important part in our lives. I know that something bad could happen to me at any time. If it did, I would want others to treat me with compassion and kindness. That's why I always try to give a hand to those in need and feel sorry when I can't do enough."

"Well, Stan, the good news is that today you are right on time at least for a celebration by all of us who are trying to make the world a better place. Let's have a shot of vodka to our friendship."

The glasses were already prepared for us. I never drank vodka, but to be polite I had to pretend I was drinking. Stas, the cameraman from the Leningrad group, noticed I didn't drink and asked if I would like champagne or wine instead. Wine was fine, and I had to join the company for the next toast—to peace in the world.

Poor Stan was trying hard to swallow vodka; it was clear he was not used to it. Everybody began to cheer him up saying that real men have no problem in drinking vodka, and that it is disrespectful not to drink to such an important cause as peace. The next toast was to our children, and then the next to the beautiful women at this table, and on and on.

Suddenly, an American woman whom I had talked with several times during the Walk came up to me and whispered in my ear, "Elena, I need your help."

"Sure, Jane, what is it?" I asked.

"It's a private matter. I need both your advice and assistance. Can you step aside for a minute?"

"I'll be glad to help you," I had no clue what she was about to ask, but I excused myself and followed Jane to sit down at another table in a far corner of the lounge.

"Do you know this man?" Jane pointed at Stas.

"Yes, it's Stas. He's been filming the Walk."

"I know he's a cameraman. Isn't he absolutely gorgeous?"

That was an unexpected statement. I did not know what to reply because I did not think he was particularly gorgeous, but I decided not to disappoint Jane. I said, "I think he's been doing his job quite well."

"No, I mean his looks. He's so handsome." Jane's eyes were sparkling with excitement.

"He's all right, not exactly to my taste, but, yes, you can say he's handsome." I could not guess where this conversation was headed.

"Elena, I may surprise you, but I want you to understand me right, and I want you to know the truth."

"The truth about what?" I could not imagine that Stas' looks had something to do with some "truth".

"We're leaving tomorrow, and maybe I'll never see Stas again in my life. I need to spend some time together with him. Can you help me?"

"I don't exactly understand what you want me to do," I hoped she did not mean to use me as a translator that last night in Moscow.

"Please ask him privately if he would like to spend the night with me in my room. I'll be frank, please ask him if he would like to have sex with me, and tell him that I'm dreaming about it."

I could not believe my ears. This was the most unusual request I had ever had on the part of anybody seeking help in translation. I was wondering if I was such a terrible snob that a simple thing like a woman's desire to love a man seemed so embarrassing to me. Should I say "no"? But why? This was none of my business. It was in my power to help this woman, who apparently was desperately in love, to express her feelings to the man she wanted. And I said casually as if it had been a regular matter, "No problem, Jane. I'll tell him. But I want to know if you are really so much in love with him."

"No, I'm not in love; I'm physically aroused. He's so hot."

That confession changed my previous thoughts about a woman madly in love. She was not in love at all. She…I looked in Stan's direction hoping to get help from a person who came from the same strange culture in which a woman could easily express her lust for a man. But he was too busy learning how to drink vodka, talking and laughing with his new friends. I thought of the famous example of the shameful behavior of a young woman described in Alexander Pushkin's *Yevgeni Onegin*—the Russian classic. The main character, Tatyana Larina, a girl from an aristocratic family, was the first to confess in a letter to a man that she was in love with him. That 'act of disgrace' has always been discussed in high school literature classes as inappropriate for a girl. In Slavic culture women were expected to be timid and shy. So it was not easy for me to agree, but I did, "I'll try my best," I whispered. "Please wait for me here."

I made a sign to Stas that I needed to talk with him. He was genuinely surprised when I led him away from the crowd to the corner of the lounge. He looked puzzled.

"Stas, I have an unusual offer for you, and I am really sorry to be in the middle of such a private matter, but I'm only an interpreter."

"Elena, I'm happy to talk on a private matter with *you*. I'm quite intrigued."

"I myself don't want to tell you anything. Look at that blonde woman by the bar, her name is Jane. I'm translating for her. She wants you to spend the last night with her in her room." I was relieved that the most difficult part of my mission was over and I could finally join Galina, Stan and the rest of the merry company. I did not expect that Stas would say, "What shall I do with her there?" He stared at me.

"Stas, just think what a man can do with a woman in her room?" I did not want to go into the details.

But Stas definitely did not get it at that point. He was raised in the same culture of 'anti-Tatyanas' where only males were privileged to express their love desires first. So he asked, "What?"

"Are you trying to give me a hard time? Don't pretend you don't understand." I was desperate.

"But I don't. Explain to me, please. What does she want? Will you be there, too? I don't speak a word of English. How will we communicate?" His eyes were wide and round—the true expression of bewilderment. I knew he was not pretending.

I sighed, "No, I won't be there, and you won't need me there. She wants sex," I said as quickly as I could.

"What?"

This "what" was so loud that the whole company looked in our direction. Stas whispered, "Are you kidding? How do you know?" He threw a glance at Jane that expressed a mixture of horror and admiration.

"She told me so. She wants to have sex with you because she thinks you're the sexiest guy in Russia."

"I am flattered, but...are you of the same opinion? To tell you the truth I'd rather have sex with you..." To my awe, he actually meant it.

"Stas, stop it. I have nothing to do with it, and I'm not going to have sex with anybody here. I'm happily married and faithful to my husband. That's it. This woman wants you. What shall I tell her?"

Stas looked funny, his eyes sparkled with excitement. He kept throwing glances at Jane. Their eyes met. They did not need an interpreter anymore. I happily joined the party at the table.

"What's going on?" Stan asked.

"I've had the most unusual request to help somebody to do something. But I can't tell you, it's a private matter," I whispered.

"Are you talking about Jane's wish to spend the night with that guy?"

"How do you know?" I exclaimed.

"Jane told me. I thought it was pretty neat."

"I don't know what you mean, and I don't have any opinion about it." I hated this stupid conversation.

"Really, you don't? Do you think it's not normal for a woman to ask a man to make love to her?"

"I don't know if it's normal or not; I know that I would never do it if I hardly knew the guy."

"And what if you knew him?" Stan looked straight into my eyes.

"Stan, sorry, I don't want to talk about it. Are you ready to go and do that translation of yours?"

"Yes, I think so. I like all these people, but I'm not sure I could stand any more toasts. While you were absent, there were toasts to parents, to nature, to pets…Thank Goodness, you are back. I don't think I can have another shot of vodka. Let's go."

We thanked our friends and excused ourselves by promising to see them the next day at the airport and say the last good-byes. Galina said they were going to film the departure and wanted to take a few more pictures of Stan.

I stopped by the elevator, "I can wait for you in the lobby over there in that cozy armchair and you can bring what needs to be translated there." After the story with Jane, I had no desire to go to Stan's room.

"No, please come with me to my room. It'll be quiet there, no people around; it'll be quicker. It won't take you long. I promise."

I looked at Stan. He was not Jane. He was a nice guy, a teacher, and a father of three children. He couldn't do any harm to me. It was even funny to think about it. I said, "Okay, but I really don't have much time. I need to get Alexei at 10 P.M. after the movie is over. He is watching *Star Wars* again with other kids. I'll have to go pretty soon."

"No problem." Stan said.

I felt that Stan was a little nervous when we came into his room. He was obviously trying to have a distance of at least two feet between him and me.

I sat in the armchair in the far corner of the room. He took several sheets of paper off the table and hesitated for a second. Then he said, "I'm sorry. Actually, there is nothing to translate right now. You might want to translate it later. But now I'd like you simply to listen to what I've written for you."

There had been too many surprises all day, so I stopped being surprised. I was tired and could not protest, so I said, "Please read it to me."

"Before I start reading, I want you to know why I've written it. The story you told me about love like salt when we went to Red Square impressed me. It was such a wonderful gift from you. Now it's my turn to give you a gift. I locked myself up this morning in this little room, and I was writing this story for you for three hours. I don't know if you will like it or not, but I did my best. Here it is:

"Once upon a time trees thought they ruled the world. The earth in those days was divided into floating islands. Each island was inhabited by only one race of trees.

"On the Island of Pines, all pines stood at rigid attention with their sharp, sterile limbs pointed up against the sky. The foolish pines thought it was their duty to keep the sky from falling. From generations to generations seedlings were carefully instructed in their sacred duty; consequently the pines had no time for play or merrymaking, only for duty. So successful was the instruction that no pine dared lower his branches lest the sky should fall. Even the most powerful wind could rarely get them to talk. They were truly a bored and boring lot.

"By contrast on the island of Birches, talk, dancing and sweet scents were in abundance. However, the dark birches were no less vain, for they believed it was only the ceaseless prattle of all their voices and sweet fragrance that charmed the sun to come each day to marvel at their festival. Each generation of little birches was carefully instructed in the arts of chatter, dance and perfume. The din of noise and scent never allowed enough time for quiet meditation or thought. Yes, birches were a noisy but shallow lot, nevertheless no birch remained silent or without perfume lest the world be thrown into cold darkness forever.

"On one edge of the Island of Pines grew a beautiful solitary tree. From his earliest youth, he had carried the weight of the sky nobly. Yet he still allowed himself to see the wider world. He enjoyed the touch of wind and the tickling feet of the gentle forest creatures.

"Being the only pine in a remote part of the island, he grew much taller than his brother and sister pines. He grew so tall in fact that one day he made a discovery that was to change the world of pines and birches forever.

"In the brilliance of a new day he saw what he had heard the winds whisper about another island. He could scarcely believe his senses. But he was even more amazed to see another tree!

"She was hidden by her brown bark against the dark cliffs, but her beautiful green leaves twirling in the wind like tambourines caught his attention. She was a beautiful wind dancer.

"She had actually noticed him first and was astonished to see a tree so unlike herself; he was so tall and handsome. She pretended not to see him and continued her twirling with a friendly sea breeze.

"She was the most beautiful of birches and had exchanged polite messages with many handsome suitors, but she chose to remain alone. Perhaps secretly she imagined herself pledged to sea, sun, and life.

"Their startled amazement quickly changed to longing stares. She greeted him wrapped in morning's twilight and sea mist, and he sent hushed messages to her with sea breezes from evening's pillared, golden palace.

"Life went on as usual on the Islands of Pines and Birches. Seasons turned over as the tides, from spring to summer then to autumn and winter. The Pine and the Birch changed and grew, but their love remained constant. From their solitary island stations they looked seaward and took joy in each other, but there was also great sadness in their separateness.

"Finally, a winter came that was colder than any one that even the oldest of trees could remember. At first the Birch stood bravely against the damp, freezing walls of winter's siege, but gradually she paled, grew sick and was near death. All the while the friendly breezes carried frantic messages between the two lovers.

"He felt heartsick and powerless. Many creatures around his base noticed his despair including one small spider who lived near the bottom of his mantle.

"The little spider knew of his love for the Birch, having eavesdropped many times to wind messages. At first the Pine ignored him, but gradually out of desperation was persuaded to listen.

"The winter's blast let up for a day and the sun again touched the Earth. On that clear winter day on the Island of Pines all but one stood holding up the sky! The single, lone Pine stood with his arms outstretched to catch small pieces of the sun's rays on his needles and many spiders (the spider's kin) worked frantically to spin sun and sap into a garment for the little Birch.

"She was so moved by his generosity that she sent most of her perfumed leaves to him. The Birch then wrapped herself in the beautiful, warm, white coat and stopped dancing, fell silent, and thought only of him.

"On that momentous day the sky did not fall, nor even budge or move, and the sun returned of its own accord to bring a new day.

"And that is why to this very day all Birches are quiet, merry, white beauties and Pines reach out with scented fragrance to celebrate freedom and love.

"The Pine and Birch still grow on separate islands."

For a long time we sat in silence. The story was so powerful and emotional that tears came to my eyes and my heart ached. Then I uttered, "Stan, you are so talented. It's a wonderful piece of literature. You must write; people need you; they need to read something noble and deep like this story."

"I think you're probably right. I've always dreamt to write, but I've never had time for it. It's very busy being a teacher in High School. Do you like the story?"

"I love it. It's also so poetic and romantic. It's beautiful. And it's also sad. I feel sorry for the Pine and the Birch that they are destined to be apart."

"Oh, well, it's only the beginning of the story. It might have a continuation." As always Stan sounded optimistic.

"Be sure to send me the next part if you ever write it."

"Agreed. There's one problem with the story though. I had no time to think of the title."

"I think I know its title—*Why Birches Are White*. . .What do you think?" I asked.

"Why birches are white. . .I like it. You know; I've always felt this writing potential in me, but you are the person who actually inspired me to write and to realize that I do have a talent for it. I'm grateful to you for this."

"I think you exaggerate. Your talent has always been there, and you finally got a chance to realize it."

"Are you sure it's by chance?" Stan asked.

"I don't know; maybe it isn't. I think there's a purpose for everything, but I can't be sure of that. Though I'm quite positive that right now I'm very late, and my poor sonny is probably worried about his mom. Thank you Stan for this delightful time and the gift, the story. It'll be a good memory of the Walk for the rest of my life. I'll see you tomorrow at the airport. We'll all need to pack and rest before a hard day of saying goodbye."

"Good night. Thank you for coming and listening to my story. And thank you for inspiring me to write. See you soon."

At this moment Stan made a strange movement as if he wanted to embrace me, but I quickly turned away and walked towards the door.

CHAPTER EIGHT

The Airport Kiss
July 8, 1987, Moscow, Russia

I put Alexei to bed after listening for an hour to his stories about his day with Andrey and his mom. She took the boys to the Space Pavilion at the Exhibition of Scientific Achievements where they climbed into the real airplanes and space crafts, touched the cosmonauts' uniforms and listened to the guide's explanations about the daily routine of cosmonauts when out in space. What especially interested the boys was the bathroom system on board the spaceship.

Alexei was so excited that long after I tucked him, he kept on talking. He confided in me that he didn't want to go to our dacha once we returned to Leningrad. Life was a lot of fun at the dacha only when his friends were there, otherwise it was just the most boring place in the world. Most of his dacha buddies were arriving only in the end of July. That's when it would be fun—fishing, riding bikes like crazy, flying kites, staying up late playing cards, or watching movies on TV together if…the weather…bad…With these words my boy finally fell asleep. I could tell the little chatterbox was tired.

I finished packing, took a shower, dried my hair and jumped into bed. It was so sweet to stretch out in bed and relax especially after the strange events of the day.

There were so many things happening this last day of the Walk. Stan's amazing story. Why did he write it for me? He is an unusual man. And Jane's strange request. She and Stas were probably having their wild sex right at this moment. I wondered if either of them was married. These Americans with their freedom of thought and speech. I would never imagine myself asking a total stranger to have sex even if I wanted it desperately. I was brought up to be a proper Russian woman. And what if the way I was brought up was not the best way?

"This woman, Jane, is not insane; she is in passion in a peacenik fashion…"

With these stupid rhymes in my head I was falling asleep when suddenly I heard someone tapping gently on the door. Did I imagine it? No, the tapping repeated, and this time more insistently. I looked at my watch; it was 1:15 A.M. Who could it be? I stopped breathing for a moment. Everything was silent; then I heard footsteps growing fainter as the person moved away from my door. Probably someone got lost and realized it was the wrong room. I fell asleep.

The next morning was the last morning that the Russian and American peaceniks spent together. The participants in the great Peace Walk began to say good-bye to each other long before the buses took them to the airport. They were hugging, kissing, embracing, and exchanging gifts in the lobby of the hotel. I had to say good-bye to many people who I would miss and probably never see again.

It was a sad day. Nadya had been right; we did become one loving family. Actually, a few people were planning on starting real families together. I heard rumors about two couples who were going to get married. That was interesting.

Finally, we arrived at the airport. I had to find Galina and Stan because I promised to interpret for their last interview. But I did not need to look for them; Stan was the first person I saw in the lobby of the airport. He looked tired.

"Did you sleep at all?" I asked.

"No, I didn't. I hadn't slept well before I left for Russia three weeks ago; now it was the same before going home," he said slowly.

"Are you afraid of flying?"

"Oh, no. I have a theory: If the flight is safe, there is nothing to worry about, and if the plane crashes, there is nothing to worry about either." Stan smiled, but it was a very different smile. Usually, when he smiled, his eyes would dance, but this time only his mouth smiled. His eyes were sleepy and sad. I said, "It's a good theory. I wish I could accept it, but I'm terribly afraid of flying, and I'm always very worried before each flight. This time I'm going home by train, so I have nothing to worry about," I tried to cheer Stan up with the happy tone of my voice.

"What are you going to do when you come home?" Suddenly Stan changed the subject.

"Alexei and I will go to our dacha. My husband's having a vacation. He's waiting for us to come and spend the summer with him. The weather seems to be really good, so it'll be a lot of fun. What about you?"

"When I come home, I'll rest a couple of days to get over the jet lag. Then I want to go backpacking in the mountains. I feel like being alone for a while to think over all I have seen and heard here."

"Will you go alone?"

"Yes, I usually do."

"Is it dangerous?"

"It can be. But I don't go to bad places, and I'll have my gun with me."

Obviously, it was easy for Stan to talk about guns. He was born in the 'Wild West' where carrying a gun was like smoking a cigarette. I heard that even children carry guns when they go hunting in the U.S. I also heard that in a number of states they had experienced a few school shootings, and that was scary. I did not want to discuss this subject and simply asked, "Is the American West really wild? What kinds of wild things do people do there except carrying guns?"

Stan laughed, "You should come and see for yourself."

"I'll never come to Idaho, maybe not even to America," I sighed, "even if Gorbachev opens the borders, it'll be too expensive for most Russians to travel. I'm only an English instructor with an average salary."

Stan shook his head, "You sound so categorical—'never' is a bad word. 'Never Say Never'—I think there's a movie with such a name."

"Well, I am categorical," I snapped. "It's either always or never for me."

At this moment Galina and her cameramen came up to us. "Here you are. How are you? Are you happy that you are finally leaving, Stan?" Galina asked.

"I'm a little tired and miss my family. But I feel sorry to leave."

"This is very good. It's exactly what I want you to show in the film; I mean that you are sorry. Now you and Elena, hug each other and show you're sad."

That was unexpected; I did not realize I would have to hug for the camera.

"Is it that necessary?" I asked and tried to put into my voice a little bit of irritation.

"Don't you want to give me a hug?" Stan looked at me and made a sad face.

"Okay, I'll give you a hug," I said shrugging my shoulders.

We hugged each other, and then suddenly Stan bent over me and kissed me on my cheek. Galina exclaimed, "This kiss is so dry, but you are good friends parting forever or at least for a very long time. Come on, show your real feelings."

Having heard that, Stan embraced me and looked straight into my eyes.

"Galina is right, we might not see each other for a long time," he said.

Then he touched my lips lightly with his. And then a terrible thing happened. I still don't know why, but I responded to his warm soft lips and gave him a long kiss, the one that is called 'French'. I heard the rattle of the video cameras around us. My French kiss was videotaped.

"This is even better than what I was hoping for. Elena, you are a great actress. Thank you. It was perfect," Galina was quite satisfied.

"So, it wasn't real but only for the camera?" Stan asked a little angrily.

"Of course it was only for the camera." I felt ashamed and confused. And then I saw a sly smile on the cameraman's face; Stas was probably still in the vapor of his wild night with Jane.

There was an awkward silence. Luckily, Alexei appeared with handfuls of big and small packages. "Mama, look how many gifts," he said, "this is a real Indian flute, and this is a bandana, and here is a tape with Native American music and also three lipsticks."

"Lipsticks? Why lipsticks?" I asked.

"I don't know. One old lady gave them to me. She said I could give them to my girlfriend."

"I did not know you had a girlfriend."

"But Mommy," my eight-year-old son said, "I might find one pretty soon."

"Oh, okay." I was hoping that Stan would say something, but he was silent. He was definitely angry with me. I said quickly, "Alexei, you need to say 'good-bye' to Stan."

"Bye Alexei. Will you come to visit me in Idaho? We have to play tic-tac-toe again so that I can win too." Stan put his hand on Alexei's shoulder.

"I don't think so. I want to go to England. Maybe after England." Alexei said.

"If you do come to my little Moscow in Idaho, we'll go hunting."

"All right." It was amazing how easily Alexei spoke and understood English.

Stan shook Alexei's hand. Then he turned to me but did not make eye contact, "Elaina, here is a little something for you, but promise not to open the package until I'm up in the air."

"What is it, Stan?" I asked.

"It is a surprise. I hope you'll like it. Take care." He paused and then added, "May I write you a letter?"

By the tone of Stan's voice I knew he was mad at me. Why would he be so upset? I told him I was acting because it was true. What else did he expect? I was not very happy about such an abrupt change in our friendship, so I said, "Thank you for the gift, and of course you can write letters. We will be pen pals."

"Sounds good to me." He waved and went through the passport control. He never looked back. Then he disappeared in the crowd.

We were standing there for a long time watching people crying, hugging, kissing, and laughing. All these people who had been strangers in three weeks became so dear and precious to each other. It was unbelievable, but real. The idea of a nuclear war between our two peoples seemed even more ridiculous than it had before the walk. We had so much in common and so much to learn from each other. If only the decency of average people could guide us rather than the ambitions of poor leaders on both sides, we would live in peace.

CHAPTER NINE

The First Letter

August, 1987, Dacha, 80 miles south of Leningrad

It was a quiet evening after a thunderstorm. The leaves of the huge maple tree, which grew so close to our dacha that its branches touched the windows, smelled freshly washed. Not a single little noise could be heard. This was hard to believe after the powerful sounds of thunder and the fast streams of pouring water. I was sitting on the porch of our dacha. It was past midnight. Alexei was asleep; he could sleep even if cannons were firing. But I couldn't; I have always been scared of thunder and lightning.

My husband was in Leningrad. His vacation was over and he was back at work. He came to visit us and relax every weekend. It was only Wednesday; Alexei and I had two more days of quiet life. It was so nice when there were just the two of us. We could sleep late, have coffee on the glass veranda, and watch cartoons. Then we would go to the lake if the weather was good, and we would spend half a day playing on the beach. We would swim, lie in the sun, tell stories, and play cards or ball with friends.

After the beach we would come home and have milk or juice and a snack, something very simple. At 5 P.M. we would watch my favorite South-American soap opera "Simply Maria" for an hour—my summer-spending-time-in-vain privilege, and then we would go for a bike-ride or for a walk. Alexei and I liked long walks together. During those adventures we would talk about life on other planets, animals, books and movies, or I would tell my son stories from the history of our family. On windy days we liked to launch a kite in the pea field. At about seven or eight in the evening we would come home and have a light dinner, a plate of salad, strawberries, peaches or apples. Then we would have tea and watch a mystery on TV, read or have friends over, play tapes and talk.

Everything was completely different when my husband was around. Our dacha life turned into a boot camp. His idea of life even during the holidays was that everything has to be on time and have productive results.

We had to wake up at 7A.M., do exercises for at least twenty minutes, take a cold shower and have a big breakfast. Right after breakfast, we had to spend all morning in the garden, weeding, digging, planting, watering, building, or repairing; there was always something to do. Then I cooked lunch. It had to be soup and salad, beef and potatoes, fish or chicken and rice. After lunch there were fifteen minutes allowed for rest. Then he and I went back to work in the garden, and Alexei had to do math problems or read a book from the list of school-recommended summer reading or listen to English tapes. At about 5 P.M. we finally went to the beach to swim and then went quickly back home to have dinner. While I was cooking, my husband would continue doing something in the garden. He always found some work there not only for others but also for himself. Alexei had to help. Only after dinner could we really relax and enjoy the evening if we had any energy left. Usually I was so tired that I could only dream of going to bed.

That is why Alexei and I loved our dacha when we were alone there and hated it when Vadim was there with his commands. We both understood it was necessary to take care of berries and vegetables, flowers and trees, but the negative side of it was that neither Alexei nor I had any freedom of choice or thought. We were like slaves meant to obey the master's directions. After ten years of married life, I got used to it and did not consider it to be too bad. It was inconvenient and irritated me, but most of the time I did not argue and did what I was told to do. I had no experience in gardening because I grew up in a city, while Vadim was raised in a small village and knew a lot about farming. Nevertheless, my secret dream was to come to the dacha only to rest and enjoy summer, and that was exactly what we did between 'Papa's week-ends.'

That August night I was sitting on the porch enjoying the freshness of the air. The sky cleared up; it was coal-black with a billion stars shimmering brightly. The full moon was like a new silver coin. It was getting chilly and I wrapped myself in my soft white shawl. This shawl was so beautiful and warm. I thought of Stan's story *"Why Birches Are White"* and the package that he had given me at the airport before his departure. As I had promised Stan, I did not open it till I came home to Leningrad the next morning; there it was in the suitcase when I was unpacking. I finally unwrapped the package and found a hand knitted white shawl of fine goat wool, like cashmere, so soft, fluffy and pleasant to touch. There was a note, but its content still puzzled me. I decided to reread it and went to my bedroom to get it out of an English book where I kept it. I read it over:

Elena,

In another world and time perhaps our destinies might have been different. Since we live on different islands I cannot always or easily comfort or love you. Consequently, please wear this white shawl when you are in need of comfort, love, and tenderness.

I was sad last night that you did not feel comfortable enough to let me hold you, but I was not then nor am I now interested in a sexual relationship. I deeply want a friendship for a lifetime; consequently, behaving respectfully was appropriate. My greatest sadness was that you could not share more, but my great joy is that you shared as much as you did—it was more than enough to win my heart. Please wear the shawl and understand that I hope fervently that our destinies will bring us together again in another place and time.

I am thankful that we are not trees after all and have some ability to determine our destinies. My time in Russia was wonderful, but our walk in Red Square will always be most precious, to be in the heart of Russia and be 'loved like salt' is the greatest treasure.

Love,

Stan

What a wonderful, warm, but strange letter. Did I understand English well enough and get it right that Stan was in love with me? Or was it simply an expression of friendship, and the man was a romantic, and therefore the letter sounded more than just friendly? Maybe he had misinterpreted my story about love like salt and had thought that I had fallen in love with him? But I had not! That was merely a story to make our trip in the subway not so boring. He did want to hold me then in his hotel room. Did he want to kiss me then? Did he hope to have more than a kiss? Was that Stan tapping on the door of my room at 1:15 in the morning? No, this could not be. He loved his wife and children; he could not be unfaithful. He knew I was married. Actually, he wrote that he did not want a sexual relationship. Yes, that was it. He was definitely not in love. He was simply a nice, kind man, a romantic at heart. He was a writer.

CHAPTER TEN

The Terrible Illness
December 10, 1987, Leningrad, Russia

Four months had passed since I was sitting on the porch of the dacha reading Stan's short note to me. It was romantic, but I decided that it was not because he was in love with me. He was a romantic at heart, and it was his writing style. So then, in August, I put the letter back in between the pages of "*Catch 22*" and forgot about it.

At the end of August I went back to work, got busy developing a new curriculum for my department and prepared for comprehensive exams for my Ph.D. in linguistics. Alexei started the third grade in September. Our life returned to its usual pace.

Then in November a tragedy happened: Alexei fell ill with severe viral pneumonia. There were three cases of this horrible disease in his school, and my dearest son was one of them. I no longer was protected by angels; I felt betrayed. I had lost my mother two years earlier, and I had thought that nothing could be worse. I was only beginning to recover after years of grief, but here came a new trial time, and it was worse than before.

The world turned colorless and dull, just a gray blur. I did not sleep, eat or think; I existed from day to day and from night to night hoping, praying, and begging God and the doctors to save my only child.

The first week was a torture, the period of the unknown, the time of tests and diagnoses. I spent most of the time at the hospital in the hall behind the glass door of Alexei's room. Nobody was allowed in that room except doctors and nurses. The best physicians were consulted, and finally, they came to a unanimous conclusion about the type of pneumonia Alexei had.

The second and third weeks were a little easier when we had some certainty; intensive treatment began, and it started to show good results. We were lucky that the medication worked well.

During all those three weeks I did not go to work. I simply forgot

I had a job, for nothing mattered but my son. I did not realize that my wonderful co-workers were substituting for me all that time, and they did it for free. Those days of fear, pain and anxiety demonstrated what really friendship is. I greatly appreciated the love and support of my colleagues, my dear Angels.

My husband, of course, was working day and night to save our child. He contacted the various specialists and made sure that we had several opinions before any important decisions were made. But he had to continue to go to work and came to the hospital only for a few hours in the evenings. We communicated by exchanging only a few words of encouragement and avoided looking into each other's eyes; we were both trying to hide our fear.

My poor father, who loved Alexei deeply, was so distraught that he was unable to help him. He had an emotional breakdown, suffered from terrible depression and cried each time I talked to him about Alexei, no matter whether the news was bad or good. He spent every day at the hospital like a faithful dog ready to give his life to save his grandson.

Those days were full of sadness and despair, but Vadim and I were encouraged by the flood of cards and flowers from family and friends. We were not alone. We also knew that Alexei was receiving the best medical care available in Leningrad. Alexei's illness gradually subsided. He started feeling better, but he was not to be disturbed by visitors. During week four of his stay at the hospital, my son and I began to write letters to each other. I saved all his letters, the heartbreaking hopes and wishes, complaints and fears of a child. One day I brought him a pile of letters and get-well cards from his classmates and teachers at school. They cheered him up. My little boy did pull through and came out of the hospital alive.

The next stage of his recovery was crucial and difficult. Alexei was extremely weak as if all the energy had been pumped out of his little body. Now we had to follow a strict daily exercise routine for at least six months. Alexei was not allowed to go to school, play ball, swim, skate or ski. He had to learn how to breathe right and eat and rest more.

Life got its meaning back; the world regained its colors. The beautiful sky and the sun were there for me again; a new flow of energy and joy gradually changed me from a tired, haggard creature into the person I had been before. I could laugh again. We had defeated a hideous disease. My baby was alive and well. What more could a mother ask for?

I took a leave of absence at work for three months and spent all that time with my boy, religiously following all the prescriptions and assignments of the doctors. After that I hired a wonderful woman who took care of Alexei while Vadim and I were at work.

When I got back to a more or less normal life, I suddenly received a letter from Stan. It was not a personal letter to me but simply a copy of a letter that he had written to all his friends in Russia. That letter completely convinced me that Stan was a nice American guy, just a friend. I was not different or in any way more special for him than other Russian participants in the Peace Walk. He addressed his letter to every friend:

Dear,

I have not forgotten you. I know that you live half a world away in a place that is both strange and wonderful to me. I see you walking in the day when I use my mind to look away from the task at hand and my dreams occasionally summon you forth at night to walk with me till morning. I find that I have collected jewels on the thread from Leningrad to Moscow. You are a living necklace of smiles, laughter, hugs, kisses, and handshakes. I know that you exist, are real, and on that account I know that the world is a better place than I imagined it to be before I left home. I love you all.

Although I have been able to send only a few letters to date, I hope now to make a new beginning and write more regularly to those of you who wish to correspond. I will take a few moments to relate what I have been doing since we said good-bye in Moscow.

I was not able to tell too much of what happened to others when I first returned home for two reasons. First, I was still processing all that went on, and second, my wife insisted that we go on a vacation. We left for Oregon a few days after I returned. We met my parents in Sisters, Oregon and proceeded to go to the Oregon coast for three weeks. My parents only stayed with us for three days there. Shortly after we returned home, to my surprise, my mother called and asked that I come home to Boise, Idaho to be with her. My mother has lupus and has not been well, so I left almost immediately for Boise.

I returned home again to learn that we were going to have a teacher's strike. Our school board was ready to fire us. We were out for over a week; consequently, I was not able to go into school to get ready for the start of the new school year. Furthermore, we have a new history book this year; it didn't arrive until the sixth week of the quarter. So, I have been busy just trying to catch up.

You might like to know that our curriculum has changed this year. Previously we spent little time on studying the Soviet Union, but now we are spending nine weeks. Also I have subscribed to the Moscow News and to Soviet Life.

Several other exciting things happened since I got home. I completed a high school correspondence course for use by the University of Idaho that has been highly praised. Also I have been chosen to develop a unit in comparative religion for my State's schools. Most exciting of all I have been chosen by the Initiative for Understanding Youth Exchange program to take students from Idaho on a tour of the Soviet Union during July and August of 1988. I hope to see all of you if circumstances permit.

I continue to work for peace. I have sent copies of two essays about my time with you in the Soviet Union to Ludmila Saharskaya so that she might share them with you. Also I started my slide show about the Peace Walk. The first presentation received a great deal of praise. People particularly loved the slides and the fact that we are 'so much alike.' I am scheduled to do many more.

I hope my note finds you and your families and friends in good health and that you have a good holiday season. My family and I are well, busy and generally happy.

Best wishes to you and yours for this and the coming year!

Stan Banks

Now I knew for sure that I did not need to worry about our relationship. It was easy to communicate with a male friend when no other emotions were involved. I had a lot of male friends in Leningrad: some of them were my colleagues, some were my friends' husbands, and others were members of clubs or associations I belonged to. My husband knew practically all of them and was friends with some of them, too. He always trusted me, knowing that I would not allow any closer relationship than friendship. All my male friends assumed that I was happy with my husband and they never acted inappropriately. Actually, most of my relatives, friends and acquaintances thought that my marriage was one of the happiest they knew. And this had been true in the past for a long time, but it was gradually changing.

Vadim and I fell in love when we met in 1977. He was incredibly handsome with blue eyes and dark brown hair; he was smart, a successful physician, talented, and polite. He knew a lot about literature and theater and even wrote poetry. We had been dating for about five months before we made love once, and I got pregnant. I was absolutely happy, and he was in the seventh heaven. We decided to get married immediately. My parents liked him a lot. His aunt and grandmother adored me, but his mother never got to know me well because she lived in Siberia and met me only at the wedding. She was not very happy with me—I seemed to be too educated and too independent. She had always dreamed of a plain village girl for her son. The good news was that right after the wedding she went back to her small Siberian town, and we rarely communicated then only by phone or mail.

In December of 1978 our son Alexei was born. My husband insisted on our moving in with my parents because he wanted to have his in-laws look after the baby so we could have more freedom as newlyweds. At first I protested. I wanted to run my own household and raise my son without any interference on the part of our relatives. I was afraid that there would be conflicts and that my parents' calm life would be disrupted; it just did not feel right. But it was very convenient to be free when we wanted to go to a theater, a party or on a vacation, so I finally accepted the situation and even liked it for a while.

Gradually, everything turned out the way I had predicted—simply bad. Vadim liked to leave the baby with my parents and supported my mom's decision to retire and be with him all the time so I could go back to work. But at the same time, he did not like to hear advice from my parents concerning the baby and when my parents expressed their opinions, he considered it to be rude interference into his private life. On the other hand, my parents thought they had the right to give us advice because they spent more time with our son than we did and they knew more about what he needed. At first it was not so bad, but I felt it would only get worse over time and asked Vadim to find an apartment where we could move. He refused to do it, pointing out that it would cost us much more to live separately. Eventually, I found myself between two enemy camps.

My parents knew that I loved my husband, and they did not want to destroy our marriage and separate us. But I felt that they did not respect or like Vadim anymore and I did not blame them for that. He had become strict, intolerant, and at times rude. The atmosphere in the family became tense and unfriendly.

I remembered that when I was little, everybody cherished each other in our family. My brother and I had never uttered a bad word or heard one from our parents. My father was the most loving person I had ever met in my life. My mom was a genuine housewife and her children's closest friend who always understood and respected us. My parents had offered the same love and affection to their new son-in-law.

I could not understand why Vadim had changed so much since he had joined our family. Later I found out that his mother had written many letters criticizing my parents and me, which probably influenced his attitude. Finally their conspiracy against us replaced trust with suspicion. Reason and common sense were also victims of my mother-in-law's campaign. As the hostility between my parents and Vadim increased, I found myself unwillingly caste into the role of peace maker. I was exhausted from trying to reconcile the many differences between the warring factions of my family. The paper cuts that we tried to ignore were replaced with open wounds.

My love for Vadim was also a causality of the war. It was at this time that Stan came into my life as an American male friend.

Stan's letter addressed to all of his Russian friends inspired me to reply. On January 26, 1988, I wrote:

Dear Stan,

Thank you very much for your wonderful words. You are a kind soul. Such people never have enemies; usually everybody loves them. I am glad my destiny was generous and gave me a chance to meet you. I want you to know that even if I never see you again, I will never forget you. I have always been lucky to meet wonderful people in my life, but you are an extraordinary person, so it is an honor to know you.

I have read your essays on Peace. They are very interesting; though, some of your attitudes and ideas seem rather strange to me. This proves that we still know very little about each other (I mean Soviets and Americans.)

I am glad you have subscribed to Moscow News. I also receive this newspaper. So we read one and the same weekly publication.

My family has lived through a great trial and worry. Alexei was very sick for four weeks. He was in the hospital with viral pneumonia. They say it's a common disease these days. His doctor says there won't be any consequences, but we have to follow certain rules of life for the next 6 months: no sports, no sun, no colds, etc. We planned to go to the Black Sea next summer, but given the circumstances, we won't be able to do it.

We have a new member of the family, a puppy. She is five weeks old, an astounding blond. We adore her. There is much work with the puppy: special food, walking 2-3 times a day, washing paws, etc. So Ricky-the-Puppy keeps us busy.

Have you seen the film about the Walk? I was a little disappointed because the movie shows not so much of the joint Walk of American and Soviet people, but rather Americans on the territory of the USSR. Though some parts of it are good, especially you at the Piskariovskoye Memorial Cemetery—a touching moment.

There is a wonderful exhibition of American paintings in the Russian Museum. I liked it a lot and I am happy that the cultural ties between our countries are being developed.

I hope you and your family are well. I am looking forward to hearing from you.

Elena

P.S. It is March already. I am sorry I did not mail this letter right away. I really don't know where the time flew. You'll probably get this letter by summer. Have a great vacation.

CHAPTER ELEVEN

Simply to Live
August-November, 1989, Leningrad

More than a year passed. During that time Stan and I wrote letters to each other every two-three months, talking mostly about education in Russia and the U.S., culture, traditions, family news, and plans. Stan also called me on the phone several times at work. It was always at about the same time when I had a staff meeting, and he was sure that he would be able to reach me. In the little Moscow in Idaho it was about 2 A.M. After a couple of Stan's calls, the secretary of the department of Foreign Languages where I worked started making hints about 'a foreign admirer with a velvet baritone.' I told her that she was wrong and that what she interpreted as an 'admirer' was simply a friend. I did consider Stan to be my friend, a person in whom I valued sincerity and a kind heart that genuinely cared about people including Russians.

Stan had planned to come to Russia with a group of students the previous summer, but the money was never raised, and the trip was cancelled. In one of his letters he wrote, "...*I would like to come back to the Soviet Union, but life is often more complex than one wishes it were. If I had a magic wand that would allow me to finish my Ph.D. and have the money necessary, I would spend the month of June in Leningrad for the rest of my life. Once the degree is complete I will be able to come more often.*"

Stan was a dreamer.

I liked Stan's style of writing. He always sounded gentle. In one of his cards he wrote, "*Dear Elena, the warmth and tenderness of precious memories makes spring time eternal between friends no matter how far they may be separated by miles and minutes...*"

Stan was a romantic.

I liked both of these features of his character and continued to correspond with Stan because his "dreaming romanticism" made my routine life less boring.

I taught and prepared for my comprehension exams. I successfully passed French and the Gothic language but had five more exams to go. It was very hard to combine work, family and classes, but I was determined to get my doctorate. So Stan's little notes, cards and letters were like a fresh breeze in a small stuffy room; he constantly encouraged me to reach my goal.

In December, unexpectedly, I got a chance to go to the U.S.A. Among several exchange programs conducted by the Soviet Peace Committee there was one called "Family-to-Family." In June of 1989 my family hosted two sisters from Iowa, two wonderful girls in their late teens who immediately became like daughters to us. We took them around Leningrad, to museums, theaters, schools; we went shopping, on boat rides and visited our friends. The two weeks passed like a dream. After Leningrad the girls went to Moscow for another week and then back home to Iowa. There were thirty Americans in that group staying with about twenty-five Russian families.

Now it was the turn of Russians to go to America in December-January. According to the rules only one person from each hosting family could go on this trip. We had a family meeting and I was chosen to travel to this far away country. My husband could not go because he had already used his vacation that year. He was not very excited about it anyway because he did not know English. Alexei after his illness was still not deemed strong enough to travel so far by himself. I was the only member of the family who could and wanted to go very much. There was just one problem—money.

In order to be able to buy the air ticket, visa, and gifts for my future American host families, I had to work during the summer instead of spending my vacation at the dacha. So all August I was in town working as a teacher of Russian for foreign students, and I made enough money to cover all the expenses. It looked like I was going to America after all.

My brother's family had hosted an American from Texas, and my brother, Vlad, was also planning to go on this exchange program. Though it was called an "exchange", we were not supposed to go to Iowa or Texas to stay with the families of the people that we had hosted. The Russian group would simply go to Washington, D.C. for the first week and to Philadelphia, PA, for the second.

I was excited about the trip. I had been to a few foreign countries in Europe, not too far from home. Now I was going over Europe and across the whole Atlantic Ocean. I was going to travel to a different world, the so-called 'New World', to the country that was so famous for its freedom, democracy, and wealth. But the most important thing was that I was about to see the country whose language I had been studying since I was six years old and spent half of my life teaching. Such a trip could be not only interesting but also useful for me from the professional point of view.

In my September letter to Stan I mentioned that I might go to the U.S. on the exchange program. At the end of November I got a letter from him in which he wrote:

"*...I do hope you will find a way to America. I thought of you these past several months when I heard about the devaluation of the ruble in relation to other currencies. First, I hope this does not make your trip impossible, but of even more importance that it will not make your day to day existence too difficult....*"

Then at the end of this letter I read:

"*Please take care; know I love you and have a Merry Holiday Season and a Happy New Year.*"

"*Know I love you...*"—what did that mean? Did he really love me? Or was he referring to all of us, his Russian friends, as it had already been in one of his first letters? Obviously, he did not mean he loved me because he wrote in his letters about his devotion to his children. His family was the most important thing in the world. A person would not write about his wife in every letter to a woman whom he loved. So, he was not in love with me and he simply meant, 'love as a friend.' This was a very satisfactory explanation, but for some reason I felt disappointed. Women are complex; they want men to love them even when they don't want those men.

By November I was sure that I was going to America. The group was formed, the air tickets were booked and the main thing—American visas were received. Now I had to exchange two hundred rubles for dollars—the amount allowed for that trip by the Soviet authorities, which was three hundred and eighteen dollars. The limitation was established because of the lack of foreign currency in the country and also to discourage the growth of the black market, which in fact was so well developed that nothing could really stop it. Nevertheless, Soviet people were used to all sorts of restrictions and limitations, and they did not pay too much attention to them and often violated them without any bad feelings or consequences. It was well known that many people tried to sneak more money through the customs than what was allowed. As for me, I was raised in the family of a naval officer where laws were respected and obeyed. If I was allowed to exchange only two hundred rubles, that was what I would exchange.

On the first Monday of November I went to the only bank in Leningrad, a city of five million people, where I could exchange rubles for foreign currency. I heard from friends that the best way to do it was to come very early in the morning and get on the waiting list. Then probably by evening I would be able to get my business done. So I got up at four in the morning. My husband thought I was insane and had no dignity. Why would a person stand in the freezing cold for 4 hours from 5:00 A.M. just to be at the bank when the doors opened? Moreover, I might spend six more hours in the line inside just for a few dollars. It seemed ridiculous to my very rational husband. I felt humiliated too, but I had no choice. They did not exchange Russian rubles in American banks, and I could not go to America without a cent in my pocket.

I left home at about 5 A.M. and came to the Leningrad Hotel, where the bank was located, by one of the first metro trains that morning. It was freezing outside. To my great surprise, despite the early hour and cold weather, there were a lot of people by the entrance to the bank. At the end of the line there was a person with a list of names, and he put down my name at the end of it by number 642. The expression on my face showed such surprise and despair that the man said, "Don't be so discouraged. This is not a bad number, and you have a chance to get your money today."

"Really? How can that be? If we calculate, it will take at least a week," I said.

"No, it won't. You probably think there's only one teller working there, but there're usually three or four. It takes about five minutes per person because each has to fill out a form, which is three or four people every five minutes." The man sounded cheerful despite the early hour and piercing cold. I doubted his prognosis was right.

"Okay, let's count. If it's an ideal situation and there're four tellers working, there will be forty-eight people served during one hour. Multiply this by an eight-hour work day. It makes it less than four hundred people a day. And my number is 642." I felt hopeless.

"That's right," the man said smiling shrewdly, "but you obviously have no experience in this tricky business. The thing is that there're over six hundred people on the list, but not everybody will actually come to exchange the money because many people put their names on the list without having an American visa. Not everyone may know that the bank exchanges money only to those who have both the visa and the ticket. By the way, do you have both?"

"Yes, I do." I felt special. At least I had something that some other people did not. Actually, I even felt lucky because I had not known that rule before I came to the bank. "Why is it like this? Is it to make the life of people more intriguing? Don't we have enough 'life excitement' without additional problems?" I was irritated.

"Oh, well, you know our stupid government. It's always afraid that the life of the Soviet people might be too easy, so they invent all possible obstacles to make it more complicated. This way you feel the zest of living by overcoming the difficulties. Once you are finished, you can experience the juicy excitement of victory." The man smiled sarcastically. Then he added, "But seriously speaking, if there were no limitations on how many dollars Soviet citizens going abroad could get, they would start selling them, and the black market would become unmanageable."

This guy was interesting. I enjoyed talking with him. He kept me awake. I asked, "Has the black market ever been manageable?"

"Sure, and it has been well regulated."

"By whom?"

"You sound as if you were born yesterday and have no life experience whatsoever. Don't you understand yourself?" He was surprised.

"Oh, I see," I said trying not to sound naive, but truly, I did not know who was managing the black market. I even did not understand very well what the black market was *per se*. I really did not care about any other kind of market but the farmers' market where I could buy fresh fruit and vegetables. And now, thanks to the new policy of Michael Gorbachev, I could travel and see the world. I wanted to go to America, and I simply wanted to get my dollars. I said to the man, "Well, thank you for explaining the situation to me. I see now that I have some hope to get my money today if only I don't freeze to death."

"You won't freeze. Since we are all "in the same boat," people here are supportive and friendly, and we take turns. After an hour or so you can go to the hotel lobby, have a cup of coffee and warm up. When you come back, other people will go to the cafeteria. We'll all survive," said the man cheerfully.

"I don't like the word 'survive'. All I want is simply to live. But it sounds like there's no other choice. I'll have to survive. Thanks again."

I moved closer to the wall where the chilly draft was not so strong, and I heard a strange song pounding in my ears with only one line: "Simply to live...Simply to live...Simply to live..."

CHAPTER TWELVE

My Best Friend
November 1989, Leningrad, Russia

One good thing about that awful ruble-exchange line was that the people there were really nice and friendly. They were telling stories from their previous experiences traveling abroad, about their jobs, friends, family members, movies or theater plays, exhibitions, and gossip. At the beginning, it was even interesting to talk, but after an hour, I got so cold that I could not concentrate on the stories no matter how thrilling they were. I thought I was well prepared wearing two sweaters, heavy pants, a long fox coat and fur boots. But nothing helped. The piercing Artic wind stabbed me right to the bone. I grew colder and colder and I felt as if my insides were about to turn into a slab of ice. Luckily, by the time when I was about to turn into an icicle, it was my turn to go to the cafeteria and warm up.

This torture lasted until 9:00 A.M. when the bank finally opened. In a moment my cautious optimism was shattered. Instead of three or four promised operators there were only two; the others were at home with the flu—there is often a flu epidemic in Leningrad around this time of the year. The line crawled forward, slower than snails, and my suffering continued till noon—five hundred were still ahead of me. By 3:00 P.M. there were still three hundred and fifty icy figurines waiting for dollars. It was at that moment that I lost hope and felt desperate.

I also heard rumors that the exchange rate was about to change, maybe even tomorrow; the ruble was going down. For the same amount of rubles people would get fewer dollars. It was so unfair but not a surprise—just another example of the countless, mind numbing actions of a government designed to preserve the status quo for the few at the expense of the many.

I needed help and advice. I knew who I had to call—my dad. He was the one I always called in difficult situations. Luckily, he was home and I told him about my misery.

My father was my best friend; I could always rely on him. Unfortunately, my husband would help me only in the cases that he considered appropriate, and he often thought that my actions were too light-minded and unimportant. In those cases he would say, "You wanted this for yourself, so now *you* solve *your* own problem." In contrast, my father considered anything I did important, and if I needed help, he was there for me.

Thirty minutes after my phone call, my father arrived and went to visit the director of the hotel who was an acquaintance of his. By this time it was 4:00 P.M., but there were still three hundred people-numbers ahead of me. There was no hope to exchange the money even the next day, especially after I heard some people talking about staying overnight because a new list would likely be made up at the start of a new business day. All my good humor and positive attitude evaporated.

Shivering head to toe I was thinking, "The curious thing about the status quo is that those who make the transition from being one of the masses to being one of the few seem to develop amnesia. Their new found privileges make them forget the lives of average Russian citizens. These so called "patriots" blinded by privilege join ranks with the few to create "their own special world" and "their rules" to make "their lives" even more comfortable while making everyone else's life miserable. Yes, it must be amnesia that makes them forget that they were once of the same "common" people."

My father came back and took me out of the line. We went to the cafe in the hotel, and he told me, "Lenochka, my little daughter"—my father always used the diminutive of my formal name, and I liked it—"I am sorry you had to suffer all day and all in vain."

"Why, Papa, in vain?"

"Because you can't get your money here, it's clear. There are rumors that in a couple of days the exchange rate will be six to one. When people start hearing the rumors, this line will become three times longer. And we cannot stay all night out in the frost to try to keep your place in the line. I don't want you to get ill. But your papa will help. I have found out something."

"What is it, Papa?" I knew it; my dad would help me; he had done so his whole life. I loved him so.

It had been my father who wanted a second child, a daughter, when the war with the Nazis was over. My mother, a practical woman, had not planned to have any more children until they moved back to Leningrad from a small sea port in the Far East. My father had been a commander-in-chief of the destroyer *"Undefeatable"* located in the Pacific Ocean. The Russian fleet had been on high alert for many years there because of the constant threat of the Japanese.

Three years passed and the tension between the Soviet Union and Japan decreased. At the same time, in 1948, my brother Vlad (short for Vladislav) turned seven; it was time for him to go to school, but they did not have a separate elementary school at the small Navy base, Chamzha. They only had a one-room school for children of all ages. My mother did not consider such a situation appropriate. She wanted to give her son a good solid education. She taught him reading, writing and math at home.

The problem about what foreign language Vlad would learn solved itself when my mom met the wife of an English Embassy officer. She liked little Vlad and volunteered to teach him English. In spite of Mom's best efforts to provide an education for Vlad, she was not satisfied. So when my father started talking about having a daughter again, she said, "If we have a little baby, I won't have as much time to devote to our son at a time when he needs a lot of attention. Moreover, I don't want my daughter to be born in this desolate wilderness. We've been here for three years already, and it's time for us to go back to Leningrad. I promise, as soon as we move back to our apartment on Tchaikovsky Street, you will have a baby-daughter." My father seldom argued with his wife; he started working hard to find a position in Leningrad. Finally, he was appointed commander of one of the Naval colleges in Leningrad, and in 1950 they moved back home.

In July of 1952 the promised, long-awaited and immediately adored daughter was born. My father was so happy that he did a lot of funny and silly things that were remembered by many people for a long time. I was born on a Sunday, at 3:15 P.M. When my father heard the news, he brought a man with a beautiful voice to the window of my mother's maternity ward. That man sang serenades for her until he and my father were sent away by a police officer because other women on the ward complained; a beautiful voice is of little comfort to women who are anxiously waiting to give birth or having given birth only want to sleep.

After that my father went to a furniture store and bought five pieces of furniture, each one decorated with a big mirror. He placed all these mirrors on each free spot in his apartment. He was sure that his daughter would be an absolute beauty and would need a lot of mirrors to try pretty dresses on and to admire herself.

Later that evening he went to the local pub and was treating every customer to drinks and lobster. The customers had to drink to the health and happiness of his newly born beauty-daughter. My father partied nearly all night, and early in the morning he sent a huge bouquet of flowers to his wonderful wife. His dream had come true; he now had both a son and a daughter.

On that day, July 27, 1952 my father and I had not been introduced, nevertheless, the strongest bond between us had been established. I treasure each memory of our lives together.

"This friend of mine is a nice guy; he told me what we should do. Tomorrow you and I will go to Vyborg by the first morning train." My dad was pleased he found the way to save his daughter from cold, humiliation and pneumonia.

"To Vyborg?" I was surprised. Vyborg is a small town close to the Finnish border. How could it be connected with my money exchange problem? I exclaimed, "Why to Vyborg? It's about three hours by electric train. But I have to be at work tomorrow. My boss won't let me miss another day."

"He will if you explain the situation to him; he's a good person; he'll understand."

"Let me go and give him a call right now." I rushed to a phone booth.

I called my department head and tried to explain to him the inexplicable. But he, being 'a product of the same Soviet system,' understood the main thing that there was the usual unpredictable meanness and stupidity of government bureaucrats. He allowed me to miss one more day of classes promising to sub for me. I was very grateful to him.

"Well, Papa, you were right, Yuri Petrovich is a nice man; we can go tomorrow wherever we need to go. Though I still don't get it, why to Vyborg?"

"Because they have a bank where you can exchange your money easily; there are not so many people there."

The next morning again I woke up at 4 A.M. and left home around five. I met my dad at the railway station, and we took the first train to Vyborg. It was even colder outside, but the train was well heated, and the trip was not bad. We arrived in Vyborg about half an hour before the bank opened. There were three people in the line—a big improvement in my situation. I felt sorry for all those people who were standing in that hor-rifying line in Leningrad that morning.

When the bank opened, there were three operators working, and I had my money exchanged in five minutes. For two hundred rubles I re-ceived three hundred and eighteen U.S. dollars. I could not believe how easy it was. With this money I could go to museums, buy souvenirs and feel more or less independent in the States during my short trip. I really did not need more money than that because the host families were supposed to take care of most of our expenses.

It all happened on November 5, 1989. That very evening it was an-nounced on the national news channel that starting with November 6th, 1989 there would be a new exchange rate between the ruble and dollar—six to one. I was shocked. The rumors became a fact. If I had not gone to Vyborg with my father, I would have gotten six times less money for my trip.

Even with perestroika and glasnost, many of the barriers of the old system remained but were hidden behind the façade of "freedom." Travel in the past was strictly regulated and controlled except for the few. The il-lusion in these new times of openness was that we were able to travel more freely abroad. Officially, the borders were open but in reality, how could people travel if they were allowed to have only thirty dollars for a trip? This was one more scam by the Russian government.

Our small victory over "the system" on that cold November morning was celebrated with a nice breakfast in a small Finnish restaurant. On that day and countless others our tender love for each other blended together like the coffee and cream the waitress brought us before the main course.

Out of all guardian-angels in my life my dad was The-Commander-in-Chief-Prime-Number-One Angel.

CHAPTER THIRTEEN

Washington Carnations
December 29, 1989, Washington D.C.

The non-stop flight from Moscow to Washington D.C. lasted for eleven hours. Our group of thirty-two people was having a lot of fun on board the plane telling jokes, playing cards, sharing our blood-chilling stories of getting our American visas, and drinking vodka or champagne to celebrate the upcoming adventures. Many members of our group had never been abroad before and were excited to be on their way to the great country of 'Uncle Sam'.

The United States of America had been idealized by several Soviet generations. It happened in part as a reaction to the merciless criticism of the Soviet press—a media we all understood to be controlled by the communists. Instead of hating Americans, most of the Soviet people admired the Americans. Obviously, all thirty-two members of the group, except for the KGB agents on the plane, were among those admirers.

About twelve or fifteen people in this group were my friends or acquaintances, and most of those were highly intellectual and knowledgeable professionals. Among them were two lawyers, three historians, a famous artist, a few college professors, several newly born Russian businessmen, and even a businesswoman—an absolutely fresh Russian phenomenon. All these people were supposed to be placed in American families of similar interests and professional background. During the long hours of the flight I got acquainted with all the rest of the members of the group. I especially liked an elderly Jewish couple. They were in their late sixties, and it was their first trip outside Russia. They were showing everybody in our group the picture of their seventeen-year-old granddaughter—a real beauty— sharing their hope to find an American boy friend for her while in the U.S. It sounded so naive, but at the same time so sincere that everybody who saw the picture promised the couple to inform them immediately if they met a nice guy of the appropriate age for this girl.

Our party continued for most of the flight. Being very superstitious (as most Russians are), I thought that something bad would happen because there was too much joy and laughter. Fortunately, everything went well; the landing in Washington D.C. was finally announced, and a few minutes later we found ourselves on American soil. It was incredible, unbelievable! Was it true? Was I dreaming? My heart was beating as fast as if I had finished a long and tiring race. It was hard to believe, but it was all real.

We picked up our carry-on bags and coats and walked through the gate into the customs area. I quickly passed the passport control and went to pick up my baggage. When I was moving toward the exit dragging the heavy suitcase overloaded with gifts and souvenirs for my future American friends, a customs officer stopped me and asked if I had oranges in my luggage. No other question could surprise me more because even if I wanted, I would not be able to find oranges in Leningrad in December, not until late February. I said, "No, I have arrived from Leningrad, Russia. We don't have oranges there at this time of the year."

"Oh, I see," the officer smiled. "But I suppose you have a lot of snow, don't you?"

"That's right, we have that in abundance." I have never seen a friendly customs officer before, so I was not sure how to react to his funny questions.

"Well, I guess you don't have snow with you." He laughed, "Have a wonderful stay in America."

"Thank you." And that was all? I was really in the free world. This procedure was extremely different from the one people experience when they arrive in Russia. The customs officers there have stone faces, piercing eyes, and they ask abrupt serious questions.

I understood this simple customs check was finished. I was in the world of easy going people who were relaxed and confident about their rights.

We entered the arrival area, and...right in front of me stood Stan. I dropped my suitcases and gasped, "Oh, no!"

Stan was smiling happily, just beaming with pleasure. He hoped to surprise me, and he succeeded. He held a beautiful and unusually large pink carnation that he handed me.

"Welcome to the United States of America," he said simply.

"Stan, how in the world did you manage to come? You didn't write that you'd be here." My lips were pronouncing those words, but my mind was still paralyzed. It just could not be true.

"I didn't know I would be here. But I am. I'll tell you later the whole story, but the main thing is that I could not miss the opportunity to greet you just the way you greeted me when I arrived for the first time in your country two years ago. Do you remember?"

"Yes, I remember. Thank you for the flower…I'm afraid I have to join my group."

My reason told me that there was nothing too special about Stan being there. He must have come on some business, and it was a pure coincidence that he happened to be at the airport. But my heart told me that there was much more than coincidence attached to this rosy carnation that I was pressing against my cheek. I was not just surprised; I was thrilled.

I saw my brother and friends standing in the distance looking with interest at Stan and me. They showed me I had to hurry up.

"I've got to go. Sorry. Everybody is waiting for me."

"No problem, let's go. Give me your heaviest suitcase; I will help you."

"I have to go to my host family, and I'm afraid I won't be able to spend any time with you."

"Please don't worry. I have arranged everything."

"What have you arranged?" Why was I so happy that he had arranged everything and what did that mean? Why did this "Potato Teacher" make me feel so protected and unafraid? For a brief moment all the excitement of the trip and our surprise meeting was replaced by a feeling of serenity that penetrated my whole being.

"You'll find out later. Now relax and don't worry. You'll be fine. Let's go." He started walking, then stopped and looked at me, "God, it's so good to see you."

We came up to the group, and I introduced Stan first to my brother and then to the leader of the group, Natasha. Stan told her that he knew where we should go and asked everybody to follow him. In the next hall we saw Joanne Benson, the organizer of the exchange. I had known Joanne since the Peace March in Russia in 1987. She was not surprised to see Stan. My guess was that these two had been conspiring to surprise me for some time.

This man, who I had written to for two years, had known for only three weeks, now had met me just as I met him at Leningrad with a carnation…my excitement was tempered with the awkwardness of the moment. I was the only one in the group of thirty-two people who was met with a flower. Since I had not hidden my surprise, many of my friends were happy for my "carnation moment". They acted as if they understood everything about the two of us.

But if they understood everything, I did not. I was more confused than ever. I knew very well that it was the time when Stan and his wife usually had a vacation together and went either to Hawaii or California. His wife used to suffer a lot in winter from the dark and cold weather, and Stan tried to help Carol overcome the anxiety by taking her to sunnier places in the winter time. What had happened this time? Why was he here in Washington D.C. instead of some sunny resort?

Following Joanne where she was leading us, I asked Stan, "Are you here with your family, your wife?"

"No, why?"

"Why? Because as far as I know you and Carol are usually in California before the New Year. What has happened this time?"

"This time it's very different. This time Ealaina, my Russian friend, has come to America. I couldn't miss seeing her."

"Really? So have you come here because of me?"

"Yes, I have. And there is also a conference on Peace and Conflict Resolution I wanted to attend at George Mason University."

"Where is your wife?" I insisted.

"She is in Iowa visiting her mother."

We were talking on our way to the bus which took us to a hotel where a welcome dinner was awaiting us. There were many families there greeting the Russians, getting acquainted, hugging and shaking hands.

There were two big tables full of various snacks, vegetables, fruit, juice, tea and coffee, anything you wanted. We filled our plates with all sorts of goodies and sat at tables. Joanne gave a greeting speech and began to introduce the host families to the Russians.

As it turned out the host family for my brother and me had not shown up, and it was arranged that another couple would give us a ride to our hosts' home.

Stan was quiet and seemed pleased. He was eating the vegetables, and

I saw him biting on a raw mushroom. I exclaimed in horror, "Stan, this mushroom looks raw!"

"Yes, it's raw; that's how I like them."

"Do you eat raw mushrooms in America? And raw cauliflower?"

"Yes, we eat a lot of raw vegetables. What's wrong with that?"

"It's not a custom in Russia. There such vegetables are always cooked."

"Well, you are beginning to learn about our customs. Americans are too lazy to cook what can be eaten fresh." He teased me.

"It's strange." It was less than an hour since my arrival in America, and my head was already spinning with confusion, and I was wondering what strange wonderful thing would happen next.

We were given lists of everybody's host families' phone numbers and addresses as well as the schedule for our tours in Washington D.C. for the coming six days. Stan received a copy of this list too. It was time to go.

I asked, "Where are you staying, Stan?"

"I have very good friends, a young couple who live about 5 miles west of the city. They are members of my church, Unitarian Universalists. I'm staying with them."

"Is it far from where Vlad and I will be staying?"

"I'm not sure; I don't know D.C. very well. But here everything is pretty far. The city itself is spread out, and people usually don't live in the city. They live in the suburbs in residential areas. Judging from your address you are going to be in a very nice place—Bethesda is a prestigious area. I'll give you a call tomorrow, and we'll arrange to do something fun together some time during these days, okay?"

"Of course it's okay."

"Have a good time with your host family. Vlad, it was a pleasure to meet you," Stan said turning to my brother.

"Nice to meet you too, Stan. Hope to see you again."

"For sure you'll see me again. Bye, I'll call you."

"Bye."

When we were in the car, Vlad asked me, "It's none of my business of course, but who is this man?"

"Stan is my friend. He was on the Peace Walk from Leningrad to Moscow two years ago. Since then we have been corresponding."

"I guess there were over two hundred Americans on the Peace Walk and all of them were your friends, but only one out of two hundred has come here to see you and from where?—from Idaho! Do you know where Idaho is?"

"Honestly? I have no idea. So many times I wanted to look at the map and never did. Where is it?"

"It's on the opposite side of the American continent, close to the Pacific Ocean."

"Really? So far away? Well, but it's not what you are hinting. Stan has not come specially to see me. It's a coincidence. He is here to attend a conference."

"Sure, and the conference's name is Elena."

"Vlad, please stop it. It's not what you think. He's married, has three children; he adores his wife; he is just a friend."

"All right, all right, don't get so fussy. He is a friend. I believe you." And then he added in a low voice, "We'll see..."

Vlad made me angry. At that time I truly wanted to believe that Stan was in D.C. not to see me but on business, and it was a mere coincidence that he was able to meet me at the airport. I decided not to continue this stupid discussion and began to enjoy the night ride by freeway to Bethesda.

In about twenty minutes we were in the house of our host family. Mark, Pam and their four-year-old daughter, Kellie, were friendly and hospitable people. We were shown to the room that my brother and I were going to share. It was a cozy little room with everything necessary in it and with a huge bouquet of pink carnations where I added the one given to me by Stan.

It was the day of pink carnations.

CHAPTER FOURTEEN

Different Blood
December 30, Washington D.C.

It was 8:30 A.M. when the phone rang and Pam was speaking with somebody for quite a long time. When she hung up she said to me, "Elena, that was your friend Stan."

"Why didn't he talk to me?"

"He was in a hurry to the conference meeting, but he wanted to know about our plans, and I told him we're going to have a party and he could come and join us. It took me a long time to explain to him how to find us. I'm sorry, I had no time to ask you—would it be okay if he came to the party?"

"Of course, but only if it's okay with you."

I was a little disappointed Stan did not ask for me, but I was happy he was coming over that night. After all, he was the only person I knew in D.C., and it would be great to have his support when our guests would be asking me and Vlad questions at this party.

"No problem," said Pam, "Actually, I think he will even make it more interesting because he promised to show the slides that he took in Russia."

"I heard about them, but I've never seen them. I'm sure it'll be really entertaining for everybody."

Pam decided not to make this first day in America too hard on us. She knew we were trying to get over jet lag. So instead of sightseeing and museums Vlad and I took it easy and lingered most of the day between our bedroom and the kitchen taking short naps and having little snacks from time to time. In the morning though, after breakfast, Pam took us for a nice little walk around the neighborhood. It was a beautiful area with lots of huge pines with crystals of icy snow in different shapes and configurations still stuck in their needles. These slender pines looked decorated for the Holiday Season. I recalled the pines in Stan's story. These pines like those who lived on the separate island, I imagined, reached out their soft, scented branches to greet the New Year.

We were admiring the big beautiful houses and sparkling, clean cars parked in front of them. People usually did not lock their cars because nobody was stealing in this quiet cozy neighborhood. The streets were amazingly still. Most people were probably at work, but if we did see somebody passing by, those people would smile and say "hi" to us—complete strangers. Vlad and I came from a different "planet", which I started to call "The Unsmiling World" after our walk around Bethesda.

Part of our little tour was a stop at the local grocery store, which was another, even more powerful shock. Tears came to my eyes when I saw a shelf about a half a mile long filled up with an amazing variety of cheeses from all over the world. My heart squeezed with pain when I thought about my poor Russian compatriots, mostly women, standing in lines for hours to buy at least one kind of cheese. Even though the time of long lines for food was in the past and more and more food had started to appear in the stores in Russia, it was still impossible to compare the abundance in this American store with what we had in even our biggest supermarkets in Leningrad or Moscow. My brother and I told Pam how our mother had spent half of her life standing in lines for food. We had an interesting discussion and in the end all three of us agreed that communism had failed primarily because it could not supply people with such simple things as food and clothes.

When we came back home, we continued our discussion at lunch talking about several generations of Russian people who had lived during the years of communism but who probably would not want to acknowledge that their ideals and lives were a failure. At least I did not think that my life was a failure. My brother though was not that optimistic. He passionately hated Communists. He criticized and blamed them for "all the sins of the world" and mostly for the lack of opportunities for the people. He felt he could have achieved more had he not had to constantly struggle with that 'rotten' system.

I was different. I simply did not notice all that 'communist froth' around me. I lived in my personal little world always trying to surround myself with people I loved and cherished, and as to politics—I never cared about it too much. For me it was like the weather; if it was cold, windy or stormy, I would simply put another sweater on to protect myself from a phenomenon I could not control or really understand.

Now, in Bethesda, living with a middle-class American family, I started thinking more about the privileged few in my country, the Communists, who I had for whatever reason tried to ignore. I thought about how they used their power and privilege to preserve a status quo that favored them and at the same time hurt so many. In fact, they were the ones who had created the elaborate maize that determined in so many ways what I could and could not do. They determined whether I should stand in line for food for several hours or use my time better but stay hungry. They even determined how many square meters per person my apartment should be, and if it exceeded 'the norm', they had the power to take it away from me. I did not choose them to make my decisions for me, but they imposed their will upon me.

I saw that an ordinary bank officer and a freelance nutrition consultant, my hosts, lived in a three-bedroom house with all conveniences, had two new cars, could afford to travel to Europe and were planning to send their daughter to a private college. I could not help but compare them with the same type of a family in Russia. Such a family there would probably live in a small one-bedroom apartment, would be saving for a Russian car for most of their lives, would not even dream about traveling to Europe, and would have only one choice of education for their children—public. They would hardly manage to buy some decent furniture; the wife would be washing by hand all her life and the husband would die from alcoholism at the age of fifty two.

I was analyzing and comparing those few things that I just started to see in America during the first thirty hours of our stay. My comparative exercise was compromised by my constant struggle with sleepiness. Just when I was finally about to doze off, the door bell rang. I looked at the clock. It was only 5:30 P.M., too early for the guests to arrive. Who could it be? I heard the familiar velvet baritone; it was Stan. I rushed to the hall as if I was going to see my closest relative whom I had not seen for years.

Stan was wearing a green and red sweater still being in the post-Christmas mood. He shook hands with Pam and Mark and handed a small box to Kellie. Then he looked at me and Vlad, "Well, how's your first day in America been?"

"We're struggling with jet lag. I'm beginning to feel better now that it is closer to my biological morning; it's 8:30 A.M. in Leningrad. From this point on I promise to be a really fun person to communicate with," I said.

"Sounds pretty confusing, but I'm glad you're waking up now."

We went to the dining room to help Pam and Mark to set the table.

By 6 P.M. we had a house full of guests. Many of Mark and Pam's friends wanted to come and look at the Russians. They had never seen a Russian before and we seemed to be the exotic item on the menu that evening.

It was a potluck. I did not know what that meant, and at first I was surprised that Pam was preparing only a salad for fifteen people. I thought it was another American custom, not to feed the guests too much. In Russia a woman would spend all day in the kitchen making many different delicious dishes. By the time the guests arrived she would be exhausted, but she would still look great all dressed up and made up with a glorious smile on her face. She would joke, laugh and entertain, and in between, by magic, new dishes would appear on the table followed by numerous desserts and drinks. The guests would finally leave way after midnight, and she would clean up the table and do the dishes. After that she would crash in bed half alive and murmur to her fast asleep husband what a great party it had been. Russian women are like that.

Here in America it was different. Soon I understood what a wonderful thing a potluck was. The American table became covered with numerous dishes too, but the difference was that Pam was not tired because every guest brought something nice to eat. I could not say that all that potluck food impressed me, but it was possible to choose something tasty.

During dinner Stan and I sat next to each other, but we could not talk, as people were asking questions constantly, and Vlad and I had hardly any time to swallow a piece of lasagna or take a sip of wine. The interest in new, democratic Russia was immense. People asked about Gorbachev, his reforms, the attitude of Russians to Gorbachev's wife, the history of the czars, the everyday life of the Russian people, their education system and much more.

Finally, Stan announced he had brought slides about Russia, and we moved to the living room. He was showing the slides making comments about his impressions during his visit. This was the first time I saw his slides. I knew Stan had been traveling all over Idaho showing them to schoolchildren and people in churches, clubs, and associations. The slides and the comments were well done. His slides were mostly about the life of common people and children that looked so much like others in the world.

He was not trying to sound superior, which often happened with other Americans; he just sounded like a simple human being deeply concerned about others. He stated that people in the Soviet Union and the United States in order to be happy and have good lives must be free from the threat of nuclear war. He was a man with a kind and compassionate heart. Everybody at the party enjoyed his slide show immensely.

Suddenly one of the guests whispered in my ear, "I'm really surprised to see that the children look very much like American kids. I'm confused because I heard that Russians have a different blood, so I expected them to look differently."

"What do you mean by 'different blood'?" I could not understand his question.

"I mean that the Russian blood consists of something different. I'm not an anthropologist or a doctor, and I don't know any details about it. I just heard that Russians don't have the same blood type as we, Americans, do."

"Like what?" I still could not get it, "Do you mean there is a lot of alcohol in it?" I tried to make a joke.

"I don't think so." The guy was serious, "There was something else that our teacher explained in school, but I don't remember what exactly it was. I remember it as different though."

I was upset. I could not believe that the propaganda in American schools could be that stupid, and that people actually believed in stories like that. I whispered furiously, "I don't know what your teacher told you. But believe me; Russians have exactly four blood types like all other human beings on Earth. As far as I remember they are A, B, AB, and O."

The man didn't reply; he just stared at me and I stared back.

By 10:00 P.M. the guests began to leave one by one, and Stan also had to go because he was staying far from Bethesda. He told me he would like to spend some time together, just the two of us, and invited me out for dinner on Friday. He was going to return home early on Saturday. I was not sure about our plans for the weekend, but he said he had talked to Pam and Mark, and they had no objections. So Friday evening we were going to have dinner together.

CHAPTER FIFTEEN

The Wish Star
January 3, 1990, Washington D.C.

The next few days were filled up with tours and impressions. We went to the White House, to the House of Congress, and to the Library of Congress, the Smithsonian, all the Memorials, the Aquarium, and the National Geographic museum. We tried different cuisines, and I decided Thai and Chinese were my favorites. We went shopping, had parties and attended a Unitarian church gathering. We met many interesting people, had numerous discussions, debates and even a press conference with the reporters of several local newspapers. We visited schools, universities, hospices, and hospitals.

At times we wondered—did Americans try to show us as much of their life as possible in one week, or were they trying to show off a rare exhibit—Russians—to as many Americans as they could?

Vlad and I hardly ever slept. We were still fighting insomnia at night and incredible sleepiness during the day. We felt and at times acted like two Zombies, but we did not want to miss anything. Maybe it was our only chance in life to see "the Capital of the World."

Every morning and evening Stan would call and ask me about my adventures. We would talk for a long time. These calls made me feel special; I was the only one to receive a regular, daily call from an Idaho friend.

On Friday morning, the day of our date, Stan had called before we left for our planned tour, "I am so happy we'll see each other tonight, and I hope you won't be in a hurry. We'll be able to spend the whole evening together. By the way, I know you'll be going places all day and probably wear casual clothes, but is it possible for you to take a nice dress with you? I made reservations for dinner in a sophisticated restaurant, and knowing you I'm sure you'll feel better if you're dressed up."

"Do you mean I have to carry my dress and shoes with me all day? And am I supposed to change in the car afterwards?"

"No, no. Please don't worry yourself for nothing. Just take your dress and shoes with you and leave them in the car while you're doing your sight-seeing and pick them up when you come to see me. I'll take you to a place where you can rest and change without any problem."

This sounded mysterious, but I trusted Stan and knew if he advised me to do so, there was some reason for it. So I replied, "I'm glad I've brought my favorite fancy dress with me. It sounds like today will be the right occasion to wear it."

"Great," said Stan, "I'll be waiting for you at 4:00 P.M. in front of the subway entrance. Pam knows where it is."

"See you at four," I said.

How I wanted that day to slip away as soon as possible so that I could finally have a quiet evening in the company of the man who had written the story of the Pines and Birches just for me. We'll talk about the Peace Walk and gossip about our common acquaintances. It'll be a lot of fun.

When my brother saw me packing my best dark blue dress, black pumps and a cosmetic bag with mascara, rouge, eye pencil and compact powder, he asked in surprise, "What's all that about? Why are you packing?"

"Stan and I are going out for dinner, and he wants me to look nice." I said trying not to look in Vlad's eyes.

"But where are you going to change?" insisted Vlad.

"Actually, I have no idea. Stan told me not to worry."

"Not to worry? I'm afraid if you don't worry now, it'll be too late to worry later." My brother was definitely suspicious and not happy with my behavior.

"Vlad, can't you simply be excited for me? I'm going to have a fun evening, that's all."

My brother did not reply. He even tried not to look at me all day, just avoided looking at me, which was quite annoying. His whole demeanor sent silent waves of reproach. I knew he felt uncomfortable as he probably thought he was responsible for his little sister, but how could I explain to him that I was a grown up experienced woman and did not need his protection?

Fortunately, that day was so busy I had little time to concentrate on my brother's feelings. In the morning, two sisters from Iowa, who had stayed with my family in Leningrad, arrived to see Vlad and me. The girls,

Pam, Vlad and I spent an interesting day in Georgetown. We also went to see the Vietnam Memorial—the mile-long black granite wall with almost 60,000 names of American sons, husbands, fathers and brothers who fought and lost their lives in one of the numerous sad wars of this poor suffering planet.

I was deeply impressed by the unusual statue of Albert Einstein. The face of this wise old man had holes instead of eyes, but those orbs conveyed the wonder and majesty of one man's mind as his mathematical genius helped us understand what we cannot even yet see completely. I thought then that if Albert Einstein could ever see this monument, he would have been very pleased. It is an incredible piece of art.

By the time of my date, I was exhausted.

We arrived at the subway station exactly at 4:00, but Stan was not there. He was not there thirty minutes later and after that another thirty minutes passed. I felt uneasy keeping everybody with me waiting out in the cold wind, but they did not want to leave me there all by myself, just in case Stan didn't show up at all. I felt disappointed and nervous. I looked ridiculous—cold and tired in my fur coat and boots, standing for an hour at the entrance to the subway with my sack of 'cocktail attire.'

Exactly at the moment when I decided not to wait anymore, Stan appeared. He looked guilty and made apologies for keeping us waiting. The problem was that he could not leave the meeting at the conference as early as he had planned, and then he lost his way. He did not expect to be so late and was in despair. When he saw we were still there, he sighed with relief, "Thank God you are here."

Finally, Stan and I let the rest of the party go home. We went downstairs by an escalator. I recalled our escalator race in Moscow. This one was five times slower. I asked, "Where are we going?"

"I guess you are tired, so I thought we should go to my hotel, rest a little, and then at seven go to the restaurant—I've reserved a table for two."

"As far as I remember you were staying at your friends'."

"I was for the first couple of days, but then they had to leave on vacation, and I didn't want to be alone in their house. It's also pretty far from the university where the conference is being held."

"I don't think I feel comfortable going to your hotel room..." I thought that my brother had been right and I should probably make my choices now before it was too late.

"Please don't feel uncomfortable. It's a nice hotel; you can see the Pentagon out of the window of my room. Believe me it's a spectacular view. You can relax and change there, and then we'll go out; that's all. Actually, there's also a wonderful swimming pool and a spa there, you might want to use them."

"But I don't have a swim suit and what is a spa?"

Stan smiled, "The swimming suit is not a problem; we can buy one. And the spa is a bathtub with bubbles and great water massage. Your tiredness will disappear by magic. The swimming pool area is beautiful; it's decorated with exotic plants, flowers and Christmas lights. You'll enjoy it, I promise."

"Will they let me in at the hotel? I'm not their guest."

"What do you mean? Why wouldn't they? And who are these 'they' you are talking about?"

"Aren't there guards at the entrance?" I asked.

It took a minute before Stan replied, "I don't think so. Anybody can enter the hotel." He was definitely bewildered by my questions, but for me there was nothing strange or unusual in them. I said, "Not in Russia."

"Really? Why not?"

"I don't know why, but I know you can't be in most of the expensive hotels unless you are staying there. Maybe it's for security reasons."

"I promise you'll be very secure here even though there're no special guards at the entrance." Stan smiled.

"Okay, if you promise, we can go."

When we came out of the subway, the hotel shuttle van was waiting for us at the exit. The driver was a beautiful black woman with her hair done in hundreds of braids intricately arranged on her head. We were the only passengers. The woman looked at us through the driver's mirror and smiled, "You are one happy couple! Ready to go?"

"We are not a couple; we are simply friends," I mentioned sternly.

"Simply friends can be a couple," she giggled and started the engine. The van ran smoothly without any noise. The seats were soft velour, pleasant to touch. After probably two minutes, it stopped.

"Well, here we are. You have a wonderful evening," the happy-faced woman said.

"Thank you. You too," Stan smiled and gave her a tip.

Suddenly I stopped worrying. I was in a good mood. The kind attitude of this unknown woman lifted my spirits. I wanted to smile at everybody too.

We found ourselves in front of a huge building probably as high as thirty-five floors, all glass and mirrors, very modern. A thick and immaculately clean carpet stretched from the street across the sidewalk to the entrance of the hotel. There were no guards as I had expected but only a man in a hotel uniform helping an elderly couple with their bags. He was very friendly. He was also smiling like the van driver. I asked Stan, "Why are all these people so personal? Maybe I don't want them to smile at me, and especially telling us that we are a nice couple." Obviously, my decision to smile back at people and actually doing it were two different things.

"I don't mind if they tell us we are a nice couple. I actually like it," Stan shrugged.

"But Stan, it's not true. I don't want to have any misunderstanding between us." I felt the warning and protective voice of my brother speaking through my mouth.

"I'm not misunderstanding. People in America are simply friendly, and especially if they are in service jobs, they try to be pleasant because they don't want to lose their job."

"Yes, I understand that, but still it's a little strange to me. A bus driver would never be so personal in Leningrad. I think, on the contrary, if he got personal, he would lose his job. And I say 'he' because there are no women bus or van drivers there."

"Is that true? Why, I wonder?" Stan seemed surprised.

"Because this job is considered to be too stressful and hard for women." I thought it was important for Stan to understand my culture where men and women had different social roles. I felt superior at least in the matter of how women are treated in Russia—protected from hard labor. But my feelings of superiority quickly vanished when I remembered how women in Russia, after working all day came home to a second job while their husbands were watching TV on sofas. Then I pictured my host, Mark, who usually after work cooked dinner, cleaned the house, did the laundry and worked in the yard while Pam enjoyed yoga, chatting with friends on the phone and reading books.

"Well, in America women have been fighting for emancipation and equality; they don't want to be discriminated against in any way. They take any job. But, unfortunately, there are still places where women are paid less than men for the same labor."

"Really? Well, we have achieved at least something in Russia. There is no such thing as less pay because of a difference in gender. Women are doctors, teachers, lawyers, school principals, road-workers; sometimes they are taxi drivers, but for some reason they never drive trucks or buses."

"Puzzling," said Stan.

We were going upstairs in an elevator, which was spacious and quiet. There were mirrors on the walls and on the ceiling and a thick carpet on the floor. Soft music was playing. I had never seen an elevator like that in my life; I even felt sorry to leave it when it stopped on the eighteenth floor. I still felt uncomfortable about going to Stan's room and about being alone with him there. I was searching for some pretext not to go when he stopped and opened the door of room number 1877. We went in.

The room was huge. Its front part was a living room with two big couches, a small coffee table and a TV set. There was a print of a Claude Monet landscape on the wall in an expensive wood and gold frame. I liked that it was Monet, my favorite among the impressionists, as if Stan knew what to choose.

In the other end of the room there was a bed. "It's not a bed," I thought, "it's a sexadrome. Could it be any bigger?" To the left there was a door to the bathroom. The opposite wall was all glass. There was a beautiful round table and soft armchairs by that wall-to-wall window.

I slowly went up to it and stood in awe for a long time as my eyes attempted to measure the dual horizons of heaven and earth—a darkening sky with newly-born bright stars and a city wrapped in millions of lights that both softened and accented the night. Among those numerous lights a pentagon shape could be easily identified. That was it—the world military center. The word 'Pentagon' had always scared me before. It meant 'threat, force, horror, and blood,' but that day when I saw it being so magnificent but quiet and beautiful, my fears dissipated. All of a sudden the feeling I had at the airport came back, I felt secure and calm in this hotel room alone with my friend. I was not worried anymore, and I did not feel uncomfortable.

Stan came up to me and also looked out of the window. He said, "Do you see that bright star? The blue one?"

"I have seen it before. Vlad and I were out walking and were surprised by its color. I've never seen a star so big and bright and silver blue. It's surreal."

"Exactly, I think Washington D.C. is the only place where you see it. I've never seen it in Idaho. When I saw it for the first time I made a wish."

"What was it? Can you tell me?"

"I'll tell you when my wish comes true," Stan said softly.

"That's right. Don't tell me, otherwise it won't."

We sat in the armchairs across from the window. We did not turn the lights on; the magic illumination came from the stars. Stan put his hand on mine, looked into my eyes and whispered, "I was dreaming about this moment so many times in the past two years. Ealaina, you must know that I love you."

My heart began to beat fast. I blushed. I felt a strange weakness in my stomach. An incredible feeling overwhelmed me. I remained silent. Stan continued, "I knew I was in love with you when I wrote that story for you in Moscow two years ago. My heart was breaking when I was leaving Russia. I couldn't imagine I would never see you again. Then I thought that it was just the spur of the moment, and that everything would change and go back to normal when I came home to my family. But it never did. My feelings for you have only become stronger. I am thinking of you day and night. I know that I love you."

He was waiting for me to say something. But I did not know what to say. Was I in love with him and did not want to admit it? I definitely had feelings for him; otherwise why would I be so happy when I saw him at the Washington airport? Why would I always be so happy when I got letters from him or heard his voice on the phone? Why would I be so proud of him when he had been giving a brilliant slide presentation about Russia at Pam's house? Why would everything in his life—his job, his degree, and his interests—be always so important to me? Why would I always secretly dislike his wife though I had never met her? Was I jealous? Why would I always feel peace and serenity in his presence?

And all of a sudden I heard myself saying, "Stan, I love you too."

His eyes brightened, and he sighed deeply, "I'm so glad to hear it. You have made me the happiest man in the world. To know that you love me...what else can I desire? Thank you for being honest with me."

"To tell you the truth I am surprised with myself, but it's exactly what I feel. I love you. I want to be part of your life. I know we are getting into a big mess, but I feel so thankful as if a huge weight has dropped off my shoulders."

"It's exactly what I feel," he said.

For a long time we were simply looking at each other. We no longer lived on separate islands. We loved each other.

Then Stan said, "You wanted to go and see the swimming pool and all the flowers and decorations there and also relax in the spa. We can go now; we still have time before dinner."

"Do you want me?" I heard myself whispering.

"Yes, my love."

It was 9:30 P.M. and it was for the second time that Stan called the restaurant and checked on our reservation. I did not want to get up; the silk of the pillows and sheets was soothingly cool. I was lying on this huge bed thinking about our happiness when I recalled that American woman on the Peace Walk—the one that had asked me to translate to the Russian camera man that she wanted to spend the night with him. I recalled how abnormal her behavior seemed that night to me, and how I thought I would never be able to do anything like that. Yes, Stan was right when he said once to me, "Never say never."

We were hungry and heavenly tired. We had to go out of the room and eat and have some fun in the outside world. I put on my elegant dress and straightened up my hair. Stan looked at me with the adoring look of a man in love and said, "Wow! You are my czarina. This dress…did you buy it here in D.C.?"

"Believe it or not, I bought it in Leningrad. Isn't it pretty?"

"You make it pretty. You make everything you touch pretty. You know, when I saw you at the airport the other day, you looked like a movie star in that fur coat. And believe me I was thrilled to see you were wearing the white wool scarf I had given you in Moscow before my departure back in 1987."

"Stan, this scarf is so dear to me. It's connected with those unforgettable memories of the wonderful time of the Walk—the time that changed our lives and eventually brought us to where we are now."

Then I asked suddenly, "Do you feel guilty?"

"Guilty? Why? No!" Stan exclaimed, but then he added softly, "Well, maybe I do a little because I've never been unfaithful in my marriage, and it's a strange feeling, but I also know that I need to be honest with myself and you, and it's ridiculous to conceal the strong love we feel for each other. If we do, it'll eventually destroy our marriages and us anyway. We both deserve to be happy, don't you think?"

"Yes, we do. But…what will we do now?"

"Let's not talk about it now. Let us enjoy and celebrate our love. We'll be fine, trust me." Stan hugged me tenderly, and this soft and warm embrace calmed me down. I thought of Scarlet O'Hara's 'I won't think about it now. I'll think about it later.' So I told myself the same and felt better, "Well, it's too late to go to the spa, I guess, but are you ready to have dinner? I'm starving."

"That's my kind of girl. I'm ready."

First we went to the lounge on the top floor of the hotel. The view from there was romantic. There was a holiday atmosphere, the music was playing softly; the people were dressed up, having drinks, laughing, and talking. We had wine, sitting at a small table by the window with a flickering pink candle on it. The flames in the fireplace brought in additional coziness and charm. Happiness radiated from both of us. We tried not to think about parting in a few hours, but we were both feeling the pain and sadness arising in our hearts.

"Remember I told you I made a wish looking at the blue star?" Stan touched my hand, "I want you to know that it has come true."

CHAPTER SIXTEEN

The Strange Dream
January 3, 1990, Washington D.C.

I arrived home past midnight. Vlad was not in bed; he was outside waiting for me. When I appeared he muttered, "You promised to be home before ten, and it's past midnight, and you did not even call. Do you think this behavior is acceptable?" His face expressed reproach, but I saw a glimpse of interest in his eyes.

"I'm sorry. It just didn't work out the way I had planned."

"Really?" Vlad raised his voice a little. His tone was sarcastic, "I don't care what relationship you have with *that* man; it's none of my business, but I do care about your attitude to your brother and the people you are staying with. Everybody was worried."

"I know I didn't do right, but the time flew so quickly. We hardly had any time to talk at all." I tried to defend myself.

"Yah, sure 'to talk'. I guess..."

"What do you mean?"

"I mean you have to remember you are a married woman. You can't simply do what you want. You have responsibilities. Do you understand how serious it is?"

"But you have just told me it was none of your business." I protested.

"Well, I changed my mind. It is my business. Your husband, my brother-in-law, allowed you to go to America, and he hopes you are okay here. I feel I'm responsible for your behavior."

"I don't understand what you mean by 'your husband allowed you to go to America.' I allow myself to do things I want to do. I'm not anybody's slave or thing." I was angry with Vlad but mostly because his words reminded me of the truth I tried not to think of.

"All right, stop being angry with me," Vlad retreated.

"I *am* angry. Don't you understand I'm a grown up person and can answer for my own actions?"

"I do understand it, but please don't do anything that you will regret later. And remember you have a son."

"What does my son have to do with this discussion? Vlad, why are you talking to me like I am a criminal? I'm not sure in anything myself."

"You see? You are already hesitating in the rightness of your behavior. I'm afraid it might be too late when you become sure. I want the best for you. I'm only trying to warn you not to do anything that can harm you, your marriage, and your life." His tone became softer.

"Don't worry, I won't. I promise." It seemed we made up. We could never be upset with each other for too long.

It was easy to make a promise, but I knew that I had already harmed at least my marriage. I felt guilty and confused. I could not understand how and why it all happened to me. My life had been so well synchronized—family, work, friends, and hobbies.

What did I do? I ruined it all. I faced the abyss of shame, whispering behind my back and lies, lies, lies every day of my life.

What was real here and now with me was an incredible sensation of happiness. Was I really in love? Or was it just the atmosphere—the stars, the lights, just the two of us in the Universe?

I loved Stan. At least I thought I did. But what could I do with my love? Where would it take me? We lived half a world away from each other. We originated from different countries and cultures. We spoke different languages. We had different customs and habits. We were both committed to other people. It was crazy. I had never been so light-minded in my life before. I had never done anything that could compromise or jeopardize my marriage. I had been devoted to my vows and had not broken them, even when there had been situations when other men expressed their interest in having an affair. But this time it was all so different. There was something about Stan that had attracted me to him since our second meeting at the dinner in Repino. I was sure it was not just an affair. What was it?

I knew what it was. Stan and I were kindred spirits. We felt the same way about people, friends, children, teaching, and simply life in general. With all the enormous differences between us, we still had the strongest spiritual bond possible. I did not want to admit it, but deep in my heart I knew that with my husband it was all the opposite—we lived together; we spoke the same language; we shared the same history of the same nation; we had a son who was the mixture of our flesh and blood, and yet our spirits were galaxies apart.

Well, everybody makes mistakes in life; I was not an exception and I was not perfect. What I did was wrong, terribly wrong, but I was in love.

Love's surprising melody takes us to places that our rational mind can never imagine, and that is why I found myself half a world away from home in the arms of another man who I hardly knew.

It was a sleepless night. I was confused; after all I had to go back to Leningrad and continue to live my life. The best thing would be to repent when I came home. No, I would never tell my husband about it. Instead, I would go to my favorite St. Andrew's Church and repent in front of the icon of St. Nicolas. If I honestly admitted that what I had done was wrong, my life would get back on track. "My husband will not find out because I will never tell him. Stan is leaving in several hours. I might not ever see him or hear from him again and if I did, I would tell him it was a mistake on his part and mine. I will have to bury my feelings for him forever." I tried to fall asleep but found myself struggling with feelings that warred with each other.

"At least there'll be something exciting to recall when I am old," I whispered in my pillow. I finally fell asleep and saw a dream:

Stan and I were sitting on a bench in the Summer Gardens in the heart of Leningrad. It was a beautiful warm afternoon, and a soft breeze from the Neva River touched our faces. Right in front of us was a little pond with clean silver water that reflected the slender figures of two white swans that were in love. The tranquility of the pond suddenly changed when I saw the reflection of my husband's face in the water. He was angry; his face flushed red with rage. I was so startled and frightened by this unexpected apparition that I thought to flee. I was afraid that he would rise up out of the pond to harm us. Stan was not afraid but held my hand and reached out with his free hand and passed it over Vadim's reflection. My husband seemed to wait for a moment for me to speak but I answered him only with silence. His image disappeared and was replaced by the reflection of the two white swans and a beautiful tapestry of colors on the water created by the setting sun.

CHAPTER SEVENTEEN

The Gardenias in the Fridge
January 6, 1990, Philadelphia, PA

It was our second day in Philadelphia where our whole group of thirty two people went by bus from Washington D.C. The trip was merry. We were exchanging our first American experiences. Some people were happy and became friends with their host families forever. A few were disappointed; they hated the days spent with their hosts—a usual situation when strangers try to live together. One of my friends, Sasha, who was traveling with his wife, was dissatisfied with their stay in Washington D.C. During our bus trip he vented to me, "Elena, can you imagine a man like me, who is used to good nutrition at least four times a day, eating little, seldom and vegetarian food? In the morning we had juice, for lunch (if any) a veggie sandwich, and then for dinner a cup of broccoli soup and pasta with squash sauce—all tasting slightly sweet. Brrr...I feel sick when I think about it. I lost my appetite. And all this is happening to me in the Country of Food!"

"Yah, I think you lost some weight." I felt sorry for Sasha.

"I sure have, and I don't need to."

"You look great." I tried to reassure him.

"I probably look great, but I don't feel that great. Instead of being interested in monuments and museums all my thoughts were concentrated on food. I have been seeing a steak in my dreams for five nights."

"Don't you tell me about dreams. I've been seeing weird dreams too." I pictured the pond and the swans...but I quickly returned to reality, "Why didn't you go and buy a steak and cook it yourself?" I asked.

"Firstly, because the nearest food store was seven miles away. Secondly, you're not supposed to eat steak if every evening you're listening to a lecture how wonderful it is 'to eat right' and 'to live right' and 'to be perfect'. Their shitty 'perfect ness' stuck in my throat instead of the steak." Sasha sounded irate.

"Come on, stop cursing. I don't recognize you," I exclaimed.

"It's because you've always seen me full. If a man is full and not dreaming of food, he won't curse. But a hungry man is an angry beast."

"I see that, and if you keep it on, you'll grow an ugly tail and horns," I teased him. "Now tell me if there was anything good in Washington." I decided to change the subject.

"Actually there was," Sasha's face lit up, "It was really neat to find the books by my father in the Library of Congress catalog. I didn't expect that; he'll be thrilled when I tell him about it." Sasha's father was a well known historian in Russia.

"How wonderful. Have you found your books or papers, too?"

"You know, it never came to my mind to check. I just took it for granted they wouldn't have mine as they're not that scholarly as my father's."

"Why not? Sasha, you were too hungry and not thinking straight." I laughed. "Next time when you go there please check."

"Next time? When will this 'next time' be? Anna and I have spent all our savings to buy the tickets. And we've been saving for many years. No, my dear, there'll be no 'next time'."

"Please don't be so categorical. You never know what life is preparing for you. Who knows, maybe in several years you'll live abroad. Never say never," I was proud of myself; what a good student I was—I remembered Stan's words well.

"What's the matter with you? Where does this capitalistic optimism come from? These Americans have done their brainwashing job well; you don't sound Russian anymore." Hungry Sasha was sarcastic.

"It's not 'capitalistic' but rather 'democratic'." I laughed, and to myself I thought—it's Stan's optimism speaking in me. It was so sweet to have my little secret thoughts about Stan.

After about a five-hour drive we finally arrived at a small place twelve miles south of Philadelphia. There were families waiting for Russian friends in the local church; the tables were set with the usual fruit, vegetables and desserts. There were 'Welcome' posters, balloons, still Christmas decorations all over the place; the Beatles' *"All We Need Is Love"* was playing. Thanks to the name tags Vlad and I spotted our host family easily. Sandy Scott was a woman of about thirty-five with three kids—two girls and a boy. Her husband was waiting for us at home.

We became friends with our new family and especially the kids right away. I fell in love with little Bryan, for I was missing my own boy terribly. I never really knew what to do with girls while boys-kids were always my favorite. I was used to boys' games: hockey, basketball, little toy cars, monsters, and kites. I knew what kinds of stories a boy would like and how to occupy a boy for hours with something that would interest him. Vlad, on the contrary, knew how to find common language with girls, for he had a little daughter. So we were happy that there were a lot of kids in our new host family and we spent a lot of time with them.

On the second day of our stay, during breakfast, Sandy saw out of the kitchen window a strange van pulling up to the house. She uttered, "A flower van in our drive way? It must have lost its way. I'll go and find out."

We all watched her talk to the driver and then saw him give her a box with a big red bow on it. Sandy came back into the house, sat the box on the table and announced, "Elena, it's for you."

"For me? What is it? Who is it from?" I was sincerely surprised.

"I don't know, but I presume it's flowers."

Vlad looked at me reproachfully and shook his head, "It's never boring when my sister is around."

"Why are you looking at me like this? I didn't do anything bad," I said.

"Come on. Open it. Aren't you interested to see what's inside?" Sandy and the kids were genuinely intrigued.

"I can help you," little Bryan was more impatient than anybody else.

"Okay Bryan, open it." I smiled.

The boy was happy—he was allowed to rip off the pretty paper and the bow. There was a white box inside. Bryan opened it. There was another transparent box with a corsage of tender white gardenias in it. The flowers were fresh and beautiful. There was also a little card pinned to the box. The boy handed me the card, "Read it, Elena."

I looked at the beginning of the note—"Dearest Elena..." I knew I was blushing. I uttered, "It's...personal."

I ran to my room, sat on my bed and waited for a long time. For some reason I was afraid to read this note. What if it was a good bye note? Would I be able to handle it?

I finally read:

Dearest Elena,

The time in Washington D.C. with you has touched my life and heart in ways I never imagined possible. Until you were by my side, I had never realized how incomplete my life has been. I was on the verge of tears on Saturday as I flew across the country away from you. I understand though that our love for one another does make us happier and more complete.

I think of you often, my Love.

P.S. In a new age birches and pines grow on the same land, a place where beautiful flowers stand in colorful chorus to celebrate and sing of dreams fulfilled and to cast promises of sweet fragrance and color that will be experienced in a life time (together) of perpetual spring.

Stan

I reread the note. It sounded so poetic. Stan was a romantic writer. His words touched my heart.

Suddenly, I thought of my husband, who had been writing beautiful poems before we had met. Then he had stopped. When I had asked him why, his answer was, "I write only when I am unhappy. Now that I am with you I am happy and I have an empty head for verses." It seemed strange. Maybe he really did not love me anymore? Or maybe he had only been in love with love and once we were married, the day-to-day grind of life had simply stolen away any romantic interest he had in me at all. Yes, exactly, that's what had happened to both of us. The sparkle of love was like a blast, strong and quick. Then we calmed down and our life together became just a routine. Was that why I responded to Stan's feelings? I had told Stan I loved him, but was that true? Did I really feel love? Or was it just a new spice added to my life that I enjoyed?

What I felt for sure was guilt. "How will I come home and continue my life like nothing happened? Should I tell Vadim everything? No, never. It will only ruin our lives, and it will make so many people unhappy. First of all our son—he needs to have a father. Stan is writing about our life 'together', but that's a poetic fantasy, a utopia. It is impossible, and he should stop writing me, sending flowers, calling. I will tell him as soon as I have a chance," I thought.

This chance happened right the very minute when I was still tormenting myself with these unpleasant thoughts. Sandy knocked on the door of my room and said there was a phone call for me. I picked up the phone, "Hello?"

"Hi my Love. How are you? Have you got the flowers?"

"Yes, I have the flowers. The gardenias are beautiful. Thank you very much. But…"

"But what?"

There was a silence on my part. I did not know how to begin, what actually I meant to say. After a long pause I finally murmured, "I feel guilty and miserable. It's as if I have committed a crime and everybody looks at me with reproach and a promise of punishment. I don't know how to explain it to you."

"You don't need to explain anything because I feel the same way. I know exactly what you mean. I do feel guilty and miserable, but when I think of living without you in my life, I feel even more depressed. I love you and I don't know how and when, but I have a strong feeling that we will be together."

"I don't have even the slightest feeling like that, Stan. All I feel is that I am bad. I'm a sinner."

"No, you are not. Every person deserves to love and to be loved. It has come to you—exactly what you deserve. If only that is true...that you love me."

"It seems that I do, but I am not sure. I think I need time to think it over, to live it through." I started to cry. Hot tears were rolling down my cheeks.

"That's exactly what you are going to have—time, my love. It'll take quite a while before we see each other again. You'll have enough time to see if your feelings for me are true." Stan's voice sounded soft and gentle. He whispered, "I miss you."

"I miss you too," I heard myself speaking, "And I love you very much. I don't need time anymore to understand it. I know it."

After a while I returned downstairs. I wanted to look at my gardenias again, but I could not find the box anywhere.

"If you're looking for your flowers," Sandy said, "I put them in the fridge. They'll stay alive longer that way."

"How strange," I thought, "I've never had gardenias in my fridge in Leningrad. America is full of surprises."

CHAPTER EIGHTEEN

The Angel
January 10, 1990, New York

The days in Philadelphia were remarkable. Like it was fascinating for Americans to see the Kremlin in Moscow or St. Peter and Paul Fortress in Leningrad, it was captivating for me to see the place where the American Constitution was born and signed by the 'founding fathers'. I learned that Philadelphia was the first capital of the United States. Our guide's story about slavery and the Civil War in America had more substance than what I read in Mitchell's *"Gone with the Wind"*.

For the first time I started to think about the striking difference between American slaves and Russian serfs. Slavery was based primarily on race in America. However, in Russia, serfdom had nothing to do with race at all. There it was based on social status. I do not know which was worse, but definitely both were evil.

Both countries managed to defeat these inhumane practices, but America's and Russia's histories took two different paths after 1861: to democracy and prosperity in the United States and to the mirage-happy-future-for-all called communism which in reality created mass repressions, terrible suffering and wars in Russia.

Here in Philadelphia, I understood that Americans skillfully tailored a system of freedom of choice for every citizen. Russians, on the other hand, had been unable to escape the cruel traditions of the past. Communists ironically used the very practices of the czars—banishment, torture, and murder—to make all of Russia bow to a new master.

On a different continent, the founders of a new country selected ideas from many great European writers such as Locke, Rousseau, and Montesquieu and from six centuries of English common law to fashion a society dedicated to the ideals of equality for all. American history from 1776 till the present is simply a story about the struggle of a people to achieve the ideals expressed in the Declaration of Independence, U.S. Constitution and Bill of Rights.

In contrast, in communist ideology, human rights were beautifully described on paper by Karl Marx, Fredrick Engels and Vladimir Lenin, but in real life for over seven decades those rights had been masterfully ignored. A Soviet individual had no face; he or she was a 'nobody'. The communist ideology was directed at some obscure *better future* for *all Soviet people* while the life of *each person* in particular did not matter.

Only in Philadelphia did it suddenly strike me why the Soviet people had not been allowed to travel abroad before Gorbachev. Simply the majority of Soviets, without knowing how people actually lived in the West, got used to the ways and rules of their native country and never imagined that life could be different. We had been skillfully brainwashed. Only now as we began to travel abroad did we clearly understand how systematically and ruthlessly we had been robbed of our basic human rights—chief among these in my mind was the right to feel special in everyday life.

Here, in the United States, I did feel special wherever I went because people were polite and friendly even with strangers; public places such as parks, beaches, and restrooms were always clean; and every public library in the country was open to any individual who was inclined to come in. All of this was exactly the opposite in Russia: being friendly with strangers was dangerous, public places were disgustingly filthy, and only highly educated people had special permissions to enter certain public libraries. The leaders hoped that the more ignorant the masses were the less they would analyze the regime and its discriminatory policies.

As I thought about all of this, I began to silently articulate for the first time an explanation of the Russian character. Given our long history of terror was it little wonder that Russians were so intensely devoted to their families? Who else but the family would cherish or care for the individual—certainly not the government or even the church that was also corrupted by communism. Family for all the generations of our existence as a people has been the only well functioning structure in Russia where a person had a chance to be genuinely cherished and cared for. Family is the place for friendly smiles and laughter; home is the clean environment; home libraries are the pride of each family. Family is where *you* are special.

Here, in Philadelphia, I knew that I had ruined my "happy harbor" I had back home—my family. I had betrayed my husband, son and father. My family trusted me and I had let them down.

Thoughts like these filled my restless brain during long sleepless nights that had been already badly disrupted by the jet lag. Finally, I tried to convince myself again, for the third time since my Washington rendezvous with Stan that I had tortured myself enough, and that nothing had actually happened. Soon I would be back home enjoying my daily routine, and I would forget my American adventure forever. I had to concentrate on my family and forgive myself for the terrible sin of unfaithfulness.

I had not spoken to Stan on the phone for three days. Vlad and I spent most of the time in the beautiful museums of Philadelphia and came home late. The biggest collection of Rodin's sculptures was the most powerful distraction from my bitter thoughts, and "The Thinker" reminded me that I should always use my reason and not my passion to guide me in life. There were messages from Stan on the answering machine, but I had not managed to talk with him. The process of our detachment from each other began. It was painful but necessary.

And then, unexpectedly, without any previous plan I went to New York.

It was quite symbolical, almost mystical when I saw Katherine, my New York friend, in her new red sparkling-clean sports car in the driveway of Sandy's house. Katherine came to pick me up and take me to New York to stay at her place for two days. Stan had no idea about this arrangement made on the spur of the moment when Katherine called and urged me to see her before I returned home. I deliberately 'forgot' to tell Sandy my phone number in New York so that Stan would not call me there. No less deliberately I left my beautiful gardenias in Sandy's fridge—one more little step to ensure the 'detachment process.' The plan in my head was simple: once back in Leningrad, I would write a nice farewell letter to Stan. I would explain that the realities of my life—my guilt and family responsibilities—were stronger than our ephemeral love. He would understand, agree, forgive and forget me.

That was my firm decision.

Katherine was a sweet and dear friend. I had met her for the first time in Leningrad where she was with a group of professionals in the field of political science who had a mission to meet high government officials in Moscow and after that had a pleasure tour of Leningrad. It was in the middle of July when I was free from my regular teaching English job, and I was working for a private company teaching Russian to foreigners. I still don't know how it happened that the American group got in contact with this company and the head of it, my friend, called me one evening and offered me the job as their guide. I needed a few extra rubles, so I agreed.

There were about twelve people in the group; four or five of them were the ones who had come on business while the others were friends and family members, just tourists. They were all pleasant, intelligent people, and we got along well. Katherine was one of the twelve, a quiet woman of my age, who knew a lot about art and admired the beauty of the Hermitage—the Winter Palace of the Romanov Dynasty and the world renown museum of Western-European art.

Among other places to be visited in Leningrad was also Our Lady of Kazan Cathedral, a majestic church built to commemorate the Russian victory over Napoleon in 1812. The fate of the Cathedral was rather sad. After the communist revolution it became the Museum of Religion and Atheism. Yes—"atheism". The church designed for worshipping God was brutally turned into a site denying the very existence of God. I personally had never been inside this building as I thought it was a boring place. But because it was in the schedule of visits for the American group, I called the museum and asked them to give us a local guide for a tour.

The building was poorly maintained, dirty and stinky. We had to wait for the guide in the basement entrance hall for at least fifteen minutes inhaling the vapors of the only small filthy bathroom located there. Then we were taken to the central gigantic hall where all the exhibits were displayed. The guide, a girl of about eighteen years old, wearing a prim white blouse and a dark blue skirt was showing us the exhibits depicting the origin of religion; she told us about different forms of worship and the variety of religions in the world. She did tell us a lot about religion but not a word about atheism. Finally, one member of the group, a professor from Stanford University, asked the girl, "Are there any exhibits in your museum proving that there is no God?"

The girl seemed to be at a loss. She was blinking rapidly with her pale eyelashes for a few moments; then she said proudly, "Yes, we have a copy of Lenin's decree stating that the new communist society was to be atheistic, free from religious ignorance, and that religion was "the opium" for the people, and that it had to be separated from the state."

"Is there any proof of the nonexistence of God other than comrade Lenin's decree in the Museum of Atheism?" The man asked sarcastically, definitely giving the poor girl a hard time. She murmured, "No." She turned red and looked away.

There were no more questions. I noticed that Katherine was upset; she had tears in her eyes. I asked her if I could help, and she whispered, "I can't stand it anymore. I want to go to Paris. Can you help me to get an air ticket for the earliest flight out of here?"

"I can try, but in the middle of July during the traveling season it'll be difficult," I whispered.

"I need to get out of here," Katharine added. I understood that 'here' was not just this pathetic museum but the whole country—a museum of "we know it all" ignorance.

I tried to imagine what Katherine was feeling at the moment—perhaps her tears were for the deliberate destruction of the sacred by a power dedicated to sully anything connected with religion. Why should it take this woman's tears to make me see how wrong this was? Why didn't all of Leningrad weep every day over the very existence of this museum and countless others like it? Katherine understood how wrong this was but could not change it so she simply had to escape from her sadness and rage.

I sympathized with Katherine's desire to leave at that moment, but I also knew that we were still going to have a few wonderful tours including the museum-apartment of Fyodor Dostoyevsky—the writer she admired, but I decided not to try to talk her out of her decision to leave and instead to help her with the ticket to Paris.

As soon as I put the tourists on the bus for their hotel, I took Katherine to the nearest Aeroflot booking office that was only two blocks away from the cursed cathedral. When we entered it, we instantly understood there was no hope. The place was packed with people in the international section. I saw despair in Katherine's eyes.

I said as gently as I could, "I understand how you feel, and how many things that you have seen might offend you. But believe me, there are hidden treasures here that cannot be seen through a bus window. Everything is not simple in my country, and it's as if there are two lives going on: one life is the imaginary 'ideal communist' future and the other life is the everyday routine of individual human beings. The main thing is that though the power is in the hands of a few wishful utopian thinkers, the majority of the people are simply living their lives. Most are not living for that promised "pink future", for they have long ago stopped believing the fairy tales about it. There are some good things in Russia created by all those 'simple' people, and I really hate to think that you will leave with disgust and hatred in your heart for them. They do not deserve it. Let's try to forget about what we have experienced today, and I promise that tomorrow I'll take you to an unforgettable place that you will enjoy. After that there will be only one more day of your stay here which we can spend in the merriest bar drinking to your safe flight back home."

"I understand, Elena, thank you for being so considerate. Where are we going tomorrow?" Katherine sighed sadly.

"To Petrodvorets, one of the most beautiful summer palaces of Catherine the Great. It'll remind you of Versailles. We'll have our own little France here." I smiled and Katherine smiled back.

Since that moment an invisible bond was established between Katherine and me; it was an amazing discovery for both of us that we were not an American and a Soviet anymore, but just two human beings, two women, who could be friends.

And now that I was in America, it was Katherine's turn to show me her hometown, New York, where she had graduated from Columbia University and worked on Wall Street. I appreciated it so much. It had been my dream to see New York and as it had not been included in the program of our visit, I had felt a little disappointed. Now Katherine was going to make my dream come true.

In the car, I closed my eyes in disbelief—was I really going to the Big Apple? Will I actually see the Statue of Liberty, the world symbol of freedom and democracy? And will I experience "the horrors of New York" described in the Soviet mass media—the hundreds of homeless people, the shootings on the streets, the oppressive skyscrapers, the dirty avenues and overpriced knick-knacks in the expensive stores for whites only? When I open my eyes, I will be in New York City thanks to my dear friend, Katherine, my kind Angel. I felt happy.

We were driving along and talking about our latest news. Katherine asked, "Well, how do you like it here, in America?"

"I love it. Everything is so interesting and different from home. Can you imagine, when I arrived in Washington D.C., Stan, my friend from the Peace Walk, was there to meet me!"

"Does he live in D.C.?"

"No, he came all the way from Idaho."

"Idaho? Is it in the West?" Katherine was genuinely surprised.

"Yes, it's in the North-West, next to Washington State. Stan says it's famous for its potatoes."

"Oh, yes, right—the Idaho potatoes. So, is he a farmer? You haven't told me about him before."

Even though I thought I had made the decision to forget Stan, I felt there would be no harm if I told Katherine about him as a friend of mine. I said, "Well, we met on the Peace Walk; actually we hardly saw each other then, just talked a couple of times. He wrote a nice story for me."

"A story? What kind of story?" Katherine sounded even more puzzled.

"It's a romantic story about a birch and a pine living on separate islands and falling in love. It's a beautiful story. He's a wonderful writer," I said proudly.

"So, what did you and Stan do in D.C.?" Katherine's question hit the right target.

I said quickly, "I saw all the major memorials; we went to the White House, to the Smithsonian. Stan came to visit at my host family's house and showed slides of the Walk. We had a party with about 14 people. It was fun. Then Stan invited me one evening to the hotel across from the Pentagon. We had an unforgettable dinner on the top floor with a fantastic view of the Pentagon lights. You know, it was so strange for me, a Russian, or rather a Soviet woman, who had been always told how evil the Pentagon—"the core of a powerful threat to the world"—had been, to admire its glowing quiet beauty in the night lights of the world's capital."

"Did you just have dinner?" Katherine wanted to know it all.

I did not know what to say, but I knew if I wanted her advice, I had to tell the truth about everything.

"We also made love, and he said he loved me and I said I loved him."

"Do you?"

"What?"

"Do you love him?" Katherine did not look at me, and I was not sure what she was thinking.

"I'll be honest with you because I need your help or rather your advice. I thought I did, but now when we are apart and I'm going back home tomorrow, and we live half a world away from each other, and he's married and I'm married and.... you know...he is American and I am Russian... There are so many obstacles..."

"Do you love him?" Katherine repeated in the same even voice.

"I don't know." I was so afraid to admit it after I had made a deal with myself—go home and forget.

"I'm sure you do." Katherine smiled.

"Why are you so sure?"

"It's simple. It's been about two hours now that you've been telling me mostly about Stan. It seems that Stan is the greatest impression you have got from your visit to America."

"Sorry if it sounded that way; I didn't mean it," I was embarrassed.

"I know you didn't, but this is the truth. You can't help it because you're in love."

"What do you think? What should I do? I'm so scared."

"I think if you, *both of you*, truly love each other, there are no obstacles. You'll be together."

"But how? It's absolutely impossible."

"There's nothing impossible if two people want to be together. All they need to do is hold on to their love. Don't ever let it go," My Angel said firmly.

CHAPTER NINETEEN

New York

January 10, 1990, New York

We arrived in New York at about four in the afternoon. Katherine was tired after the long drive. We decided to go to some quiet place to rest and have a drink or two. Later that evening we were supposed to go out for dinner at the Tavern on the Green; Katherine's boyfriend had invited us. He had been granted the title of "boyfriend" quite a while ago and was now at the intermediate stage before becoming a fiancé—what would that be called—pre fiancé? Katherine was telling me about him while we sat in the lounge of the President Hotel, which was richly decorated with gold and marble. We were drinking tasty sparkling champagne from elegant crystal glasses, talking, giggling and feeling happily silly. We were becoming quite tipsy.

This was an enjoyable time. We were recalling funny things that had happened to us in Leningrad when Katherine was there with the VIP group visiting the parliament of the USSR. We were gossiping about the people we both knew, and meanly added new details to old stories.

I was telling Katherine about my dissertation; what in particular I was studying in the English language, and how I had been overwhelmed by the process. So many ideas had sprung into my head, but unfortunately they had just as quickly been forgotten. To that Katherine said a very simple thing, "You silly, don't you know how to keep the ideas alive?"

"How?" I laughed, "My ideas are not very important if they escape me as easily as they visit me."

"I'm sure you have plenty of those, but a few of them may be of some significance. Just write them down each time they come to your pretty head." Katherine was for the moment surprisingly serious.

"Do you mean I have to carry a note book and a pen everywhere I go, sit, sleep, or take a shower? The thing is these ideas arise at the most inconvenient moments of my life," I sighed.

"I don't see any problem. I'm sure you carry tons of make up with you no matter where you go. You can fit a little notebook in your purse as well. Am I right?"

"I guess you are. I think I can deal with a notebook and a pen in my cosmetic bag. I can glue the notebook to the back of my little powder case. The most valuable ideas strike my brain when I am looking at my shiny nose." I began to feel the influence of alcohol and enjoyed being funny.

We kept laughing, happy to be simply silly that evening. Katherine was usually such a serious businesswoman at work that a few laughs were good for her.

Then we went home to clean up, change and get ready for the dinner. I unpacked and presented the gifts I had brought for Katherine. Among the different things I had prepared were some typical Russian treats—a can of black caviar and a bottle of Soviet Champaign. Katherine looked at me in astonishment, "Are you crazy? It's so expensive!"

"No, it's not. But even if it were, I'd like to bring something very Russian for you. Don't you like black caviar?"

"I love it. But it's terribly expensive here."

"Well, this can is from *there*, and it's not *that* expensive there. Don't worry, I'm not bankrupt."

"Thank you, Elena; it's nice of you. I'd like to give something to you too. Here, take this gold chain. It was a gift from my ex-husband, but I don't want it. It reminds me of a time that I don't want to remember. It'll be better if it finds a new life on your neck."

"I think it's you who is crazy. By no means can I accept it." I tried to put the chain back in Katherine's hand.

"Don't be silly. It's yours." She threw the chain over my head. It landed very graciously around my neck as if it were specially designed for it.

"Thank you. I'll always remember your kindness," I said.

But that was not all. She said, "Before we get ready to go out for dinner let's make another quick shopping trip."

First she took me to the nearest fish store to look at the caviar displayed on the counter. There were lots of different cans there. To my surprise I felt as if I were at home in a fish market—the cans looked exactly the same. We found a can similar to the one I had given Katherine. I could not believe my eyes. The price label was $100.99. I had paid only five rubles, say three dollars, for it in Leningrad.

"See? I told you it was expensive." My friend looked at me triumphantly, "Now follow me, I want to show you something else."

We went out to Lexington Avenue and walked a couple of blocks up to a department store. I have never seen a more beautiful store in my life, not even in Washington D.C. I could not believe there were so many things in one place. We went to the perfume section and found the Estee Lauder counter. Katherine said to me, "Please choose what you want."

I felt embarrassed; I knew most of the Estee Lauder products were pricey. But Katherine was insistent, and I gave in. I chose a powder, an eye pencil and a lotion. Everything was packed in a nice make-up bag. Katherine mentioned, "Don't forget to put your notebook in this bag."

"I will, I promise."

We laughed.

The bright lights and the smell of the hundreds of beautifully packed cosmetic products from world famous companies excited me. The cosmetics department was one of my favorite places in any department store. I could stay there for hours, but my curiosity about Katherine's pre fiancé was stronger. No matter how much I wanted to stay longer in Bloomingdales, we had to go home and get ready for the date.

I put on my navy blue dress, the one I was wearing when Stan and I had gone out for dinner in D.C. and had a flashback—we are in the elevator, Stan touching my sleeve tenderly and whispering how beautiful I looked in the dress. It was such an intimate moment. I closed my eyes...

"Are you sleepy? Is it still the jet lag?" Katherine was wearing a small black dress and a beautiful mink coat. She looked stunning.

"No, no; I think my head is swinging from all the excitement. Gosh, you are beautiful!" If I had been a pre fiancé, I would have asked Katherine to marry me right that second.

We took a cab and in about five minutes arrived at the Central Park. We entered the restaurant where sparkling Christmas decorations still richly ornamented the windows, doors, walls and the trees and bushes around the building. It was like a fairy tale. Soft music flowed into the room from somewhere above us. The music combined with strings of twinkling white lights woven around the interior and reflected by mirrored walls created a magical space for us.

He was in the lounge waiting.

"Hi, Roger, please meet Elena, my Russian friend. Sorry we are a little late." Katherine smiled and hugged the man who rose up to greet us.

"Pleased to meet you." Roger and I shook hands.

"I'm glad, too. I've heard a lot about you. And all only positive." I smiled.

I liked Roger. He was tall and handsome with pleasant manners. Katherine had told me early in the evening that he was as busy with his law practice as she was with her consulting company. They were typical middle aged business people who had never taken time for their private lives, but who both desperately wanted to start a family. The way they were looking at each other told me that they were in love, and I felt happy for Katherine.

I thought, "Am I in love too? Do I miss Stan? Is he still thinking of me? He is probably at home making love to his wife right now." This last thought was painful and at that moment I hated him. "But when I come home I'll have to pretend that nothing happened and then…I'll have to make love to my husband…I'll have to? I've always loved to do it with him and have never had to make myself love him; it has been my desire, not my obligation. But now…I feel as if I'll have to…what have I done to us?"—not very pleasant thoughts in a spectacular place in the company of good friends. I made myself stop thinking about Stan.

The people around us, the third glass of champagne, the lights and the mirrors, the fact that I was in the Big Apple—all this made me feel a little dizzy and happy. I did not have to solve any problems, but I could simply enjoy the moment.

Unexpectedly, Roger, like Grandfather Frost—the Russian Santa Claus—took out from under the table a big package wrapped in beautiful paper with a gold and red bow on it. He said, "Elena, this is a little gift for you to remember New York City when you return to Russia."

"Thank you so much, but it does not look like a little gift. It's so heavy I can hardly lift it," I exclaimed as I put it on the table and started to open the package. It was a wonderful album with pictures showing New York at the beginning of the 19th century and today. What a thoughtful gift it was. I was glad I had brought a present for Roger, "And this is a really small gift for you from the Russian Santa. It's a military watch."

"Oh, Elena, how nice of you; thank you!"

Katherine was smiling as she watched us enjoying our gifts like two little kids on Christmas morning.

"I'll never forget you and your beautiful country," I said softly, "I've met here so many really generous and openhearted people."

"And please remember that the best place in this country is New York City!" Roger teased me.

"And the best place in my country is Leningrad!" I said.

We laughed again, praising ourselves for being such great patriots. We had a good time.

Finally, we were invited to come into the dining hall. Our table was at the window facing the park with hundreds of trees sparkling with lights. It created a festive holiday mood. We ordered wine and lobster. Roger and Katherine asked me many questions about what was happening in Russia, what "perestroika" meant, and my personal attitude towards Mikhail Gorbachev.

"Mikhail Gorbachev is my hero," I said, "If it weren't for him, I wouldn't be able to come to the U.S. Before Gorbachev, visiting countries like the U.S., Germany, Great Britain or Italy was possible only for big party bosses—"shishki"—that's how people call them using slang. In translation it's "pine cones". I couldn't even dream about traveling here before Gorbachev's Perestroika. For me, a teacher of English, it seemed a necessary but unattainable goal to actually visit an English speaking country. Now, after this trip, I'll give presentations and workshops to my students and colleagues so that they can better understand your country and the language. I've learned so much about the English language and American traditions and culture here in just a few weeks."

"Really? Can you give an example?" Katherine asked.

"For me, a linguist, it's very interesting to observe how the language is developing. Every language is changing, and the American language is not an exception. I've noticed some metamorphoses that are appalling from the grammar point of view, but they steadily creep into the language and become standard norms. For example, I was shocked when I saw a sign in a grocery store "Ten Items or Less." I've taught my students they should use "fewer" with countable nouns, which 'items' is and "less" with uncountables, with words like 'milk, snow, anger', and here I come to America and read in some grocery stores an official sign where "less" is used grammatically incorrect. Another example is "there is" with plurals like 'There's books on the table.' One more example will be what linguists call "hypercorrection" when people say 'between you and I' instead of the correct form 'between you and me'."

"Elena, this is so interesting. I've never paid any attention to all these language peculiarities, but you are right. Is there anything like that happening in Russian?"

"Sure, it is. I think it happens in any language. Languages are like people—they change."

"Who is among your favorite American linguists? Have you heard the name Chomsky?" Katherine asked.

"Of course, I had to read lots of his books and there were several questions connected with some of Noam Chomsky's theories during the comprehensive exams I had to take last year. But I personally don't agree with lots of Chomsky's ideas and truthfully, some of them are so complicated, I just fail to understand them. I like when theoreticians express their thinking clearly so that any person can see their point. In this respect Otto Jespersen, a Scandinavian scholar, is probably my favorite."

It was unexpected for me that Katherine, a businesswoman from Wall Street, would know the name of a linguist. Later I stopped being surprised at her knowledge about everything, but I never stopped admiring her intelligence. On the other hand, for Katherine it was strange that a Russian woman would not only be familiar with the name of a famous American linguist, but would have read his books. That evening was the time of many discoveries about who I was and about my place in this world. That evening I didn't think about Stan anymore, and I felt great.

CHAPTER TWENTY

Taste My Meat
March 8, 1990, Leningrad

When I returned home after my first visit to the U.S., it was extremely hard to go back to the Russian way of life. The Russian consumer unlike his American counterpart had to deal each day with the unpredictable Soviet system of production and distribution in the grocery store, pharmacy, bakery, or any other business. For instance, all of a sudden, certain food products might disappear. Imagine going shopping and having in mind to buy, say, mayonnaise or mustard, and not being able to find any—"surprise!"

In such fashion, one spring day in 1990, there formed long lines for butter. The next day people were standing in lines to buy milk. Each day brought new surprises, and after a short while special coupons for dairy products were issued and distributed among people. One coupon, for example, allowed every citizen of the U.S.S.R. to buy two pounds of butter a month. As there were three people in my family, we could have six pounds of butter every month. Of course, we could not eat so much butter, but I bought all of it anyway and froze it just in case the coupons would disappear, too, in the next stage of the 'well planned' Soviet economy.

After a while some other products were rationed: sugar, flour, cooking oil, vodka, and soap. By this time people were more or less used to the idea of the coupons, and nobody was surprised or irritated—it was 'the Soviet prototype of the game Monopoly'—the difference was that the game was a reality, and in this reality people were manipulated like game pieces, but instead of becoming rich the majority of those game pieces became even poorer than they had ever been. For most people the only way to survive and not to lose their mind was to accept the rules of the game and to participate as unwilling actors and actresses in the Soviet "Theater of the Absurd" that had been forced on all of us since 1917.

Every month my husband would go to the local housing office to get the coupons. They were long strips of paper of different colors—pink for soap, blue for vodka, yellow for butter, light purple for sugar, and so on. At least those colors, unlike the Soviet darkness, added to our bleak existence. A pink coupon, for example, allowed us two bars of soap, and a blue coupon—two bottles of vodka, per person a month. My family could definitely use more soap and significantly less vodka, but the rules were universal for the population of the country where every person had 'equal rights' as Lenin declared in his famous decree of 1918. Unfortunately, the current system ignored the obvious fact that this population had to wash and take showers more often than two bars would allow for, but then again our great socialist "engineers" seemed to think this inconvenience could be compensated for by an abundance of drinking. As nobody in my family drank vodka at all, in just three months we accumulated eighteen bottles. At the same time, there were people who needed a bottle of vodka a day—poor them. Those were very important participants in our 'monopoly' game. I could trade my vodka coupons for their sugar or soap coupons. As a result, a lot of people would gradually acquire hundreds of pounds of sugar and hundreds of bars of soap in one household. That was close to winning a real monopoly on essential goods—and consequently, the dynasties of the Soviet Sunflower Oil "Rockefellers" or No Scent Washing Soap "Vanderbilts" came into existence during these days. The vodka coupons were valued more than anything, and the vodka coupon holders had financial power like Bill Gates on the big board of Monopoly at the New York Stock Exchange.

Thus, with time, my family became vodka 'rich and independent'. We had the most powerful currency in the country, which allowed us to improve our quality of living significantly. The service of a plumber, a carpenter, a taxi driver, any repair or craftsmanship could be paid for with 'the golden' blue coupons.

It was also the period when the Soviet black market flourished for those who were selling the magic blue coupons and at the peak of the Coupon Era the price of one vodka coupon was equal to the price of a Panasonic boom box or a Kodak camera.

Those who could not afford to buy the coupons on the black market but suffered without a daily drink started using some herbal drugs mixed with alcohol and other ingredients. As a result, the drugs so necessary for the old and the sick disappeared from the pharmacies. The same thing happened to cheap perfume products and lots of cleaning substances. Russian men used Mr. Clean instead of "five o'clock whiskey." Consequently, more and more reports of deaths from poisoning among men at the age of 45-50 appeared in the press.

At first the coupons seemed to be a reliable method of distributing needed essentials but with time this system like the previous "planned economy" was destroyed by inefficiency, unpredictability and corruption. It became simply another failed attempt at centralized economic planning that eventually brought more pain and suffering to everyone, especially those who were not "pine cones". It was another national tragedy.

Finally, people stopped buying the stuff with coupons; they simply had no place to store all the coupon products; furthermore, they could not fight the bugs that started nesting in sacks of flour, cereal, and pasta.

With or without coupons, life's routine continued.

Spring was coming to Leningrad. One of our favorite spring holidays—the International Women's Day celebrated on the 8th of March—arrived. According to tradition my family was planning to picnic in the park with our friends, a couple and their two sons. There was still a lot of snow everywhere, so the kids wanted to ski or sled. The grown-ups were going to drink lemon vodka—a famous coupon product and the best warming-you-up substance on a winter picnic—and eat ham or tuna sandwiches.

Usually on that day husbands gave their wives flowers and chocolates, and later in the evening they would also cook dinner and even do the dishes. I supposed the 8th of March would be the same this year.

But that was not the case.

That morning, when I woke up, my son brought a sweet little picture of the sea and a beautiful sunset that he had drawn for his mommy. In the lower right corner he wrote, "I love you, my dearest Mama." Alexei was a caring boy and always liked to make me feel special. I loved the picture and his attention. Now it was my husband's turn, but…nothing followed. There were no flowers, no gifts, no breakfast or coffee in bed.

When our friends called and asked if we were going to meet in the park, my husband seemed to be surprised. He had completely forgotten about the holiday. I felt neglected and offended given that the 8th of March was just once a year. I got upset and decided to cool off my anger by taking my dog out for a walk.

On my way I checked the mailbox and found a pretty envelope from America in it. My heart started to beat fast. I recognized Stan's handwriting. In the envelope there was a beautiful card with warm 8th of March greetings. It was such a contrast. The man living thousands of miles away from me in the country where nobody even knows about this holiday remembered and showed his affection for me. The other man, living in the same apartment and sleeping in the same bed with me forgot about an annual celebration and demonstrated his indifference.

When I came home from my walk, all my husband said was, "Sorry, I forgot, but I didn't mean it. Next year I'll be better." Then he lay down on the sofa with a book.

It might seem a small matter, but it was a big deal for me. I did not want to wait for the next year to feel special. I wanted to be loved and cherished and understood and given attention every single day of my life.

I closed my eyes. Suddenly a set of horrid pictures from my past revealed themselves. They were images I had tried to forget, but one, in spite of my best efforts, crawled into my consciousness occasionally.

It happened on July 14th 1985.

That was the darkest, saddest day of my life. My mother had been very ill for several months. She came home from the hospital in June after an operation for cancer. At first she felt better, and all the members of the family hoped she would be all right. The only person who knew the real truth was my dad. He knew that Mama had probably only a few weeks left. He knew, but he did not tell anyone because he wanted to conceal the truth from my mom. He could not bear to think that a word or even a glance from anyone who knew the truth would give his horrible secret away and cause his wife even more pain. The doctors said not to tell her she had cancer because sometimes not knowing helped people live the last days of their lives in a better state of mind. I still don't know what I would have done had it been my secret but that was my father's decision because he loved Raisa more than anyone in the world.

For the first two weeks everything seemed fine, but then her condition became worse with the passing of each day, and it was clear that something was wrong. At first I was very angry with my father. I could not understand why he was not trying to find better doctors, put Mama in a better hospital, and find some better medicine.

One day my anger and disappointment both vanished in a moment as

I watched my dad standing vigil over his beloved who was sleeping peacefully. The pain and anguish in his eyes told me everything; my mother was going to die—die no matter what we did or did not do. He stood beside all of us but he was so alone at that moment, consumed by the grief that there was nothing he could do to save her.

We pretended that she would be fine, and that it was just a normal relapse. It would just take a little more time to recover. Those days were the most difficult days for my family, but we simply stuck to our normal routine. What else could we do?

It was the middle of the summer. The weather was warm. Alexei was living at the dacha. My husband and I took turns staying with him during the week. I would come to the dacha in the morning at around eight or nine after spending the night helping my dad take care of Mama. I would stay with Alexei during the day until my husband arrived from work around 5 P.M., and then I would rush back to town to spend the evening and the night with my mom. It was hard but necessary to insure that Mama would never be alone without care or attention.

That Sunday, July 14, I planned to come home around noon, and my husband was supposed to arrive at the dacha at the same time. Alexei had to stay with my friend at her dacha a few blocks away from our place until his father came to pick him up. My friend's husband, Sasha, was going to town by car, and he offered to give me a ride home.

We left at 11 A.M. The day was beautiful, sunny and warm. Sasha was an excellent driver, but he liked to drive a little too fast. Usually I felt nervous, but on that day I did not care. My thoughts were far away with my poor sick mother; I was imagining that when I arrived, she would look healthy and happy—the way she used to be.

The road was empty; very few cars were going to the country that Sunday morning. Sasha knew I was going through a difficult time in my life and was trying to cheer me up by telling funny stories and jokes on the way. Then it happened. It happened in a wink. A car was approaching us very fast, and from quite a distance I felt there was something wrong. Then we both knew it was going too fast, and it had crossed the center line into our lane. On our right the deep ditch that had run parallel to the road for miles had suddenly been replaced by a little forested area. At the very last moment when it seemed that the other car would crash head on into us, Sasha made a sharp turn to the right and slammed on the breaks. I saw the car passing only half an inch from the window on the driver's side and quickly disappeared into the distance. Our car stopped with a jolt. I will never forget the piercing silence after that.

We did not move for a long time. I saw Sasha's shaking fingers still clutching the steering wheel as if he was afraid to let it go. Then I whispered, "Thank you, Sasha. I think you have just saved our lives."

He looked at me; his lips were trembling too. Finally, he asked me, "What is the date today?"

"It's July 14th."

"Well, remember this date. It's your new birthday. You and I were born today ten minutes ago. This little stand of pines saved us. It's as if an angel was watching and arranged everything exactly on time so that those guys would miss us. They are driving right into the jaws of death. Did you notice? I saw there were a lot of them in that car."

"Seven or eight," I murmured. "And they were young, noisy teenagers. I can still hear the loud music and their laughter; the windows were open."

My fear about almost being killed was suddenly replaced by another. I got a strange feeling that something had happened at home and I knew I had to be there. I felt as if I was needed there now more than ever. It was not my destiny to die that day on a highway between our dacha and Leningrad. Sometimes destiny calls us to a worse fate than death. Once our car began to speed towards the city again each telephone pole that passed by the passenger's window signaled that I was coming closer to what I feared the most.

When I arrived home around noon, I rushed into my parent's apartment, "How is Mama?"

My father did not answer but simply sighed. I understood she was not doing well at all. Before I went into her bedroom, I went to my room to change. To my surprise my husband was there. He was smiling, "Great! You're here. I waited for you."

"Why is that? I hoped you would be at the dacha by now. Alexei is waiting for you to go fishing together."

"Well, he can wait a little while longer. I haven't seen my wife for a week, and what a wonderful chance to have some time together now."

He tried to kiss me. At that moment I would have appreciated a hug, but I also knew that my father was exhausted after a sleepless night, and I had to go—my dying mother needed care. I had to see her as soon as possible. I wanted to tell her how important it was for me to be with her that even accidents avoided me. I whispered, "Please, let me change and go to see Mama. Dad told me she had a bad night."

"*She* had a bad night! And what about me? How many bad nights have I had? Do you care? I'm a man and I need you. Please…" He started kissing me and pushed me lightly until we both fell on the bed. I wanted to yell out, "Vadim, stop, my mother is dying in the next room. How can you possibly be so insensitive and uncaring at a time like this? Stop!"

My father was in the apartment; I was afraid to make any noise. I whispered in despair, "Please don't touch me; let me go right now."

"I've been waiting for you all morning, and I can't think of anything else but *my* feelings right now. I don't have any more patience. It's been hell lately. I never see you. You are either with Alexei or with your parents. But I am a man; I need a woman."

"Do you need a wife who is a friend, a companion and a mother to your child, or do you need just a woman to have intercourse with? My mother is dying! Can't you understand?"

"Oh, she's not dying. She's always sick with this or that. You'll see that she'll be as healthy as a bull by the fall. And I can really get sick. Don't you know how important it is for a man of my age to have regular sex?"

"I don't want to know it. You may think anything you desire. You haven't seen my mother for months, how can you say she is not sick? Would a healthy person be secluded in her room for weeks? You never even ask me how she has been, how can you say she is okay?"

All I was feeling at that moment was fear and anger. I was going to say that…

But I could not pronounce a sound anymore. He grabbed me and started to undress me. I could hear my father going into the bedroom where my mom was. I did not want him to hear noises, so I simply submitted to the rape. I hated every move, every sigh, and every glance of that man who had become a stranger—a rapist, a brutal vandal, and an enemy.

When everything was over, I quickly put my clothes on trying not to look at the man I despised. On my way out I heard him say, "You could give me a grateful kiss for the pleasure of fulfilling your spousal duty."

I did not turn my head and only whispered, "Hurry to the dacha;

Alexei is expecting you to bring his favorite book about Nusmumriks. Don't forget it."

"When will you come to the dacha?" He sounded disappointed.

"I don't know. I'll be here as long as my mother needs me."

I went out of the room and took three deep breaths to fight back the tears coming to my eyes. I did not cry. I was too full with rage and hatred.

Then I slowly entered my mom's bedroom. My dad was sitting in the armchair. His eyes were closed, but I knew he was awake. He whispered, "I'm so happy you are back. I think your Mama is waiting for you."

I sat by the bed. She seemed asleep. She looked very pale.

"Papa, did she eat anything?"

"She has not been eating for two days."

"What? Why? It's terrible! Did you call the doctor? We must do something immediately!" I felt cold with fear.

"Stop it please. We can't do anything. She will eat when she wants to."

I knew that part of the foundation of my life, of our family, was about to collapse. Beyond the immense sadness I felt knowing that Mama was about to die was even a greater emotion—a terrifying fear about what would become of all of us without Mama.

I whispered, "Papa, go to the kitchen and fix something to eat for yourself. I'm not hungry. I'll stay with Mama. Don't worry."

When my dad left, at first I felt uncomfortable in the room. It seemed so empty and terrifying with Mama lying motionless, so thin and grayish-pale. But gradually I felt calmer and relaxed in an armchair. The warmth of the sunrays penetrated through the heavy curtains. I was so tired after the near-death experience on the road and the humiliation my husband had just subjected me to that my body could not take more. I fell asleep.

I did not know how long I was there in that warm soothing silence when suddenly I felt that Mama was moving. I asked, "Mam, how are you my dear? It's me, do you recognize me?"

My mother opened her eyes and slowly turned her head in my direction. She was looking at me, but I had a feeling that she did not really see me. Then her lips began to move, but I could not hear anything. I knelt over her and heard a strange coarse voice, "Please...not a crematorium..."

"Mama, my dear, let's not talk about such things. Everything will be fine. Let's now think about what you would like to have for lunch. I know you like French fries; I'll make them for you."

I was talking and talking, but I knew she was not listening. Then she looked at me and suddenly her eyes changed their color. They became dark, almost black. She made a strange movement with her hands as if she wanted to touch her chest, and then she became very still. I felt my heart become ice cold. I opened the door and yelled, "Papa, rush! Oh, Mama, Mama, Mama…"

My father appeared in the room right away. He looked at his wife, fell on his knees and began to sob. I was still whispering "Mama, Mama, Mama…"

My father lifted up his face wet with tears and clearly articulated each word, "You don't have Mama anymore. She is gone."

I had Sasha's words ringing in my ears, "Today, the fourteenth of July is the day when you were born again. Don't forget this day…. You were born again…. You were born…"

Did angels sent by God give me a new life so that I could be with my mother at the moment of her Departure?

Why should I remember so vividly all of these terrors at this exact moment when my husband was offering his fake apologies? Why relive all the pain of the day of my new birth? Whether it be angels or devils that controlled that day and my destiny, I still remember every detail and will never forget the day my mother and my marriage died.

The pain of the loss of the dearest person in my life and the accompanying grief has subsided and given way to deeper emotions, to warm memories and gratitude for all the wonderful things that my mother had done for us all.

The pain of the loss of my husband was with me also. The rage I had felt at the moment had been transformed into a numbing emotion that left no room in my heart for the father of my child. Although I tried to forgive and forget, I had not been able to do either. I did manage to repress the memories to make life bearable in a marriage without real love, but from that very day my bitterness toward Vadim had really never left me. I was unable to hide it.

I wondered if he really did not notice or just pretended not to notice how our relationship had changed from that day to the present. How could he not notice the "yes" and "no" answers to most of his questions, my frequent absence from his bed and my absence from his life as I spent more and more time with our son, my friends, and at work? But in spite of all this and more he did not ask questions. Our relationship became a game played by strangers. The goals and strategies for each of us were vastly different. He wanted to control everyone and everything about our family, and I wanted to be free of his control. I wanted my freedom.

That 8th of March attitude of my husband was another sign of his indifference and coldness. I knew definitely that love between us had been lost forever.

I called my friends and said we were not joining them at the park because I was sick. The holiday was spoilt. I was cooking and cleaning all day—what a special quality time on a holiday for women.

While cooking I was gulping hot tears and thinking about Stan. What a difference. He did love me. I was thinking of him all that day.

The next day I got a package from my friend Edward, who lived in London. It contained several books. One was especially interesting. It was an anthology of British poetry. I opened some page at random in the middle of the book and read:

"Love bade me welcome: yet my soul drew back,
Guilty of dust and sin.
But quick-eyed Love, observing me grow slack
From my first entrance in,
Drew nearer to me, sweetly questioning,
If I lacked anything.
"A guest," I answered, "worthy to be here."
Love said, "You shall be he."
"I, the unkind, ungrateful? Ah, my dear,
I cannot look on thee."
Love took my hand, and smiling did reply,
"Who made the eyes but I?"
"Truth, Lord, but I have marred them; let my shame
Go where it doth deserve."
"And know you not," says Love, "who bore the blame?"
"My dear, then I will serve."
"You must sit down," says Love, "and taste my meat."
So I did sit and eat."

George Herbert wrote this poem in 1620. It was over three hundred and seventy years old and yet it spoke to me, a woman living at the end of the twentieth century. I felt so reassured that centuries ago people had lived through the same passions and worries, hesitations and victories. George Herbert's words were the real 8th of March gift. I did not hesitate anymore and decided to have my 'feast of Love.'

And Edward, my seventy-year-old London friend, had joined the procession of Angels who were helping Stan and me to find our way to each other.

CHAPTER TWENTY ONE

The Letters
Spring 1990, Leningrad

After March 8, 1990 I felt strong emotional threads connecting Stan and me. If I had a bad day at home, at work, or elsewhere in town, while commuting or shopping, I would take time to think of the one person in the world who I knew loved me—Stan, and feel better. If I experienced confusion or felt insecure, I thought of what advice Stan might offer. His spirit prompted me to calm down, to love and respect each person around me, even when I was mistreated and hurt.

I felt an even more powerful support when I regularly started to receive letters from Stan. The first one came at the end of April.

April 14, 1990

Dearest Elena,

Your letter finally arrived on April 10th, my Love. Its content lifted all my stress and anxiety about our friendship and love away. Your friendship is my greatest treasure. I am so glad that you feel the same way. Your sense of frustration about our separation 'for days, for months' is my own as well. I too can accept the reality of our situation with my mind, but my feelings (my heart) are in a daily state of rebellion. The expression of honest emotion is neither 'silly' nor restricted to 'female creatures' as you put it.

I am elated to know that you like me to call. At first when I called, I thought that perhaps you were displeased and hung up, but as our relationship continued, I imagined that perhaps the place, time, or presence of others made you cautious and restricted (limited) your ability to speak freely. I can certainly relate to this feeling of frustration because when I am near you in the presence of others, I purposefully hide my real feelings to protect you from any embarrassment or harm that might happen to you because of our love. I can tell you that greeting you in Washington D.C. at the airport was a great test of my discipline. I wanted so to hug and kiss you; but then again the surprised, happy look on your face when you first saw me was worth many hugs and kisses. As for the expense please do not worry. I promise not to bankrupt my family with calls to the Soviet Union.

It is strange but I must say that I feel you also understand me as well or better than any other person I have ever known. In English the term "kindred spirits" is used to describe two people who automatically seem to know and understand each other in a way that others who live together for a lifetime will never achieve. The miracle of all this to me is that relationship has so quickly and easily been achieved in spite of the formidable barriers of language, culture, politics, time, and space. One example that comes to mind is a comment you made while we dined in Washington D.C. that last evening. You looked out at all the elegant ladies and handsome men and remarked that these Americans were indistinguishable from other men and women, just happy people having a gay evening. My heart thrilled at your comment. I had a similar feeling in Moscow, Russia when my friend Al and I went out to dine in one of the great hotels.

As for "clouds of recollections and dreams" you are writing about, I am equally blessed. I frequently sleep alone both at home and on the road. I feel pain and pleasure when I imagine you by my side. The pleasure of course is having memories of being together. The pain is having you so far away.

I plan to come to Leningrad in summer. I will have spoken with you by phone about my summer schedule before you receive this letter. The good news is that I have been selected as one of fifteen university teachers to participate in a program sponsored by a Fulbright grant. I do hope as the time approaches that I can have more exact information about dates and places that I will be staying in both Moscow and Leningrad this summer. I certainly want to be with you every moment, but you can appreciate that a trip of this type will have, like your Washington one, some expectations about what one is to do. I will certainly ask for a single room so that we might have some time to be alone. I must share with you that I am elated to receive a Fulbright—one of the most prestigious grants—and at the prospect of seeing you so soon. I am however distressed by your explanation of the difficulties this may pose for you. I hope whatever barriers there are that you can find a way to overcome them.

This summer I will be working on a new slide show—"The Emergence of Democracy in the Soviet Union", and I am sure you could be of great help in developing it.

Thank you for taking the time to read my curriculum. I recently received a letter from Valentina Krymova who works at the Pedagogical Institute in Moscow, USSR. She informs me that my curriculum units will be used by some Soviet teachers this fall. I was so happy to learn of this because like you I dearly love children. I am thrilled to know that some Soviet children will be touched in hopefully a positive way by what I have written.

The other good news is that the United Nations American Association (a national organization designed to encourage Americans to support the good work of the UN) has consented to publicize four new curriculum packets I am writing for use in schools all across America for UN Day on October 24th. This year's theme is on illiteracy. I must confess that I am a little frightened by the great responsibility I have taken on, but I will do my best. As for "children's letters" I am working with an organization in Washington D.C.—Peace Links that has provided me with several hundred letters from Soviet citizens of all ages (9-90) who want pen pals. I am sending you two maps of Idaho. One has a blue star by each community I have given programs in the past two years. I have left pen pal letters in over forty communities this year with students and teachers.

I am delighted to know that Alexei has completed his "novel". By all means send it along. In this age of glasnost anything is possible. If you might have a copy for me this summer, I will also try to help get it published.

I understand being "tired of parties" because I am growing tired of giving the same program over and over. I will leave for this evening to do ten programs in that many places over the next two weeks. By the time I return home, I will have 2,000-3,000 more miles on my car's speedometer.

I am happy to know that you had a good time in America and had "no negative impressions." You know of course that my time in the Soviet Union was equally pleasant. However, we are both realistic to know that both great nations, sad to say, have many negative characteristics but none so great I think that they cannot be overcome by people of good will and character who are willing to work to make their special place in this world better.

I must confess that when I read your entry (in the letter of Feb.15th) that I was very alarmed and sad almost to the point of tears regarding your problems with the dissertation. A similar thing happened to me when I was working on my M.A. in anthropology. I too, however, luckily changed advisors. Then I wrote my thesis (three hundred sixty five pages) and graduated. I am glad to learn that you have a new advisor and hope that your interview has gone well. Perhaps having an advisor who is seventy-five will prompt you to complete the dissertation as quickly as possible. I found and sent to you the best dictionary available on scientific terms (Russian/English), and I hope you have received it by now and that it will be of help to you in your work. I wanted you to have something that you might touch, as I touch the clean, smooth, hot side of the samovar that reminds me of you, so that you would think of me.

I am glad you waited to send your letters. I dread the thought of your letters ever being lost in the mail. I treasure each one so. I certainly agree with your thinking and that of your friends (members of the Leningrad Peace Committee) regarding the necessity of dealing with the problems of ecology, starvation and diseases. I would be happy to discuss the possibility for more professional exchanges and activities for children this summer. I could secure an official invitation from the Peace Committee or Leningrad University with specific suggestions about topics for discussion that might result in exchanges and the development of cooperative programs that would almost certainly make a return trip possible later in the fall. I am glad to hear there is more food in the shops than in December/January. I hope to speak in more details with you about the "multiple party system." I can understand how one can grow weary of words (rhetoric) especially when realities remain generally the same in spite of great promises. We experience that here also. I always enjoy the sanity that my classroom and students provide when trying to cope with some of the insanity that abounds in the world.

Yes, I know that at any moment should tragedy strike we might not see each other, however, I am inclined to be positive and imagine that we will live a long time and that even age will not diminish the love we have for each other. If the worst should happen, even death, it will only have a small victory, for our love exists and if there is an existence beyond this one, I will find you.

I am happy to know that you had a good time in New York with Katherine. It was quite a surprise to learn that you might be coming to New York in summer. I love you and want for you only that which brings you well deserved happiness and success and perhaps one such trip at the right time might in the long run guarantee many other such opportunities for you to be here, advance in your profession and of course for us to be together. I will no doubt speak with you and have some better understanding of your summer plans before this letter reaches you, but I thought it important to state my opinion on this matter for your future reference should such situation arise again.

Please don't worry about the calls (expense). I promise I shall not call so much as to require that you send me a "benefit". If it is impossible to call, certainly letters are always a great gift and treasure. We cannot know the future, perhaps there will yet come a day when what is impossible will become possible. I hope to have the exact dates for you when I call on April 17th for my time in Moscow and Leningrad. As I reread your letter I have discovered that you will in all likelihood be home from New York before I arrive in Leningrad. Perhaps you shall "have your cake and be able to eat it too."

I am glad you think of me, Elena, because I think of you each day. In fact I have started telling time in two worlds—yours and mine. When I am up at 5:00 A.M., you are finishing a day of work and as I have morning coffee, you are preparing an evening meal.

Do not feel you are a "criminal". I had no idea nor did you that we would fall in love. Each of us simply followed our hearts to what now seems a natural, beautiful conclusion and to our destiny. Certainly we may have existed in another time and place and perhaps even together but as a practical matter I only concern myself with one life at a time. Professionally and personally, I have been raised to be a problem solver. The problem in our case is how to be together as much as possible for the rest of our lives while still maintaining the status quo of our lives before we met. I do suffer and have pain over this dilemma, but more than ever I have accepted the challenge that our situation presents and promise to find ways and means that will allow us to be together as much as is humanly possible. Certainly once I have finished my degree and have my summers free, that will allow for more such opportunities.

Thank you for the beautiful post card with the picture of the birches.

I love you,

Stan

The spring of 1990 was full of Stan's letters, cards, little gifts, notes, phone calls and all sorts of surprises. And yet that was a very sad spring— the spring of learning how to live with two heavy burdens over my heart: first, it was the love for an unreachable man who lived thousands of miles away over the oceans and continents, and second, I felt guilty about putting my son and marriage at risk. The letters had to be carefully hidden in a small box in the apartment of my best friend Nina. That was easy. But it was much more difficult to hide my confused feelings, my anxiety and fear. And yet those letters were important like air to breathe and water to drink to live.

May 20, 1990

My dear Elena,

Your letter of March 20, 1990 touched me so, especially your account of the tears of joy you shed upon reading my letter as you traveled home on the bus. Your first short note from Washington had the same effect on me. Your words then confirmed what I wanted to believe about our love for each other both thrilled and comforted me. I loved the image you created about our "waves" of thought and feelings meeting "maybe somewhere over Europe" and that such a union of thoughts makes our lives rich with feelings, bright with hopes, and happy with the knowledge of love. As time has passed and I have gained perspective, I am more inclined to agree with your assertion that our love for each other is certainly "the greatest gift of destiny." Please don't "hurry time". I fear you will make me into an old man before my time, and you won't love a grandfather with white whiskers as you love me now! Ha! Please don't worry about not writing in a way that I can understand. You do a superior job of communicating in the written and spoken word and your body language, I might add, is elating.

As for our star, the blue one, I will find out its name one day. I did honor our little star by using only blue stars on the map of Idaho. I think of you a great deal when I do the programs. There is a great difference in learning with the head and heart. I can memorize many facts about any topic. But in learning about one beautiful gentle Soviet woman with my heart, my understanding of just how absurd the nuclear arms race is has been increased a thousand folds. As our two lives have been woven together by the fates, I now understand by my real personal experience how the destinies of all people are one as we live in this fragile, finite sphere in space.

I am excited about the opportunity that the summer holds for being together. I long to hold you close again and feel your soft skin beneath my fingers and to hear the rhythms of our hearts and breaths moving together.

CHAPTER TWENTY TWO

Together Again
August 1990, Moscow-Leningrad

The year of 1990 turned out to be a happy one.

I had planned to go to New York in August to a linguistic conference; however, my department failed to come up with sufficient funds to sponsor my trip. I wasn't sad but happy about this "disappointment" for that was exactly the time Stan was coming to Russia. I wouldn't miss him for anything in the world.

That summer Stan and I saw each other three times. It was quite a difficult task. We knew that with careful planning, perseverance and a little bit of luck we could find ways to be together. We were also more convinced than ever that our desire to be with each other was no mistake. Our destinies continued persistently to show that we were meant for each other.

As Stan mentioned in one of his letters, he really had won a Fulbright grant to go to the Soviet Union with a group of twenty-five Americans working in the field of peace studies and conflict resolution. Their program included visits not only to Leningrad and Moscow but also to seven big cities in western Russia, central Ukraine, and southern Georgia, which were all at that time republics of one huge country, the USSR. The group was planning to come to Moscow first, after which they would travel to Volgograd, Kiev, Pyatigorsk, Tbilisi, Sochi and Leningrad, and then back to Moscow. The chance of seeing each other at least three times—twice in Moscow and once in Leningrad—sounded so tempting. But how could I go to Moscow in the middle of the summer? Why would I 'need' to go there? What could I possibly tell my husband?

It seemed impossible but then again an "invisible door"—a portal that allowed us to pass through an impenetrable wall—opened. It was Angel Nadya that came to our rescue again.

On one of those magic White Nights in Leningrad, the time of inspiration for poets and artists and the most romantic time for lovers, I was racking my brain about how to arrange the trip to Moscow when the phone rang and Nadya asked if I wanted to join a Peace Committee delegation going to Denmark to the All-European Peace Festival. My first response was "no", but when I heard that the delegation would go to Moscow for a three-day orientation, exactly during Stan's first visit, I jumped up on the sofa with excitement. No, seriously, our Angels were at work; otherwise I had no explanation for such a precise coincidence. What was even more incredible was that our delegation was supposed to return home to Leningrad from Denmark the day after Stan's group arrived in Leningrad.

It was destiny.

In early August, our small group of eight active members of the Peace Committee arrived in Moscow. I did not tell anybody that I was planning to see Stan the next morning, but I had to think of some excuse to miss the first session of the orientation. I only mentioned to Nadya that I wanted to visit my two cousins, and she simply said, "Listen, my dear, I don't think you have to be at this orientation. I'll write everything down and let you know if there's anything important. I understand what fun it is for you to see your relatives. Have a good time and call me if you need anything. Please don't forget that we are leaving on Thursday at noon."

Instead of saying thank you I gave Nadya a kiss on the cheek and a long hug of gratitude and rushed to my cousin's place to leave my baggage. My relatives were as usual happy to see me and not in the least surprised when I disappeared shortly after I arrived. I had to get to the airport on time to meet Stan.

I was both nervous and excited. It had been eight months since we saw each other in Washington D.C. How would we act in the presence of other people? What would Stan explain if somebody asked about our relationship? What if we ran into some person who knew my husband? And the most painful question torturing me was: What if my mind was playing a trick on me? What if the man I thought I loved was nothing like the real person? What if…?

My thoughts were interrupted by the announcement that the airplane from New York had arrived. It seemed to be an eternity till I finally saw Stan coming through the customs gate looking anxiously around. Then he stood waiting for his friends to join him. This was the man I hardly knew and had seen only a few days in my whole life—the man, who in some staggering way had become so dear in my life and for whose sake I lied, made up stories, left my family during the summer vacation, and traveled away from home. I did not move, questioning myself, *do I really want to see this man?* I hoped that my common sense would correct the strange zigzag path that distorted my straight life line—when suddenly our eyes met.

Stan's face lit up and his open engaging smile changed everything. My question was answered with a smile and a glance—"Yes!"

Still looking in my direction Stan said something to a man who came up to him and then started moving slowly up to where I stood. When he got closer, he said softly, "Hi my true love." Then he stretched forward his hand and said in a louder voice, "Elaina, it's very nice of you to come to the airport. I was nervous about being in this huge city without an interpreter. Now I feel much better. I know you will help me a lot."

I immediately picked up the rules of the game: I would be introduced to the rest of the Fulbright group as an acquaintance from the Peace Walk who was willing to be Stan's interpreter in Moscow. I thought it was a good idea and shook hands with Stan politely.

"Welcome back to big Moscow," I said, "How was the flight?"

"Pretty good," Stan said loudly and then added very softly, "I've missed you terribly. Boy, I'm happy to see you."

At this moment a man came up to us. Stan introduced him, "This is Phil, our group leader. Phil, this is Ealaina I told you about. She is going to act as my interpreter when I meet with the teachers who have been using my Peace Curriculum in Russian Schools."

"Oh, yes. I do remember. *Zdrastvuite. Kak vy pozhivayete?*" Phil spoke perfect Russian. He said *hello* and *how are you* without any accent. I was impressed. I said, "Wow! *Vy govorite po-russki?* Where did you learn this difficult language?"

Phil laughed, "I lived in Moscow for eight years. My father worked in the Embassy, and I went to a Russian school, but you are right, it's a very difficult language."

"I see. Well, it's a pleasure to meet an American who speaks my mother tongue so well."

"Nice to meet you, too. I'm afraid I've got to count the people to see if everybody is here and ready to go to the bus. Please excuse me."

Before Phil left, Stan asked him, "Is it okay if Ealaina goes to the hotel in our bus, so that she knows where we'll stay? I'd also like to invite her to dinner tonight."

"It's fine." I did not really like how Phil said it, but then why should I care one way or the other about what he said. So I simply said *thank you*.

After Stan had introduced me to the other members of the group, we sat in the back of the bus, and finally could talk over our plans. It was such a good feeling to have Stan so close to me. He touched my hand, and I got an amazing sensation all over my body. Just a touch. What a touch.

The two days in Moscow flew by "as if in a mist"—according to a Russian saying.

Stan and I had a wonderful time: we went around the Kremlin Wall like we had done in 1987; we had lunch and dinner together; we made love in his hotel room while his roommate was out visiting a host family; we went to the strip show in the Cosmos hotel—an innovation in a new dem-ocratic Russia; and...we ran into a woman from Moscow, Idaho. That was a phenomenal encounter. I was the one who was constantly alert because I was afraid of being seen by someone who knew my husband. Stan, on the contrary, was relaxed; there was no way that any of his wife's friends would see him in Moscow with a Russian woman. He was dead wrong.

We were going downstairs to the lobby in his hotel when a woman with a suitcase literally bumped into Stan. When she raised her head, she could not believe her eyes. She screamed, "Stan? What the hell are *you* do-ing here?"

"I could ask you the same question," he said, "Jeannie, I'm here on the Fulbright trip. What about you?"

While they were talking, I quietly continued going downstairs and sat down in an armchair so that Stan could see me. In a minute he joined me, "Ugh! That was close. Just imagine if I was holding your hand or giving you a kiss at the moment she saw us. This lady is from our church. She is actually a good friend of Carol's."

"Well, there's nothing to worry about. I'm leaving today, so she'll never know."

"I can't let you go. These two days were magical. I love you so much. You are the love of my life. But this time it's not too bad. We are going to see each other in Leningrad in three weeks. I am happy."

Those two days of reunion in Moscow were encouraging. We both had a good time in each other's company. We loved; we laughed; we did not quarrel; it was easy to be with each other. We did not see much of Moscow, choosing to stay in the hotel most of the time. We were experiencing and enjoying true togetherness—such a rare delicacy. We were happy.

My trip to Denmark was interesting and fun. Our little group went to a small island of Bornholm to participate in the International Peace Festival in the city of Ronne. First, we went to Finland by train. By that time in Russia it was against the law to drink alcohol in public places. A train was considered a public place, but only until it reached the Finnish border. As soon as it crossed into the territory of Finland, people could drink anything they wanted.

Because of this new ridiculous law, people created many funny stories and jokes about it. Among the members of our group there was a talented joke-teller. He was the major performer during the trip. One of his famous jokes was especially popular:

A man calls his friend and asks,

"Ivan, how are you?"

The friend answers, "Oh, Pete, not very well."

"Why so?"

"Guess what, yesterday I went to the "book store" to buy some "books", but they had all been sold out. So I had to go to the "library" and "read magazines" and I don't usually learn much from them. And what about you?"

"It was even worse. When I went to the "library", all the "magazines" had been checked out. So I had to go to my mother-in-law's and "read her manuscript" in her company."

A person who had never lived through a time of alcohol prohibition would probably not find anything funny in this joke, but those who had been through the hardships of imposed sobriety enjoyed it and laughed till they cried because the "book store" meant a liquor store and "books" meant vodka; the "library" was a pub while "magazines" were beer or wine, and "my mother-in-law's manuscript" was the strong home brew called "samogon", which has an extremely unpleasant flavor.

As soon as the train had crossed the Finish border, the male part of the Russian delegation decided to "read some books," and the female group wanted to "read magazines." We were a merry group of people who knew how to have a good time.

From Helsinki we took a ferry to Stockholm. We spent two days in that beautiful city visiting museums, friends, and various peace groups. Then we took a train and then another ferry and finally got to Ronne. We lived in tents in a park, had barbecues, sang and danced, had discussions and lectures, went to saunas, attended concerts, and made friends. It was a real festival and celebration of life and peace.

One day was free from group activities. The weather was warm, and we decided to spend most of the morning on the beach, but some people preferred to go shopping first, some wanted to sleep longer, and I was the only one who wanted nothing but the warm sun, the sea, and the sand. So I went to the beach alone, and my friends promised to join me later.

When I got there, I took off my dress and stretched out on my towel on the white, almost flour-like soft sand. After so many busy days, I finally attained comfort and peace of mind and could devote all my thoughts to my wonderful memories of Stan. I felt a little guilty that all the time spent in Denmark I had so much fun that I had no time to stop and connect with him in my thoughts. Here, finally, was the right time. But the heat relaxed me so much that I could not concentrate on my thoughts, and instead I shielded my eyes from the bright sun with my hand and watched the slow, leisurely life of the beach.

Gradually, I understood that I was probably the only woman wearing a full—top and bottom—swimming suit. Most of the women of all ages were topless. This was very unusual for me. There are nude beaches in Russia on the Black Sea, but those are separate for men and women. I was not ready mentally to expose my 'topless top' to strangers, and especially to male strangers. On the other hand, I began to feel a little uncomfortable being the only female with more than my birthday suit on; I began to feel like "a white crow," as the Russian saying has it.

I was absorbing the tender warmth of the sunrays thinking about different customs in different cultures. Suddenly I heard a voice, "Hey!"

A handsome man of about thirty was standing in front of me screening the sun with his broad nicely tanned shoulders. I said, "Pardon me?"

He said something in Danish; I could not understand. I asked, "Sorry, do you speak English?"

"I do. Are you English?"

"No, I am Russian, and if you can speak Russian that would be even better."

"Unfortunately, I can't. But I have always dreamed of learning Russian. Actually, I've never seen a Russian person so close before."

"Well, I haven't seen a lot of Danish people until I came here."

"May I sit by you, do you mind?"

"No, I don't mind, you are welcome."

"I'm Bengt. And what is your name?"

"Elena."

"Eleena? What a beautiful name." As usual my name was barbarously mispronounced. It certainly did not sound beautiful in the mouth of this Danish man. But I did not pay any attention.

All I said was, "Really? My older brother gave me this name. I happened to be born at the time when he'd been reading Greek mythology, a story of Helen of Troy. In Greek and Russian Helen is Elena."

"How interesting. Did your brother want you to be a beautiful woman for whom nations would be fighting?"

"Oh, I doubt that. All he wanted was to have a Trojan Horse in which he could hide with his friends from their teachers."

We both laughed

And then two unexpected events happened. On the right, I noticed Nadya, Nina and three men from our group approaching us; they had just seen me and were coming up slowly. On the left, my new acquaintance started to undress, and when my friends had reached us, he took off the last piece of clothing—his swim shorts. Standing with all the 'beauties of Apollo' right in front of my eyes, Bengt said, "Take off your bikinis and let's go swimming."

My friends froze dead. They were staring at the naked lower part of Bengt's body with obvious shock. I could not help looking, either, because his private parts had suddenly become the center of public attention. I blushed and shouted, "No, thank you, I can't swim!"

"You can't swim? I'll teach you. Let's go!"

"No, no. Thank you, I really prefer to stay in the sun."

"Okay. I'll be back soon." He finally left.

Now the torture began.

"Of course, we left this young woman alone for some thirty minutes, and look what she has done. She has undressed a man with her glance. Well, well, well...We could not expect that you—a mother, a teacher, a Russian Perestroika Peacenik (!) would compromise yourself and what more—us, your comrades, with such light-minded behavior."

And on and on and on...

Everybody was laughing happily. It was unusual for Russians to see naked women and men on the beach. Oh, the free manners of Scandinavia.

Later, when Bengt came back, dried himself with a huge green towel and finally put on his shorts, I introduced him to my companions, and we had a long and interesting conversation. He turned out to be a pleasant person, an architectural engineer, a divorcee with no kids, a man with deep feelings for beauty in both nature and art. He also asked me why our group was laughing when he had left to swim. He could hear us even in the water. I had to tell him the truth. He was genuinely surprised because in his culture it was not a big deal to see a nude man or woman on the beach or in a sauna. I told him that I could not understand why men did not feel aroused at the sight of nude women.

To this Bengt said, "Oh, no, seeing a nude woman on the beach does not inspire any sexual desire in a man. But in the evening, when everybody goes out to a restaurant or bar, that's where all the excitement is!"

"You don't mean they are topless at the restaurants, too?" I asked in astonishment.

"No, no," Bengt started to laugh, "of course, not. Eleena, you are so funny. No, no!" He kept giggling, "In the evening, at restaurants women wear formal evening dresses exposing their nude shoulders, backs, necks, arms of beautiful peach color from the sun tan. That's when men begin to imagine more than what they can actually see and become aroused."

It was an unexpected discovery for me, and it seemed quite reasonable. But what did we know? We were "peaceniks" living in tents in a park. Nobody was wearing formal exposing dresses there, but "wearing tents" seemed to be cause for plenty of arousal.

Bengt became a close friend of all the members of our small delegation. He even gave us his car to go to several small, ancient and beautiful villages, tourist towns, and parks. He treated us with the famous and absolutely delicious Ronne ice cream, which is served in portions of three sizes, and even the smallest scoop was as big as the dome of St. Peter's Basilica in the Vatican.

He took pictures of us and wrote down Danish names which were too difficult for us to spell. He was the perfect host. Thanks to Bengt we learned a lot about this little fairytale country, and we felt sorry to part when it was time for us to leave. He came to the airport and to our amazement he cried, hugging each new Russian friend goodbye. In the end he told me, "Eleena, you can't imagine how grateful I am to you and your friends. You actually saved my life. I was so lonely and devastated after my divorce that I was even thinking about suicide. But I met you, and I understood how stupid it was to try to solve my problems that way. Life is not easy in Russia, and yet you and your friends are full of energy, happiness, and excitement. You know how to value every moment of life. You breathed new hope into me. Thank you. I'll never forget you."

It was an unexpected confession. During the days that we spent with Bengt, we had not seen the slightest sign of his miserable state of mind. He always looked happy and full of energy, while we, on the other hand, had complained about Russia's economic and political problems a lot. And yet, we were a happy bunch of peaceniks who felt inspired about life. It was not the first time I had discovered that people in the West despite their freedom of choice and great opportunities to succeed in life, were often insecure and vulnerable, but did not complain or show their bad moods to other people. Russians, in contrast, liked to sound pessimistic and complain about everything, criticize relatives, friends, co-workers, bosses, neighbors, and high political figures, but, generally, they were strong emotionally and happy spiritually. What a strange paradox.

When the Peace Festival was over, we went to Copenhagen for sightseeing. The place amazed us by its cleanliness, its many porno shops with nude pictures in the windows, and its high prices. The street artists, clowns, sword swallowers and jugglers on every corner downtown made me feel that the city was celebrating a permanent holiday.

At the Royal Palace during the changing of the guards I tried to walk by the guard's side and make him smile. I don't know why I did it. I felt like one of those clowns and wanted to entertain the big crowd by performing for my friends mostly. Many people were laughing, whistling and trying to help me make the guard at least grin a little. But no, absolutely not. He was like a rock, a monolithic image of a faithful royal soldier. I was impressed and a little ashamed, but not too much because the atmosphere of the city invited everyone to be playful.

After the sightseeing, we still had several hours before the departure of our ferry to Stockholm. Some people from the group wanted to go shopping, but Nadya, Irina and I decided to go to Little Holland, a famous embankment with hundreds of cozy coffee shops, restaurants and pubs. We found a pretty place with tables outside. We ordered espresso and talked about the city. We were sitting right across from an anchored boat, all white, red and blue with the romantic name "My Dream" written in English.

Suddenly a young pretty woman came out from downstairs followed by a handsome young man, her boyfriend as we presumed. At first they were talking and kissing each other lightly. We were watching them with delight. Then the man began to lift the girl's blouse. She did not try to stop him; on the contrary, it was clear she enjoyed the game. In a minute, she was topless, but that was obviously not enough; he started lifting her skirt up. The rest happened so quickly that we did not even manage to exchange glances or comments; the pair was making love right in front of us. They didn't seem to notice anyone, fully giving themselves to the pleasure of lovemaking. It did not look bad or disgusting; it looked natural and beautiful. After they achieved their climax, they began to laugh, and at this point it looked as if they did notice that there were people around. The man waved at us. We blushed with embarrassment and began to talk trying not to look in their direction. When a little later I looked at the boat again, there was nobody there. Was it only a mirage? My Dream? I could not tell for sure.

That very night we arrived in Stockholm, changed ferries and were soon on our way to Helsinki and then back to Leningrad. I became nervous because there had been something on my mind all those days in Denmark, but I could not tell anybody. The secret that was keeping my attention during the trip was connected with Stan. He was supposed to meet me at the railway station, and I had to think of a good explanation for my friends why Stan and not Vadim would be meeting me. I could not think of a single one.

CHAPTER TWENTY THREE

The Empty City
August 1990, Leningrad

I decided not to tell Nadya about Stan until we arrived at the railway station. If Stan was there, I would not have to explain anything right on the spot because everybody would be surprised and preoccupied with greeting him, and I would be able to think of a good story later.

Finally, the train slowed down as it entered its designated track, and I stepped out of the compartment into the corridor to look out of the window to see if Stan was on the platform. There were a few people meeting their relatives and friends, but Stan was not among them.

We started walking along the platform towards the exit of the station. Stan was nowhere to be seen. I had mixed feeling; on the one hand, I was delighted I did not have to explain anything to Nadya, but on the other hand, I was disappointed and worried. I desperately wanted to see him. What could have possibly happened?

"Are you looking for somebody?" Nadya asked, "Are you expecting Vadim to meet you? I thought he was at the dacha with Alexei."

"You're right; he is. I was just wondering if maybe my dad would come," I lied.

"I see. If he doesn't come, will you need a ride? My friend, Alla, should be here with her car."

"No thanks, I'll take a taxi. Thank you so much for an absolutely fantastic trip and enjoyable company." I gave Nadya a hug.

"It was a pleasure to have you in our delegation. Enjoy the rest of your vacation," Nadya smiled.

I said goodbye to the members of the group and went outside. Stan was not to be found anywhere. I kept looking around slowly walking towards the taxi stop. My heart was beating fast. I was still hoping to find him somewhere outside on the square in front of the railway station. I stopped at the red marble wall under the big clock—the place where people usually wait if they get lost. I waited for ten minutes, but it was all in vain.

I decided to go home.

I came to the empty apartment and looked at the silent ivory phone. It was like a little enemy—stiff, indifferent, and almost hostile. The clock showed 8:40 A. M. Suddenly the phone rang. I grabbed the receiver, "Hello?"

There was silence on the other end.

I repeated, "Hello? Hello?"

Again there was no answer. Then I heard short buzzing. I sat down and stared at the phone. Who could it be? If it was Stan, why didn't he talk to me? Could it be Vadim checking if I was back in town? But why didn't he talk to me either? Definitely, somebody dialed a wrong number. I waited for a few minutes, but it did not ring anymore.

I decided to take a shower and get into a better mood. I enjoyed standing under the streams of hot water, but I was still thinking about possible reasons why Stan was not at the railway station. He could have been lost. He could have simply forgotten the time of my arrival. He could have been sick. Or something terrible could have happened to him in one of those cities he was traveling to. He could be drowned in the Black Sea. Or maybe he was robbed and killed. The showers of warm water did not warm my cold, dark thoughts. I was surprised how I let my imagination run wild. I was known for my rational approach to life by my family and friends, but this was about love after all. I drove myself to such a state of mind that when I was drying my wet body, my fingers trembled so much that I hardly managed to hold the towel. I felt really sick.

Suddenly, the phone rang again. The sound was so sharp in the silence of the apartment that I was startled. Momentarily, I rushed to the phone and heard an unknown female voice, "May I speak with Elena, please?"

"This is she."

"Please don't hang up. Someone wants to talk with you."

My heart beat madly. I was about to pass out. I was now sure that something very bad had happened, and an official person was going to inform me of the terrible news. Then I heard, "Elaina? Is this Elaina?"

"Stan? Thank Goodness you are alive. Where are you?"

"My dearest," Stan's voice was as always—quiet and velvet, "Why shouldn't I be alive? Of course I am alive, and now I am even in seventh heaven—when I hear your voice and know that you are here. I want to see you immediately. Where can we meet?"

"Where are you? And why didn't you come to the railway station?"

"I'll explain everything when I see you."

I decided not to ask any more questions but instead find out where he was so I could go to see him right away. He was on the Moscow Prospect not far from his hotel Pulkovskaya right across from the famous memorial to the victims of the 900-day siege of Leningrad. I told him to stand right by the monument and wait for me.

Life was not that scary after all. All my fears vanished. All of a sudden I noticed how beautiful the late summer morning was. The sky was clear bright blue, and the sun was already generously warm. Once every three-to-five years August could be fantastic in Leningrad, and this was one of those summers. I put on a new light-blue open summer dress that I had bought in Copenhagen, white pretty sandals on high heels, styled my hair and used some light makeup. I reserved a taxi by phone, and in half an hour I was on Moscow Prospect.

I got out of the taxi on the opposite side of the street from where I could see Stan sitting on one of the granite slabs of the monument. I felt so good. There he was—my love, my man, my friend, my lover, and my very important person.

Our reunion was happy. First we went to his hotel room and satisfied the love thirst for each other. It was wonderful to feel his arms around me; it was so natural and pleasant.

Then we talked. There was so much to tell each other.

Stan was full of impressions after visiting so many different places in my big country. He was fascinated with the magnificent Volga River and the white sturgeon steak he had in the restaurant in Volgograd. The next day he was astounded by the size of the Mother Russia monument there, and his heart was over flown with sympathy, pain and tenderness for the lonely women who came to the monument with tears in their tired eyes. They were coming to that monument like a silent river of people. Those women lost their fathers, husbands, sons, and daughters in the ugly war, and now their destiny was to come to the foot of this enormous hill with the monument on top of it. Their pilgrimage was a clear testimony that not even time could fully erase the pain and suffering that the loss of their loved ones had brought into their lives decades ago.

Stan told me about the holiday mood of life in Pyatigorsk—a picturesque mountain vacation site in the Caucasus. It is famous for numerous mineral springs that according to local legends have magic healing power and whose waters are used in love potion. Stan drank some of the cold bitter-sour water and confessed that only my image had saved him from its taste of this 'love elixir.' Oh, the power of true love.

Another interesting memory of Pyatigorsk he shared with me was his relaxing one-hour massage, complete with an audience. The little daughter of the masseuse kept peeking from behind the curtain to catch glimpses of a half naked American.

Stan especially enjoyed telling me stories about the hospitality of Georgian people in Tbilisi where he drank red sweet wine out of a bull's horn for breakfast, red sweet wine out of a bull's horn for lunch and red sweet wine out of a bull's horn for dinner. There he danced in circles of twenty-thirty men, and even kissed men on both cheeks right on the streets—the custom he learned quickly and easily to his surprise.

He also told me about the gentle Black Sea waters in Sochi where he wanted to go to the beach but was astonished by the sign "Unisex Nude Beaches" and decided he was not ready for that yet—oh, yeh, here I interrupted him with my Danish beach story. My experience was more interesting than his because no woman in Sochi took off her bikinis right in front of Stan. Instead, he had to admire the beauty of the flowers and plants of the tropical varieties in the Dendrarium and spend sad evenings enjoying the gorgeous red-purple sunsets, sitting in the armchair on the balcony of his hotel room alone. Sochi was the romantic paradise for lovers where Stan painfully wanted me to be by his side.

He told me about the gold cathedral domes glittering in the hot and dry Ukrainian sun and reflected in the waters of the calm Dnepr River in Kiev. The soul touching tunes and voices of the Ukrainian choir left an unforgettable mark in his heart. He also loved the real *vareniki* and *golubtsy*, *pirozhki*, and *galushki*—all the genuine varieties of the Ukrainian cuisine.

And all those days—the wonderful days full of events, new friends and experiences, he was still longing to finally go to Leningrad where he could see me. When his group eventually arrived in Leningrad, he immediately asked the guide to call me. He had misplaced the little piece of paper on which I had written the date and hour of my arrival and the name of the railway station where I expected him to come to meet me. The thought that he could fail to see me in Leningrad terrified him. Then it became even worse when the guide told him that nobody answered the phone for two days. Today, after breakfast, he was hoping that the guide would tell him the good news that I was found, but the guide did not say a word when she took the group to the bus. Stan unwillingly got on the bus. He was looking out of the window at all those people walking on the streets and riding in cars and buses. He was in a place with a population of five million people, and yet this city was absolutely empty—empty without his Ealaina. He was desperate when suddenly the guide came up to him and said, "Stan, by the way, I called your friend in the morning. She picked up the phone, but I did not talk with her. I'm pretty sure that was her."

"Really?" Stan sprang to his feet. "Please stop the bus. I have to get out immediately."

"What's the matter, Stan?" Phil asked with unconcealed irritation, "Aren't you going on the tour to Petrodvorets? If you don't go there, you'll regret it afterwards. It's probably one of the most beautiful places in the whole country."

Stan did not even look in Phil's direction. He was pleading with the driver to stop at the nearest cross section. The bus stopped with a jolt, and Stan rushed out. He found himself on the street alone; he did not know where to go. He was bumping into people, but he did not notice that. He had not found his Ealaina yet...the city was still empty.

He finally stumbled onto a phone booth, but there was another obstacle—how to dial the number? What coins to use? He tried to talk to passers by, but they did not understand what he wanted. After maybe ten minutes, a young woman stopped and asked him in good English, "Do you need a coin to make a call?"

Stan smiled happily, "Yes, please help me call a friend. I'm an American, and I've never used a Russian pay phone. This call is very important."

The woman dialed the number.

Stan found me and Leningrad was no longer an empty city.

CHAPTER TWENTY FOUR

The Fish Pie Wish
August, 1990, Leningrad

Stan and I had two days together in Leningrad. I wanted to use the opportunity and show him *my* Leningrad so that he had a chance to see where I lived and what I valued.

The first day we spent mostly outside. Early in the morning we went on a boat tour along the rivers and canals of the city. As it was in the middle of the week, there were few passengers on board the tour boat. The guide was not tired yet and told us all sorts of fables, legends and true stories about the mansions built along the numerous rivers and canals of the city.

When we were passing by Count Stroganoff's Palace on the Moika River, our guide, Vera, told us how the cook of the palace was ordered by the master to make something tasty and unusual for an unexpected foreign guest, and how he used long elegant pieces of beef sautéed in a special sauce, the cook's personal pride and secret, and how he served it with mashed potatoes. Stan was surprised to hear what the original recipe was because he thought that 'beef stroganoff' was ground beef and sour cream sauce served over noodles. The recipe apparently suffered a lot of modifications by the time it arrived in America.

When our boat was passing by Count Yusupov's Palace, Vera told us the story of Rasputin, who had been a serious threat to the Russian bourgeoisie and the throne due to his enormous influence on the Czar's wife. He was the healer of the little prince, who had suffered from hemophilia, and had become a sort of an angel-savior for the Czarina. He, a peasant by origin, possessed some kind of extrasensory power and thought that he could actually be the czar himself.

The leading aristocrats of the country could not allow that to happen. Knowing that he was a womanizer and loved to be introduced to beautiful noble ladies, count Yusupov and a few of his close friends decided to invite

Rasputin to a party where he was supposed to meet Yusupov's incredibly charming wife. The woman was not even in the palace, but instead a deadly dinner had been planned for Rasputin. For dessert Rasputin ate six cream puffs filled with poison, but he did not seem to be influenced by it in any way. The assassins had to then use a more extreme measure; one of the 'guests' shot Rasputin. The man did not seem to be harmed in the least, just a little surprised, and the desperate killer fired nine more bullets in the body of the peasant giant.

Finally, presumably dead Rasputin was packed in a sack and thrown into the river. Later, the 'heroes' of the plot read a newspaper report of the autopsy performed on Rasputin. To their great astonishment it said that even though the man had ten bullets in his body, none of them had been fatal, and that the cause of death was actually drowning. The poison was not even mentioned. Many years later it was proven that the Madera wine Rasputin was drinking at Yusupov's party had acted as an antidote for the poison used in the cream pastries.

We passed the palaces of many other wealthy Russian aristocrats of the 18th-19th centuries. Some of those buildings had been turned into museums; others housed local communist party committees, trade union organizations, or culture centers—the equivalents of American community centers. In addition we saw many beautiful churches, opera and drama theaters, banks, department stores, and restaurants.

The boat finally went back along the Moika River before it entered the deep waters of the Neva—the major and biggest water artery of our Venice of the North. When we were passing by the mansion where the great Russian writer Alexander Pushkin lived, Vera told us the official "tourist" version of a sad and complicated story of the short life and senseless death of this talented poet.

Pushkin became famous among both the rich, highly educated and the poor illiterate people of Russia early in his career as a writer. The reason for Pushkin's fame was his ability to embed philosophical and romantic meaning within his lyrical poetry and rhyming fairy tales both of which were easy to memorize and retell. He was one of the rare literary masters, who was able to express the "mysterious Russian soul" in simple and exquisite words.

He married one of the most beautiful women in Russia of that time— Natalia Goncharova with emerald green eyes and the thinnest imaginable waist line. Pushkin adored his beauty-wife, had four children with her and considered himself the happiest man on the face of the Earth. But unfortunately he was an acquaintance of a few young intellectuals who were part of a plan by a group of aristocrats to over throw the government of czar Nicolas I. These men hoped to assassinate the czar and turn Russia into a Republic. The uprising was a catastrophic failure. Five of the leaders were executed and dozens of others were exiled to Siberia for life.

Pushkin's bitter satirical criticism of the czar did not go unnoticed either. He was secretly declared *persona non grata*. The Royal Court devised a sophisticated way to get rid of this dangerous famous poet. The fabricated anonymous letter informing Pushkin of his wife's secret love affair with a young and handsome French émigré in Russian service, d'Anthes, did the job. Pushkin did not believe the dirty rumor, but he was a man of honor, and he challenged d'Anthes to a duel. A loud shot sounded in the silence of the freezing January morning of 1837. Its brutal simplicity was in stark contrast to the exquisite word tapestries created by Pushkin in life.

His writings survive him to this very day; he is the greatest Russian poet of all time.

In the end of her emotional story Vera recited one of Pushkin's poems, which later Stan found in the English translation by Walter Arndt:

This valedictory effusion
Pleads in a tongue you do not speak,
And yet for it by fond illusion
Your understanding I would seek.
My dearest, till a pall may smother
These senses while we are apart,
While I can feel, you and no other
Will be the idol of my heart.
On strangers now your gazes bending,
Go on believing just my heart,
As you believed it from the start,
Its passions never comprehending.

Our guide was definitely a Pushkin's fan and seemed deeply touched by her own recitation of his poetry. So much so that she remained silent for some time seemingly savoring the meaning of the romantic verses she had just recited. In contrast, Stan and I knew exactly what Pushkin was talking about in these poetic lines as if the great poet had written them just for the two of us. Stan lightly touched the middle of my back giving me the sign "it's about us" and I brushed his knee with my fingers responding "yes, darling, I know."

Then she treated us to another fascinating story as we passed under the hanging bridge-connection of the Winter Palace, the former residence of Russian czars. It was the sad place where one of the heroines, Liza, in the famous Pushkin's *"Pikovaya Dama"* ("The Queen of Spades") committed suicide when she was waiting in vain for her lover to come. She suffered so much from the humiliation of being forgotten and abandoned that she took her own life. This fictional story was so powerful that the residents of Leningrad always refer to this spot as the place where Liza's soul dwells.

As we passed under this hanging bridge, we found ourselves in the widest part of the Neva where its tributary, Malaya Nevka and the major river Neva converge. A panorama of astounding architectural beauty and harmony opened to our view: The Peter and Paul Fortress, the former Stock Exchange, the spit of the Basil Island with two Rostral columns-light houses, the minarets of the blue-tiled Mosque, the Winter Palace known in the world as the Hermitage, and the Academy of Sciences. The boat turned right, and in a minute we were passing by the exquisitely simple fence of the most romantic place in the city—the Summer Gardens. Here was the end of our tour. We thanked Vera, the captain and the crew of the boat and stepped down on the old cobble stone road leading to the entrance of the Summer Gardens.

By this time of the day, the sun was up in the sky, and the air was still and hot. It was the right place to hide from the heat in the shade of the two-hundred-years-old oak and maple trees.

Stan and I found a quiet path among the marble Roman statues of gods and goddesses and sat down on a wide comfortable white bench. Stan looked at me, and in his eyes I could see tender love. He whispered, "This city is exactly like you—gentle, beautiful and strong. Now I see where your spirit comes from, and I also think that I'll probably never solve the famous mystery of the Russian soul. But for sure this culture attracts me like a magnet. You are my magnet."

"Oh, my dear, I've heard about this mysterious soul stuff, but I don't think I can solve the mystery either. That is why it's a mystery. And let it be that way. As to my soul, it's open to you and my heart has no secrets. I enjoy sharing my culture with you and I hope you don't feel bored."

"Bored? Are you kidding? With you I experience lots of emotions, but for sure there is no place for boredom," Stan put his arm around my shoulder.

"Well, I hope there's at least some place in your stomach for lunch. How about having some fish in the best seafood restaurant in Leningrad. It'll be my treat."

"I can never say "no" to such a tasty proposition," Stan smiled.

We were about to set off to the restaurant when an elderly lady appeared carrying a short ladder and a bucket with soapy water in her hands. She gave us a warm greeting smile, arranged the ladder by the marble statue across from our bench, climbed up and started washing gently the figure of the goddess with a soft sponge. Stan was staring at this statue taking a bath; then he muttered, "I don't think I can stand looking at this sexual bathing any longer. The soft strokes with which the lady is touching the breasts of the Roman goddess and the streams of the bubbly soupy water flowing straight into her groin are very arousing."

"Stan! How can you say such things?" I could not help laughing. Then I said, "Okay, I think it's time to take you away from this erotic scene. Let's divert your attention from the stiff stony groins to hot nourishing food."

"Oh, yes, please, please take me away from this pornography."

We laughed, waved goodbye to the elderly cleaning lady and headed out to the street where we caught a taxi and went to the restaurant "*Demya-nova Uha*" ("Demyan's Fish Soup").

The name of this restaurant was the line from the title of a famous Russian fable written by Andrey Kryloff. In this story Demyan was a pushy host who kept feeding his visiting friend the *uha* (fish soup), which was very tasty, but because there was too much of it, it became a disgusting experience for the guest. The lesson was clear: everything is good in life only in moderation. Stan said, "It's interesting that in Russia so much is connected with literature and old culture of the country. It seems like a name of this sort for a restaurant implies that everybody knows this Kryloff's fable. Can that be true?"

"Absolutely, I assure you every person of the age of seven and up does know. The education system in this country is based on the universal curriculum, and all over the eleven time zones from West to the Far East in all elementary schools all the children not only read Kryloff's fables but also memorize them and remember them through their entire lives."

"Amazing. I don't think it could be possible in the United States. In our education system teachers are free to work out their individual curricula and choose the stories to read to their students. And memorization of poems is not emphasized as a method of teaching at all."

The waiter gave us the menus, and Stan looked bluntly at the Cyrillic letters. Having watched him for a while and seeing how desperate he was, I finally said, "Do you need my help?"

"Always," said Stan sighing with relief.

After a long translation and discussion, Stan decided to try the pot pie with the filling of three different types of white fish: halibut, sturgeon and lightly smoked cod. I ordered pancakes and black caviar. We drank the traditional soft drink '*kvas*' made of rye bread and spices.

When Stan tried the pie, he looked satisfied; he obviously loved it.

"Can we ask the cook for the recipe? I love it. It's delicious," he said.

"I guess we can ask for the recipe, but I don't think you'll be able to make it without the sturgeon. As far as I know it's expensive and rare in the U.S."

"You are right. Forget about the recipe. Elaina, if you keep feeding me like this, I might never want to go back to Idaho."

"That's the plan. I know that the way to a man's heart is through his stomach."

"It's a shame, but it's true," said Stan, and we laughed.

After this enjoyable lunch, we walked slowly in the park that stretched along the walls of the Peter and Paul Fortress. It was a beautiful summer afternoon with a light breeze from the Gulf of Finland. The seagulls were flying around looking at us with open interest: what an unusual couple— they were thinking—a Russian woman in her mid thirties, blond and slim with green-hazel eyes and an American man in his early forties, hairy, huge and blue eyed—such different creatures and so much in love.

We were enjoying the quiet company of each other. We both knew that we would have to part soon, and we were absorbing the last hours of togetherness. We were both silent for a long time.

Then I asked Stan, "What are you thinking about, my dear?"

"Remember you told me Russians believe that if they eat something for the first time in their lives they make a wish and it comes true? When

I was eating the fish pie at that restaurant, I made a wish. I am thinking about the wish now."

"Can you tell me what it is?"

"Sorry, you taught me it should be a secret or it won't come true, my love. I'm telling you nothing."

But for me it was enough to see the look in Stan's eyes—the same wonder they expressed in Washington D.C. when he had made a wish looking at the blue star.

I thought I could guess what his wish was.

CHAPTER TWENTY FIVE

The Squirrel and the Crocodile
August, 1990, Leningrad

We did not want to part that evening. I invited Stan to come to my brother's apartment. Vlad, his wife and daughter were in Pennsylvania. He had received an invitation to teach physics in Penn State University in 1989. He was successful and got an extension of the contract, so the family was not coming back for another year. I was in the process of looking for nice renters, but so far the apartment was empty, and it was a good place for us to have a few hours of privacy.

When we arrived, Stan was genuinely surprised to see such a huge apartment. There was a large entrance hall with a few book cases along the walls. To the left there was a kitchen. A dining table for twelve people, a long sofa, a refrigerator, a stove and a double sink found room there easily. There were about twenty hand painted lacquer trays collected by my sister-in-law hanging all over the kitchen walls. Further down the hall on the left hand side there was a bathroom with a deep and long bath tub and sink and then a separate room with the toilet. Next to it was a storage closet full of all kinds of junk.

On the right hand side of the hall there were two rooms. The first one was about five hundred fifty square feet and the second room was over four hundred thirty square feet. The apartment was not typical. Usually a family of three people had an apartment of three hundred fifty square feet with tiny rooms in it. But this one was unusually big with beautiful vaulted ceilings. It was also in a convenient location a few blocks away from the Neva River and one subway stop from Nevsky Prospect—Leningrad's down town.

The sunset reflected in the windows of the rooms, and the space was filled with warm rosy colors. Stan whispered softly, "Everything is so unusual here: all these Asian carpets on the walls and on the parquet floors, the icons in silver frames, the sparkling crystal glasses and vases in the breakfront, and the mahogany piano—it feels like a museum. Is this the way most Russians decorate their homes inside?"

"Yes, I would say so. The custom to hang thick colorful Persian carpets on the walls was probably brought to Russia by Tatars and Mongols in the thirteenth century. Their three hundred years of occupation impacted not only Russian culture but heredity. Russians also got some of the Asian facial features, and lots of straight long Slavic noses turned into shorter aquiline forms, cheek bones became higher and more square in shape, and even blue eyes developed all shades of darker brownish colors."

"Really?" Stan exclaimed in surprise. "And what about blond hair?"

"What about it? Hair is not a problem. It's the only part of the human body that can be changed any time and very easily thanks to the cosmetics industry, so it's really hard to say what the real Slavic hair color should be. My mom, for example had dark brown bronze hair; my dad was very light brown before he became all gray; Vlad was born with red hair, and I have always been blond. So we've covered all the bases."

"You belong to my family more than to yours as everybody in mine is born with blond hair," Stan teased me.

"Well, who knows, maybe my great-great-great-great-grand mother had a romantic relationship with a blond American who brought potatoes from Massachusetts to Russia in the year say...1790, only two centuries ago. I have one cousin who's also a blond jewel among all her relatives with dark hair and eyes."

"I like that, Elaina. It would be fun if we find out one day that we are actually related." He smiled but then added seriously, "No, I don't want to be related. I want to be able to love you and have you in my life as a love, not as a cousin."

"Don't worry. I am quite sure it's hardly possible that we are related."

We were sitting close to each other on the wide soft sofa. The colors in the room changed into light bluish purple. Stan touched my hair with his lips, then his lips moved slowly towards my ear, and I felt the warm wet breeze of his breath. His tongue scanned the tip of my ear lobe. A thrilling sensation crept all over my body. His fingers stroked the nipples of my breasts, slowly and gently, yet firmly so that I could not escape. I did not want to escape. I wanted more fondling and caressing, more lusting touches and strokes. And he did it all. He knew exactly what to do to make me feel ecstatic. There was no world around me at that moment. All I was feeling was the sensation of my sexual desire.

Now we were lying on the sofa kissing and undressing each other. The light had changed to dark violet—almost sinful—shades. Our desires were free and daring; our movements were strong and without a single flaw. We fit each other as if our parents had used the exact matching patterns designing their babies. The firmness, the wetness, the rhythm of the strokes, the gentleness of the kisses and the passion of the love whisper—everything was gratifying to an extent almost unbearable. It was beautiful.

Now we were lying in complete darkness and silence close to each other feeling the heat of our bodies, the breathing of our lungs and the beat of our hearts. And suddenly Stan began to sing:

Once a monkey climbed a tree

He saw a banana in the leaves

The banana was yellow, and the leaves were green

And the monkey was happy like a summer bee...

I started to giggle. The song was silly and funny, but the melody was capturing. I knew he was making it up on the spot:

The monkey was flying like a bee

Up and down the big banana tree

Its tail and its soul were happily free

And its heart was in love—in love...

We laughed, and we kissed, and we sang silly words, and we were happily in love. We lit all candles that we could find in the house and played soft Bach and inspiring Mozart. We drank Armenian cognac—the only alcohol we found in my brother's bar. We made love again and again. And we talked.

That night was a charming dream, a fairly tale planet with only two happy people living on it.

I woke up with the bright sunrays beaming into my eyes. I jumped up onto my knees on the bed panicking, not understanding where I was. And I saw Stan lying on his back smiling widely. I finally realized where I was and calmed down. I wanted to get out of bed, but Stan grabbed me gently by my arms. He whispered, "Please don't move. Stay like that. The sun rays are shining through your hair so beautifully. You are my golden haired goddess—my goldilocks princess."

"And you are my big hairy bear," I laughed, "No, I actually think you are a *zaichik!*"

"Zaickeck? What's this Zaickeck about?" Stan looked worried.

"Oh, my dear, not zaickeck, but zaichik. It means bunnie."

"You think I am a bunnie?"

"Of course you are. You are my little beloved and very fluffy bunnichka."

"What's this bunniechka? You are scaring me again."

We laughed even more.

"Don't be scared," I said, "Bunnichka means a little zaichik."

"You have completely confused me, my dear. Just tell me if I am an okay animal."

"Oh, yes, you are a very okay animal. Have you ever been any animal before?"

"To tell you the truth I've never been an animal until I met you. And now I am all these animals that you call me: a fox, a bunny, a bear."

"Yes, I love all these animals in you, but I hate the one that you haven't mentioned—the camel. Remember when we ran into a woman from Idaho at the hotel in Moscow? You immediately turned into this disgusting camel pretending you did not know me." I felt angry.

"I'm afraid I'll have to be a camel for quite a while yet. Everything is so uncertain. I know we love each other—this is the only thing which is crystal clear, but everything around it is vague and unpredictable. We don't know what'll happen tomorrow. But I also know that I can be one more animal—a very important one—a crocodile."

"A crocodile?" I was horrified, "Why a crocodile? I hate them."

"No, no, my dear, you shouldn't hate me-the-crocodile. I am a very patient crocodile who seems to be asleep, but who in fact has a very sharp sense of reality and can patiently wait for the right moment."

"For the right moment to do what?" I asked still not sure I understood Stan's allegory.

"The right moment when I can catch you, my squirrel, and we can be together forever."

"Stan, how can we be together forever? It'll never happen. Think about our situation: you and I are both married and committed to our partners; we have children whom we'll never hurt; we live a world apart and are from two different cultures and speak different languages. No, we'll never be together, and you'll be my sweet pain for the rest of my life. It's awfully sad, but it's the truth that we have to admit."

"My dear, you are saying all this because you are only a squirrel—not a simple one of course and with a very pretty fluffy and inspiring tail—but sorry—only a squirrel, so please don't argue with a Bunny-Fox-Camel-Bear-Crocodile. I assure you that a combination of all these creatures will think of the way for us to be together. I don't know when it'll happen and how, but I do believe that it will."

Tears were streaming down my cheeks. I knew only one thing at that moment—I was in love and I had a few hours left to be with the man of my heart. I had an intuition that we would not be together again. I was sad, but at the same time I felt happy. I remembered the line from one of William Shakespeare's sonnets "...love is an ever-fixed mark..." Even if Stan and I would never meet again, our love will not fade away.

My eyes dried. I did not cry anymore. I said, "Are you hungry, my crocodile?"

"Always," he said, "But before we get up and have breakfast, I want to ask you a question. I'm leaving for Moscow tomorrow morning, but I'll be there all this coming week and leave for New York only next Monday. Will you be able to come to Moscow for the weekend?"

"I've already arranged everything. I'll come on Saturday morning and leave at midnight on Sunday. We'll have two more days to be together."

"How wonderful. Thank you, my love. I know it's not easy for you to do it, but the idea of being in Russia and not seeing you is unbearable. Do you remember I made a wish when I was eating the fish pie? It has come true. My wish was to see you again in Moscow before I leave Russia."

"Now I see. It was a magic fish pie. Okay, I will cook something even more powerful so that all our dreams come true. And you should help me."

"I'll be happy to do it."

When we got up and looked at the clock, it was clear that it was too late for breakfast; it was past three in the afternoon. We decided to cook dinner.

"What would you like for dinner? Do you have anything special in mind?" I asked.

"Yes, I do. Can you teach me how to make Russian borshch?"

"There is nothing easier and probably healthier because it has lots of vegetables in it."

Stan put on a pink and blue apron with lots of ribbons and ruffles.

He looked ridiculous in it, but apparently he loved it because he constantly peeked in the mirror in the kitchen. He peeled potatoes, carrots, beets and an onion while I put a piece of beef and a chicken breast in the pot with cold water and let it boil for about thirty minutes. Then Stan cut all the vegetables except potatoes in small long pieces and sautéed them in olive oil. We put the potatoes and the rest of the vegetables into the pot and simmered the mixture on very low heat for fifteen minutes. After that we added thinly cut green cabbage, sweet pepper, three big tomatoes and a bunch of fresh parsley and dill and let it simmer for another fifteen minutes. In the end we dipped a leaf of basil in, added salt and pepper, turned the heat off and let the soup stand for about an hour to saturate.

As we had no bread and sour cream, we went shopping. This was a new experience for Stan. He was looking at everything with wide-open eyes. When we finally came back home, he asked me, "Why is the shopping system so complicated here?"

"What do you mean?"

"I find it all puzzling: first people enter the store; then they come up to the counter and look at the display. After that they go to the cashier and stand in line there. The cashier makes calculations on the abacus which I have not seen since I was five. Then finally people pay and get a receipt. With this receipt they go back to the counter and stand in another line to get the products. They also have to have some sort of a sack of their own because the stores do not provide customers with plastic bags. People spend so much time even if they need only one item to buy. And it's a complete mystery how in the world they can remember all the things they want to buy if it's a list of more than five items. And also the sales person cuts cheese and salami for each customer separately; this is one of the reasons why they have long lines at each counter. I'm quite sure if there was something like that happening in the U.S., people would have stopped shopping and the stores would have to close. "

"You're probably right; it's pretty irrational," I sighed, "but what is rational in the socialist system? I think people are used to this shopping ritual, and as they don't know any other one, they consider it's the only way."

Finally, by 6 P.M. we sat down to have dinner. We were both hungry and borsch tasted absolutely delicious. I taught Stan to add sour cream in it and eat it with brown rye bread. After the third portion Stan said, "It was my first homemade borsch. As it was for the first time, I think I'm eligible for making another wish."

"Go for it. It never hurts to make a wish."

CHAPTER TWENTY SIX

He Will Never Marry You
1990, Moscow/Leningrad

A week later, at 8:30 A.M. sharp, the night express *Red Arrow* arrived in Moscow. I was walking along the platform listening to the melody of the national anthem—an old tradition to greet 'the guests of the capital of the Soviet Union' solemnly with pomp. I was in a happy mood anticipating seeing Stan again though I was a little worried if he would be able to find the place where we were supposed to meet. But there he was, standing under the huge arrival-departure announcement board. His face expressed anxiety, but as soon as he saw me, his worried face vanished. He gave me a warm hug.

"My dearest, I thought this day would never come. The week seemed endless," he sighed.

We were both delighted to see each other again—what a treat, our third rendezvous in such a short time.

Saturday and Sunday flew by. We went to visit some friends, who were Peace Walk participants. We had a tour of Ostankino and the Kremlin.

Of course, we went to Red Square—the place so full of happy memories. This time there was a long line of tourists waiting to get inside the Mausoleum. I refused to go to see the remains of Lenin, and fortunately, Stan did not insist on it. I had always thought not burying the body of Lenin was a terrible violation of his privacy. Everyone should finally be able to rest in peace at the end. Stan did not want to look at a corpse, any corpse. So we had a perfect consensus on that issue. Actually, we seemed to share the same or similar attitudes about the most important things in life. We had no bitter arguments or quarrels. Stan's aura radiated such soothing calmness that I always felt relaxed and free from any tension.

On Saturday evening we went to the Bolshoi Theater to see *"Karmen-Suita"*. The passionate music and dancing impressed us a lot, but Stan did not like the sad tragic end of the love story. He told me after the ballet, "I don't want our love story to have a sad ending. We should do everything in our power not to let it happen."

I did not answer then; it was useless to have the same old discussion about: how to be together, how not to hurt our children and other important people in our lives, how to survive the separation, and how to live our lives without any guarantee that we'll ever see each other again and then the idea of actually being together...

After the ballet we wanted to go to a nice place for dinner, but it was late and most restaurants were closed. We finally stopped at a hotel and entered the restaurant hall. It was empty; there were no customers or waiters to be seen anywhere. We were tired and hungry, so we found a cozy corner and sank into soft chairs. Stan stretched his hands across the table, took my hands in his and squeezed them gently. He said softly, "Finally, we don't have to be cautious. The theater was great, but the fact that I had to be a 'camel' and pretend I hardly knew you has completely worn me out. Here it doesn't look like anybody you know could see us. It would be super if someone would come and feed us."

At this very moment a waitress appeared in the doorway. Her face did not promise anything good, but when she came up closer to us, she smiled and said, *"Aha, Ya vizhu dva vlublyonnyh golubochka."* I translated to Stan, "Here, I see two little doves in love."

I tried to free my hands from Stan's grasp, but he kept holding them. The woman said, "Hey, girl, don't refuse a guy like this. If a man looks at you the way he does, you should stick to him forever."

I smiled, "I'm trying to, but it's not easy."

Stan looked at me with this painful 'please translate it to me' look. I translated. The waitress said, "Ooh, now I see what the problem is. Yes, girl, I don't envy you; you must have to make a tough decision. Does he want to marry you and take you with him? Where is your foreigner from?"

"He is an American." I told her and translated to Stan what she had said.

Stan smiled widely but said nothing.

The woman sighed deeply and said, "Here's the situation: the cook has already gone home; the kitchen is closed, but I can probably find a couple of cold sandwiches in the bar fridge. What would you like to drink?"

"Do you have champagne?" Stan surprised me with this question. He usually did not drink because of high blood pressure. Then he added, "I want to celebrate tonight."

The waitress left, and I asked what we were celebrating.

"We're celebrating our love, our wonderful summer with so many blessings given to us by our kind destiny, and we're celebrating our future when we won't have to hide, to separate, to cry and long for each other." Stan sent me an air-kiss.

The cold salami sandwiches, black caviar, smoked salmon, cheese and some vegetables appeared on the table as if by magic. Champaign played in the crystal glasses. The candle was lit. For a second the waitress-Angel admired the still life created by her on the table; then she said, "Enjoy your meal, and the company of each other. You are a wonderful couple, and I hope you'll be happy together. Take your time. I'm on duty to close the place tonight, and I'm not in a hurry. I have lots of things to do before I go home. So please take your time."

I translated everything to Stan and we thanked the kind woman. She knew she would get a really good tip that night.

The next day I could not stop crying. Wherever we went, I constantly had to fight my tears. I had a headache and a heavy feeling of a severe loss. Stan said nothing to calm me because he knew that if he only started, I would cry even more. We both remembered that day forever as "The Crying Day."

My train was leaving at midnight; the weather that evening was awful—it was rainy and chilly, so we had to spend the last two hours in the subway. We simply rode the subway trains back and forth for two hours. The trains were empty; there were not many passengers on Sunday night. We did not talk. We were simply together, and that was enough.

I tried to send Stan to his hotel before midnight, but he insisted on seeing me off. Finally, we came to the platform. My train was there. We found my compartment. It was clean and cozy for two people, but apparently I had no neighbor. Stan said, "I wish I could go on this train back to Leningrad with you, my love."

I burst into tears again. We did not talk but only looked and looked at each other as if it was for the last time and we wanted to remember the features, the eyes, the hair, and the touch. The conductor announced that the train was leaving in five minutes. Stan and I went outside. He kissed me.

It was a heartbreaking farewell kiss. I could not stand it anymore. I went back to my compartment. I did not look out of the window.

I hardly slept that night. Again and again I imagined that scene in the restaurant, and the words that the waitress had said were ringing in my ears: *"Hey, girl, don't refuse a guy like this. If a man looks at you the way he does, you should stick to him forever.......Does he want to marry you and take you with him?"* Why did Stan say nothing to that? He simply ignored the whole idea. But then how could he say anything at all—we were both married. It never crossed my mind, and of course he never thought about it. It was an unexpected idea for both of us.

I was glad when the train pulled up to the railway station in Leningrad, and now I was walking along the platform listening to the anthem of the city of Leningrad. I thought the music by Glier was solemn but down-to-earth in contrast to the pompous national anthem played in Moscow.

I had always thought everything was better in my native city compared to Moscow. I hated crowds of indifferent people on the streets and huge distances in Moscow—no matter where you were going, it always seemed you had to spend at least an hour one way. In Leningrad everything was different: the people were proud of their special city and would never ignore strangers if they needed some information or directions; the service was usually friendly and casual, and the size of the city was manageable; the city plan and the architecture were in practical harmony. My own personal "Tale of Two Cities" was probably tainted by some bias, but it was based on the studied, objective conclusion of a lifetime of observation when comparing Moscow to Leningrad.

After I graduated from the university, I had a few excellent offers to go to work in Moscow, but I could not imagine my life in any other place but my beautiful Leningrad. Some of my cousins in Moscow laughed at me saying that I lived in a world of illusions and museums while missing out on the bubbling business life of Moscow. But for me it was exactly what I wanted—a world of harmony between nature and manmade structures, enchanting history, high culture and exclusive taste. So when I was walking along that platform, I was thinking how fortunate I was to be born and raised in this wonderful place.

It was the last Monday in August, the day of the first faculty meeting at my department when we usually gathered to discuss pedagogy, curriculum and other important issues for the coming school year. My husband and son were still at the dacha where I planned to go right after the meeting and spend the last week of vacation with them.

According to a tradition, this morning I was going to join four of my friends and colleagues for breakfast. We usually gathered at Alla's apartment and each girl brought different delicious pastries and fruit while Alla provided coffee, tea, milk and juice. I had special treats, famous poppy seed pastries from Moscow.

All five of us had been very close friends. Two, Larisa and Irina, were German teachers; Alla and I taught English, and the fifth person, Tamara, was the department secretary. We gossiped about other colleagues and students, discussed professional matters and talked about our private lives and problems.

When I arrived at Alla's apartment with a small suitcase, my friends were surprised. Alla asked, "Lenochka, are you leaving or have you just come back from somewhere? Why do you have a suitcase? What's going on?"

"I came back from Moscow by the *Red Arrow* express just twenty minutes ago," I answered.

"What did you do in Moscow?" There came the question in chorus.

I could not speak. I sat down on the chair and burst into tears.

My friends were definitely puzzled with this strange behavior. Usually, I was a merry person with lots of fun stories and laughter to share. None had seen me cry so publicly before. The girls surrounded me and started calming me down asking if they could help me. Finally, I whispered sobbing, "Nobody can help me. I am the unhappiest woman in the world."

"Why?" Asked my girl friends, "Why?"

And here I told them everything: how Stan and I fell in love; how we were corresponding and talking on the phone; how we met in Washington D.C. and in Leningrad and Moscow; how I knew that my life had been ruined and there was no way for me to live in peace because my heart was tearing apart, and loneliness was destroying my soul. I told them how I felt guilty because I knew that my relationship with another man was wrong, and how I considered myself trapped not knowing what to do in the future.

Alla was genuinely astonished, simply stunned and could not say a word. She was a much younger woman recently married, and my story horrified her.

Irina and Tamara were sorry for me and surprised to find out that my marriage was not the one it seemed to be.

As for Larisa—she was a mature woman with a vast experience in life being married for the third time. She said, "You know, Elena, I think you should stop crying and begin thinking about the whole story as a nice fun adventure. Look at it as a little spice in your life, enjoy it, but please don't be so serious about it because it's not a real thing."

"But it is!" I exclaimed, "You don't understand how serious it is for both of us."

"No, my dear. You maybe think it's serious, but trust me, for your American 'friend' you are only a toy, and he's only playing because it's fun. It's clear he'll never marry you, so why would you cry and devastate yourself with the unknown 'ifs'? Have him as a lover; it won't hurt because in your relationship with your husband you need something different to make you feel a worthy person, but other than that—don't stress yourself out. Consider yourself a lucky woman."

"A lucky woman? Why am I a lucky woman?"

"Because your lover is far away, and your husband will never find out. So you can have a fun secret life neither harming yourself nor your family."

I suddenly felt a strange emptiness inside: "he will never marry you", "it's not a real thing", "you are only a toy." Could she be right? This was all so wrong and so different from what Stan and I felt. These women could not really understand what we were both experiencing. But then maybe Larisa was right. Maybe I was the one who tortured myself, but for Stan it was like a game, and I was his toy. He did not react in any way when the waitress at that restaurant mentioned marriage. But what marriage could we think about in our situation? Larisa was right: I had to get used to the idea it was just an entertainment in my life, and I ought to enjoy it instead of crying.

We were drinking coffee; the girls were asking me questions about my trip to Moscow. I calmed down and told them all the details focusing on funny episodes during my trip. Tamara thought my story was cool and that I did the right thing living my life for myself. Irina was happy for me because she had never really liked my husband and thought he had gotten what he deserved. Our breakfast turned to be a fun time, and at noon we all went to the meeting.

That very evening I went to the dacha and spent a wonderful week with my family. I did not think of Stan, not even once.

CHAPTER TWENTY SEVEN

The Thirty—Mile Walk
November 1991, Monterey, CA

Another year passed.

I was extremely busy finishing my dissertation. I had to publish two final papers and give presentations on the main research results at three different linguistic conferences. I literally moved to the Public Library where I spent all my evenings and days off. My husband tried to be supportive, but at times he would lose patience and tell me that he thought the dissertation was tearing us apart. He was right—we were mentally and spiritually apart, but the dissertation had nothing to do with it. My heart was closed up for the feelings towards this man, and the dissertation was the pretext that could always explain why I was not the same person I used to be. I could not forgive him his indifference when my mother was dying, his assault, his stubbornness in our relationship with my relatives and his overbearing attitude and harsh treatment of our little son. But even more—I could not forgive myself for being an unfaithful wife, a double-faced deceitful manipulator, who had let my emotions override both my reason and principles. I knew I would have to pay for these horrible mistakes for the rest of my life.

With all this in my mind and heart, being busy was the only way to survive.

I still tried to give every spare minute to Alexei. He was growing up fast, and he was copying his mom a lot. Often I would come into his room and see him writing something. To my questions about what he was doing, he would say, "I am writing the dissertation," or "I am writing the agenda for the faculty meeting." Although only a boy, he had heard all of these adult words so often in his family that they had become the main themes in many of his games.

Every now and then I would feel guilty that I did not spend more time with my son, but I did know that every minute when we were together was quality time. I took Alexei to tae-kwon-do practices, to a chess club, to ballroom dancing, ice skating and piano lessons. Eventually, the piano lessons and ballroom dancing ended—they were not 'cool enough' for a twelve-year-old. I felt sorry that my son was not going to become a great pianist or dancer, but I wanted him to do what he really liked, and he preferred martial arts. These classes were good for his health and helped to build a good character. Later Alexei took karate, and it was excellent for developing his will power and self-discipline.

The only thing we still did regularly together as a family was going to the theaters two or three times a month. All three of us loved to go to the ballet, opera or drama theaters. Each time when we went to see Tchaikovsky's *Nutcracker*, I would tell Alexei the same story about what he had to say when he saw it when he was three years old, "It was your first ballet performance, and you were very serious and watched the show with great interest very quietly. After the ballet your dad and I asked you what you liked in it the most hoping to hear something about the music, costumes or a particular dance. You thought for a second and said, "The big dagger of the grey mouse."" We always laughed at this funny story—it was our little ritual.

The spring of 1991 was exciting for me because I was invited by my good friends Edward and Irene, who lived in London. I decided to go there for two weeks during the spring break. Stan and I had been talking about going to London together one day, so that might be the chance for us to get together. We were still corresponding and talking on the phone, but our relationship had become different. After our last meeting in Moscow and my realization that it was impossible for us to have any future together, I decided to be only friends with Stan. Of course, it was not the first time in four years of our relationship that I made the same decision. It was my usual state of my mind once Stan was away from me. So I saw nothing bad about two friends meeting in London and having a few fun days together.

On April 20th, 1991 I arrived in London where Edward met me at the airport. I hoped that Stan would come five days later. As soon as we came to Edward's house, the phone rang. Edward gave me the receiver and said, "I think it's your husband."

I said, "Hello?"

"Hi, my beloved squirrel. How was the flight?"

"Oh, hi!" I was happy; it was Stan, "I'm fine. When are you coming?"

"I am sorry, dear, but I won't be able to come."

"Why not? You told me you would come by all means." I was disappointed.

"I know I did, but believe me, I can't. My family circumstances do not allow me to do it. My wife and I are going to Hawaii. We're leaving tomorrow."

My tears ran uncontrollably down my cheeks; I was only grateful that I was alone in the room so no one would see. I could hardly breathe. I felt abandoned. I did not want to talk to Stan anymore that night. I said,

"Sorry, I've got to go. I have to be polite to my hosts. Have a great time in Hawaii with your wife." I hung up. The tears changed from drops to streams. Could people cry like that if their friends failed to come to London?

I had wiped most of them away when my host appeared in the doorway. Edward asked me, "Are you all right?"

What could I tell him? "I have something in my eye; I'm fine." I lied.

The next morning during breakfast, Stan called again. He was trying to explain why he could not come, and that he would come to Russia soon, and that we would see each other again. I wanted to believe him, but his unexpected trip to Hawaii must mean that our relationship was coming to an end. After all, I was only "his toy."

Edward and I made a plan where to go and what to see during the next two weeks. I was busy every day from early morning till evening visiting museums, castles, more museums, and more castles.

In the Westminster Abby I imagined how Stan and I could be listening to the organ sitting in the corner of the cold Cathedral.

In Hyde Park I was picturing us walking holding hands, smelling the spring flowers and listening to orators speaking strange British English.

In Tate Gallery I visualized how Stan would be bored in fifteen minutes looking at nude bodies in the paintings and would lure me to a nearest hotel to make love instead.

In Madam Tuso's Museum of wax figures, I imagined how Stan would fake poses with wax Lenin or King Henry VIII and how we would laugh like crazy attracting reproachful glances of the other tourists.

But I was absolutely alone in all those fantastic places, and now London was as empty for me as Leningrad had been once for Stan.

To make things worse, every morning during the breakfast time Stan called to say "hi" to me. And on the tenth day of my stay at Edward's I got a big and heavy box. Edward was both suspicious and interested. We opened it together. It was a wind chime. It was made of mahogany plates and black metal pipes. It sounded divine. I loved wind chimes, and Stan knew that. Edward was smart enough to understand that such a beautiful, expensive gift would not likely come from a casual friend by DHL from America, but he was very tactful and did not ask any questions.

I brought the beautiful chime home from London along with my bitter feelings of disappointment. Again and again I wanted to start a new life—a life without Stan in it as our relationship did not lead us anywhere but to frustration and disappointment.

We did not keep in touch all summer.

In November of the same year I went to California with a group of five English teachers and fifteen high school students on an exchange program. When Stan had called me in October, I mentioned I was going to Monterey and Carmel for twenty-one days. At that time I did not ask him to come or even if he would consider coming. I did not want to be disappointed again.

We arrived in San Francisco where our host families met us. I was invited by Janice and Mike Walton to stay in their home in Carmel for ten days. Then I was supposed to move to Monterey to stay with James and Barbara Keyson. After the first two days of rest and getting over the jet lag, we started the program. It was filled up with lots of activities, meetings, school visits, press conferences, potlucks, and tours. My crazy dream to walk all the way across the Golden Gate Bridge came true—I did it.

During the first two weeks I did not have any communication with Stan. I was a little surprised because usually he would be calling me wherever I was, but it did not happen this time, and I thought that finally, he let go of his 'toy' and time had shown that our relationship had been just a game.

On Friday of the second week we went to a local high school to observe English teachers' classes and to talk with the school principal and students. In groups of four or five we were assigned to go to different classes. When I entered the classroom, the first person I saw there was Stan. He was sitting in the corner by the window. He was dressed up in a suit and a tie, and he had a small brief case on his lap. He had this intriguing expression of a cunning fox on his face. It was difficult, but I did not show I knew him. I was not sure if we were supposed to be 'camels' or not.

Our group was seated in an opposite corner of the room so that I could see Stan very well. He kept smiling probably because he was so excited about surprising me again. He had done it again. I was surprised.

The lesson started, and it was interesting to observe the interaction between the teacher and the students. The entire demeanor and behavior of the teacher was different from those of Russian teachers. It was strange to see the teacher wearing jeans and a T-shirt, sitting on her desk and sipping coffee while teaching. It was even more unusual to see students wearing hats in class, eating and chewing, sitting with their feet up on desks, calling their teacher Susan instead of Ms. White and talking to her without standing up.

Maybe because of the strange ways the students and the instructor behaved, or because the teaching method was not very efficient, I did not feel that the lesson was successful since it was hard to tell what the students had learned.

Finally, the class was over, and we were invited to go to the school cafeteria for lunch. In the hall Stan came up to me. He said, "Hi; how are you? Are you surprised to see me?"

"Hi," I answered, "I was surprised not to hear from you for quite a long time, but yes, I'm happy to see you."

"I'm sorry I didn't call earlier. I didn't know till the last minute if I would be able to come, so I didn't want to disappoint you again."

"How long are you going to be here? And where are you staying?"

"I am leaving on Sunday, so we'll have two days together. I'm staying at a nice little motel; it's not far from downtown. Will you come and visit me there?"

"Stan, I really don't know because every minute of my stay here is scheduled. There'll be a little farewell party at my present host family's house, and then in the evening I'm moving to my other host family. I don't think I have time to see you."

"Don't you worry, my love," Stan smiled, "I have already arranged everything."

"What have you arranged?" I was worried that my host families might be unhappy with me.

"You'll see; everything will be fine."

When Stan said that, I knew it would be fine. His calmness always affected me like a soothing balsam. In the cafeteria he told me that he was in this high school to do slide presentations about the Peace Walk. He had been doing those presentations all over Idaho, Washington and Oregon states in the past year. He took a leave of absence at school and worked as an assistant to the Director of the Peace Institute at the University of Idaho. The slide show about the life of the Soviet people was the one he had given for the Institute to make people aware of its existence at the University. This short trip to California was simply designed to see how people outside the Northwest would react to his presentation.

He was scheduled to do the shows all afternoon in the school where we did our observations. The authorities of that school thought it was a good idea to combine the visit of the Soviet students and teachers and the presentations by an American expert on Russia. Modest Stan did not think he was 'an expert'. He had always introduced himself simply as someone who had had the good fortune to travel to Russia on two occasions and who was happy to share his impressions with those who had never had his luck and might gain some new information and insights about the Soviet Union.

Stan had also contacted the Waltons, my hosts, and was invited to join us at the farewell party where he promised Janice to show the slides, too. Well, it looked that we would have some time together after all.

Everything worked out great. After a successful party at the Waltons', Stan helped my new host, James, load my suitcases into his black Ford Mustang and discussed with him our plans for Saturday. Stan wanted James to let me be away for the day. He explained that we were old friends since the Peace Walk, and that it would be fun for us to spend a day together talking about our past experiences. We hoped to visit a few mutual friends who lived in that area. It turned out to be fine with James since that Saturday he was unexpectedly hired to do a wedding photo shoot and his wife was supposed to help him. They thought I might like to go with them and watch the wedding, but it was perfectly okay if I spent that day in the company of my friend. So, as usual, destiny's invisible door opened, and Stan and I had another opportunity to be together.

On Saturday morning, James took me to the restaurant where Stan was waiting for me to have breakfast. He and Stan talked for a while about the places where Stan and I could go. James told us it would be a good idea to take a walk along the Monterey Beach, and we agreed to do exactly that. My gracious host was supposed to come to the same restaurant to pick me up after dinner at ten in the evening.

It was a wonderful morning. We were sitting on the terrace facing the ocean. The blue sky and the water with boats with sails created an atmosphere of fun and adventure. Those sails could be the ones that made dreams and wishes come true like in Alexander Green's Novel *"Red Sails"*; only the color of the Monterey sails was white—a bad sign for my wishes. I did not know any happy love stories about lucky white sails.

How did it happen that again Stan and I were together? Why couldn't I keep my promise to myself not to see Stan anymore? My desire to be with him was obviously stronger than my common sense.

We had coffee and blueberry muffins and talked. An hour later Stan said, "I have brought something to show you. It's in my motel room. Would you like to see it?"

We went to his room. It was a cozy place with a king size bed, two armchairs and a round table. On the table was a big dark red photo album. It was the album of Stan's pictures from the time he was a baby to the present days. His mother had compiled the album. Not only did it have his pictures but also locks of his blond baby hair, some of his school report cards, newspaper clippings about him as a college student, and the copies of all his awards; he was an outstanding senior in his college graduating class. It was an interesting book about Stan's life.

I learned he liked to play cowboys and Indians when he was little. There were pictures of his dogs and cats—he loved pets. Stan was a winner of several competitions—and really different ones—such as a University Speech Contest and a Watermelon Eating Contest that did not allow for the use of hands. It was funny to see him with his nose buried in a watermelon.

There were pictures of a thin slender Stan in cap and gown when he received his Bachelor Degree, and I saw pictures of a much larger Stan in his Master's cap and gown.

There were pictures of Stan as a member of the Executive Board of the University of Idaho Student Body Association.

There was a picture of Stan wearing a white tuxedo, playing a dulcimer at a friend's wedding.

There were lots of pictures of Stan with his son and first wife and with his daughters and his second wife.

It was exciting to see Stan's life in all those pictures—a life full of events, achievements, changes, and promises. Finally, I said, "Stan, thank you for bringing the album. It gives me a good image of your personality. I thought I knew who you are, but this scrap book tells me more."

"So what do you think? Who am I?"

"I think you are a decent human being with a lot of potential who has had a successful, happy life. You are a person who is not indifferent to the world around you, one who tries to make a difference by being an active, responsible citizen. You are also a good son and father."

"I'm trying to be a good son and father, but it's not always easy. I didn't have a good relationship with my father when I was young. He was always critical of everything I did. When I graduated from High School, I chose a place to go to school three hundred miles away, so I could be free and make my own way. At that time my parents did not have enough money to help me very much. I helped myself by working five different jobs, working every summer and taking out school loans to get through school. I could have had issues with my parents about that period of my life, but I don't. I love and respect them because I know they did what they could. I love my parents.

As for being a good father, I have always tried my best, but I haven't always been successful. I still have trouble in the relationship with my only biological son. After the divorce, his mother did not want me in his life for a long time, and I went through terrible stages of suffering, hatred, confusion, and despair. But eventually, things got better. My son has grown up enough to be able to understand more about the relationships among people, and I think he wants to be part of my life. So we are in a much better place now. In fact, he is dreaming about going to Moscow, Russia to study theater. He's interested in the Stanislavski approach. Have you heard about it?"

"This is the core of the Russian drama theater," I said.

I was a little surprised to hear about Stan's problems in life. We had talked about them only once long ago on the Peace Walk, and he had never mentioned them again. His life always seemed to be so trouble-free. I was wrong; he was not different from any other person on the planet, for life could not be all rainbows and honey, no matter who you are or where you live.

I asked, "What about your daughters? Do you have good relationship with them?"

"I think so. My older daughter is a serious girl. She's a little shy, but she's like that with everybody, and I'm not an exception. She was eight years old when I married her mother, and I think she had never really figured out what to do with me, so we have never been as close as I would like. But we are friends, which I think is enough in a daughter-step-father relationship. I have never tried to take the place of her biological father. He is a great guy and loves his daughters very much.

"My younger daughter is my best friend. She was only two-and-a-half years old when I became her father. She is the only one of three children who actually calls me Dad. And she was the first one of my children to know about you."

"What? I don't understand. What do your children know about me?" I was astonished.

"Please calm down, my dear. There's nothing bad about it. You should try to understand that I have always been honest with my kids about everything and of course I had to tell them I am in love with you."

"Stan, I really don't get it. Don't you think this news hurt their feelings?"

"Maybe it did, but don't you think it's better that they know the truth? They have been aware of the fact that my wife and I are different people, and we've been becoming more and more distant in the past six-seven years."

"Am I to blame for that?" I felt bad. I was sorry that I could be the source of grief for the children who loved Stan and cared for him.

"No, you are not. I had been far away mentally and spiritually from Carol long before I met you. You have to believe me; it's the truth. Ashley knows. When we talked about all of this, I told her that my concern was that I might not be able to take care of her mother anymore. She told me that that was not my job but rather something that she and her sister were responsible for."

"What will you do then?" I asked thinking how much I did not know about this man, and how much sorrow and sadness he had in his life.

"I'll be happy with the woman I love—you." He smiled, "Of course, only if the woman I love wants to share her life with me."

"Stan, I don't know what you have in mind, but my life has been planned for centuries ahead without you being included in it. You are actually an invader, an intruder, a nuisance."

"Wow! These are serious words. I'd rather remain animals like a crocodile or camel instead of a nuisance," Stan's eyes were serious though he tried to joke.

"Sorry I'm using all these unpleasant words, but they reflect the reality. Just think about it. I had my life pretty straightforward and arranged. I probably don't have the best marriage, but I think what I have experienced is the symptom of where most marriages end up. I do have problems in the relationship with my husband, but I also know that I loved him when we met and got married. I loved him for many years and a lot of good things happened between us. I am adamant about the fact that my son was conceived in great love, which is not a small matter."

Stan was listening intensely with great interest.

I continued, "I'm sorry to admit that before you and I met things happened that permanently damaged my marriage and destroyed my feelings for the man I thought would be the love of my life forever. I don't want to talk about what happened, but the simple truth is after that each day has been part of a continual erosion of my feelings for him and now I am left with nothing. It was during this process that you appeared and added to my general confusion. Does what I say make sense to you?"

"I think so. Please continue," Stan said softly. His eyes were sad.

"Well, today my marriage is obviously not what I had hoped for. My expectations have changed about marriage and my relationship with my husband. Consequently, I have changed and so have my priorities. Right now I'm focused on bringing up my only child, and I'm interested in my career. I don't know if my marriage is going to last, but I think I can find a way to live with my husband for the sake of my child. I'm sorry, but there is no place for you in this picture, and I don't think we should continue our relationship. I'd definitely like to remain friends. Do you think it's possible?"

"Sure. I always like to be friends with people. As you know, my profession is peace making. But please don't forget that it's also conflict resolution. I do see a pretty significant conflict in your life—you deserve to be happy and live a full life. I believe you will find a way to help your son become a successful young man with his own career. I also think you'll find happiness as a woman, wife, companion, and friend with a man who will value and cherish you. All this is possible if you open your mind and heart to your personal goals instead of focusing only on other people's needs. One reason that you are so conflicted is that you are thinking about everyone else's needs and not your own. I am not advocating selfishness here but focusing on one simple truth. Until you are happy with your life no one that loves you will be happy either. It's time for you to think about yourself."

"Stan, but to see my son grow up as a kind, healthy and happy person is the major satisfaction for *me*. And to achieve what I want in my career—to get a doctorate in linguistics and lecture at the university and maybe write a book later on—is also just for *me*. I don't even have time for anything else in life."

Stan was silent for a long time. I had nothing to say either. After a while I added, "But you are right, I have a big conflict in my life, but I see it differently than you do. I consider my relationship with you to be the major conflict."

Stan was still silent. He was looking out of the window. His mind was wondering somewhere far away. Suddenly, he smiled. His face expressed eureka. He said, "Did I tell you about my big award that I had received this summer?"

"You received an award? No, I don't think you told me about it. What is it?" That was a skillful change of the subject.

"My school district nominated me for a peace prize. It was a national competition. I won the award for my work in the field of Peace and International Understanding last summer. I went to Orlando, Florida where I received it at the annual conference and gave an acceptance speech in front of ten thousand delegates from all over the United States. Our union has 2.5 million members. I have it on a video and will show it to you some day."

"Congratulations, it's pretty impressive."

"Yes, my dear, and you should believe me now that I'm an expert in conflict resolution and especially in international understanding. You're as international as it can get, and I'm sure I can help you to resolve all your conflicts."

Stan had an amazing ability to spin things around, and troubles would turn into small concerns, problems would become just simple questions, and life would take a more cheerful orbit.

We talked and talked all day and evening, and finally it was time to say good-bye. Before we left the motel to go to the restaurant where James was supposed to pick me up, Stan put a big square shaped box wrapped in colorful bright yellow, pink and blue paper with a green bow on top of it in front of me, "This is a small gift for you in memory of our Monterey adventure. But please don't open it until you are on the plane."

"Another surprise? Can you tell me what's inside?"

"No, of course not. If I do, it won't be a surprise anymore." Stan loved to torture me with secret surprises. I lifted the box; it was feather light. At least I did not have to carry a heavy surprise.

On our way to the restaurant, I asked Stan what I should tell James if he asked me where we spent the whole day. Stan said, "Remember he told us about a walk along the beach? Tell him we did that."

"What if he asks me the name of the place?"

"No problem. We'll find out the names."

At the restaurant we asked the hostess about nice places to walk along the Monterey beach, and she gave us a few names. I memorized one of them.

James came at 10:00 P.M. sharp. Stan and I said good-bye and shook hands. We parted like good friends.

On our way home James asked me what we did and where we went. I said, "We followed your advice and walked along the beach to Pacific Grove."

"Do you mean you walked to Pacific Grove and back?"

"Yes we did. It was wonderful. I like long walks."

James was silent for a minute. I thought he was politely amused about something. Then he said, "But it's about thirty miles round trip. You must be absolutely exhausted."

"It didn't feel like thirty miles," I said thinking what a stupid squirrel I was. I should have asked the girl at the restaurant about the distances. Now I could not take my words back, so I said, "Stan and I are well trained walkers. We walked from Leningrad to Moscow in 1987. Thirty miles in California is nothing in comparison with four hundred and fifty miles in Russia."

James smiled but made no comment.

CHAPTER TWENTY EIGHT

The Babushka Mission
Summer, 1992, St. Petersburg

On board the plane on my way home to Russia I unwrapped the big colorful box—Stan's surprise. When I opened the box, two fluffy light-gray bunny ears sprang out. The people sitting across the aisle laughed. The bunny was handsome with a little red heart instead of a tie. There was a note in the pocket of the bunny's jumpsuit. Stan wrote:

Elena, My Love,

Thank you for bringing magic and miracles into my life. My spirit will reach out to you in the gentle glow of the stars that will accompany you on the way home to Russia. I find great joy and comfort in loving and being loved. I send this little bunny to touch you gently as I would if I were there.

Love,

Stan

P.S. Our star, the one we saw in Washington D.C., is still in the heavens. Neither of us can be sure about where or when we will be together again, but I am confident that there are many places in the world where we will share time and love together.

I loved him. I knew I did, and it was so hard each time to see him and then to be separated again and again. There was no war or Iron Curtain anymore—things that could separate people in the past, and yet, there were even stronger barriers between us—things like obligations, other people's opinions, traditions and limitations. Stan was able to be hopeful. He was a patient and optimistic person by nature. He knew what he wanted, and he could wait for a gift from destiny for as long as it might take once he believed. But I was a different creature. Patience was an unknown category for me. Optimism was my greatest enemy; it was bad luck to be optimistic about the future. In my little personal world it was all now or never. If I could not have my love when I loved, it made me miserable and helpless—the worst state of mind.

I was looking at the smiling bunny petting him between his ears. The bunny moved closer to my cheek and pocked me gently with its nose. It was a "hi" from Stan. I already missed him.

I returned home right before Christmas. St. Petersburg, which had finally received its original name back a few months ago, was decorated for the holidays. Nevsky Prospect was sparkling with millions of lights. The days were filled with gift hunting, cooking delicious meals, and partying. Life was busy, but I always had time to stop and think about my Big Bunnie who lived half a world away. I did not sweep thoughts about Stan away anymore. I knew that at the very least we would always be friends. Every day before I went to bed, I talked to my little gray bunny while touching the red heart on his chest.

Days went by, and spring arrived. I had to finish the dissertation and submit it to the committee for the approval in May. I slept four hours a day, but I did not feel tired. I found the extra strength to do what was necessary to finish. In May the dissertation was approved, and by June my abstract was published. The defense was scheduled for October 22.

I could enjoy a free summer for the first time in eight years.

As always, Nadya had an idea, and I joined a group of nine Peace Committee members to bike for peace around Finland. I was not a good biker, but I was an excellent peacenik. I had to support Nadya's peace mission. So I biked for peace for seven days.

We had a great time enjoying saunas every evening, savoring famous Finish grilled makkarras (sausages) with beer, dancing at parties. We had no accidents and came back home alive and healthy. Alexei was proud of his mom as he was the one who had taught me to ride a bike when he was seven, and he thought it was cool how I had used this skill to support world peace. He felt special.

After my trip I stayed at the dacha all July. Alexei and I flew our kite, swam in the lake, picked strawberries and raspberries in the garden, and made jam. My friend Tatyana and her son, also Alexei, spent the summer in their house six blocks away from our dacha, and we had a lot of fun time together. That was a wonderful summer—my free summer.

In the end of July I got a card from Stan. On the cover it had a picture of a camel and words: *"I'm like the camel from Moscow, Idaho."* And inside it was hand-written: *"I can do without water but I can't do without YOU,' Love, Stan."* It was funny. There was also a note on a separate piece of paper. Stan shared great news—he was coming to St. Petersburg on a 'Babushka Mission' and he asked me to help him and be his interpreter, for money.

I had no clue what kind of mission it was, but I knew Stan, and I could be sure that the 'babushka mission' would not be boring. I explained to Alexei and Vadim that I was hired to work as an interpreter for several days and left for St. Petersburg on August 10th.

Stan came in the company of an Episcopalian priest by the name of Father John. He was a priest at a church in St. Petersburg, Florida. That church congregation was in touch with the Orthodox Seminary in St. Petersburg, Russia; they were something like sister churches in sister cities.

After the beginning of political and economic changes in Russia, powerful religious forces that had been repressed since 1917 began to resurface in Russian society. The Russian Orthodox Church was again an important institution in my country. The religious nature of the Russian people was finally free from communism and for the first time in decades people were able to express their beliefs openly. The churches that had been ignored and abandoned for over seventy years during the communist era started to revive thanks to the enormous support of both Russian Christians and their brothers and sisters in faith from all over the world.

Father John was one such supporter. He had visited St. Petersburg Seminary a year ago and found out that there were a lot of lonely elderly women (*babushkas*) fanatically devoted to God who volunteered all their time to do different necessary chores in their local churches. These women had a great deal in common: they had no children or relatives who could support them, and they had little or no pension to live on. God and the kindness of people alone helped to sustain them.

Father John talked to his congregation about these amazing Babushkas and their great courage and faith. The members of his church wanted to help them. They collected stewardship money to purchase soap, shampoo, detergent, lotions, canned fruit, cookies, and chocolate. They decided to send Father John to St. Petersburg with packages of these goodies—special gifts for these brave souls. This is how the *"babushka"* mission started.

Later another idea came to Father John's head—not only to bring the gifts to the women, but also to take pictures and even to make a video to show later in his church so that the congregation would be able to actually hear some of the life stories of the women and see how the gifts were delivered. He started to look for a person who might be interested in doing the video work for him and contacted his friends, Audrey and John Palmer—the Palmers-Angels, who had been on the Peace Walk in Russia.

He hoped they might be interested in his project. Neither of the Palmers could do it as they both worked that summer, but they promised to help to find a person who would be able to assist him. They contacted many friends and one of them was Stan. When Stan heard about the opportunity to go to Russia with such an honorable mission, he immediately gave his consent. And of course the idea that it was also a chance for him to see his beloved squirrel, Elena, crossed his mind, too. Stan called Father John up, told him he was free in August to do the job and could recommend a Russian teacher of English who could act as an interpreter. Thus this Episcopal priest hired both Stan and me.

I met Father John and Stan at the restaurant of the Pulkovskaya Hotel where both men stayed. Again Stan and I turned into 'camels'. This time it did not irritate me, but it added spice to our new and unusual venture.

Father John seemed to like me and agreed to let me help with the project. When I found out all the details about the mission, I was fascinated with the idea and impressed with Father John's commitment. I was excited about being part of such a splendid humanitarian effort.

We were supposed to meet the next morning. Father John left and Stan and I went to the lounge for a drink and a talk. Stan as always ordered diet coke, and I had a glass of red wine. We were finally alone. Stan said, "Well, my dear, are you excited about the prospect of seeing me every day for the coming two weeks?"

"Two weeks? I thought Father John said it was just one week!" I was surprised.

"That's right. His project will last only one week, but I'll stay for another week as I have a few important things to do while I am in Russia."

"What are these things?" I was puzzled and just a little irritated because I wasn't sure I was ready for any more surprises. I thought I would be back at the dacha in a week and have another ten-day vacation with my family before our summer vacation was over.

"I need to do some research in terms of children's summer camps around St. Petersburg because I'd like to organize a summer camp exchange between Idaho kids and the children in this area," Stan beamed.

"It sounds promising. Do you have anybody here in town you are going to work with on this project?"

"Yes, I do—the director of the Palace of Youth Creativity, previously known as the Pioneer Palace. She is ready to assist me with it. I have bought a new automatic slide projector as a "good faith gesture" for the director to let her know I am serious about developing a joint venture."

"I see." What an amazing person Stan was. He was thinking about so many people and trying to help them in any way he could. I knew he was not a rich man, and he had three children to support, and yet Stan was trying to help those who were in greater need.

"I have one more project in mind," he added, "I'd like to go to Moscow to visit a couple of people and talk with them about an opportunity for my son to come next year and study theater there. Could you go to Moscow with me and help me out there?"

"Stan, it's all very unexpected. I did not realize you had more than this 'babushka mission' in mind. I have to think about it and see where I am before I can tell you for sure." At that moment I was both startled and a little worried about this sudden avalanche of projects that threatened to consume the rest of my summer vacation.

"It's okay, I understand. Please think it over and let me know so that I can book train tickets. It's always been my dream to ride this *Red Arrow* express with you."

We talked more that evening, and I was pleased that we were like real friends: there were no kisses or embraces, no romantic glances or hand holding. I thought, "Maybe we have finally gone through the romance stage and now we can be simply friends. It feels so much easier this way." But my feelings for Stan warred with this rational idea that we would now be simply friends. Disappointment walked hand in hand with relief in my mind.

The next morning all three of us met at 8 o'clock. Father John had a list of addresses of the babushkas we were supposed to visit. We had a car and a driver to work with us all week. There were about fifty names on the list, so we planned to visit ten or twelve women a day. First, the driver and I sat down for a few minutes and drew a little map of our routes so that we could save as much time as possible. We loaded the trunk with about fifteen plastic bags full of nice goodies for the babushkas. And our journey began.

What we experienced that first day and for the rest of the week was so unusual and powerful that it deserves to be described in a separate book, but I will only touch upon some important events very briefly.

Each babushka had a unique life story full of turmoil and personal tragedies that left them absolutely alone. No husband, no children, no family, no life long friends…the war and time had robbed each of what most people of a different era simply might take for granted. God alone and His infinite love was all that lifted each of these women out of the depths of despair and loneliness that their fate had cast them into. Their solitary lives, poverty, and declining health had stolen away much of their beauty, and dignity.

But with the passing of each minute heralded by the clocks in their small apartments, their heartfelt testimonies about their many blessings and their sincere belief that God was with them in even the darkest moments literally transformed them before my eyes. They were beautiful strong women who had survived the loss of everyone and everything in their lives but who could stand before God and man and give thanks for their good fortune. They were alive. They were not forgotten. They felt especially blessed when we visited them because their Angel, Father John, had brought soap, shampoo, toothpaste…. none of which they could afford on their pension of $20 a month.

Most of our Babushkas lived in communal apartments. These apartments were shared by several families. Each had only one bathroom and kitchen. No matter how small or simple their 'homes' were, these women, all of them without any exception, were glowing with happiness to see us and expressed warm hospitality to 'their savior Father John, and two Angels—Stan and Elena'. Until that time I thought only my friends and relatives were Angels and I had never considered myself to be one. "Ms. Elena Angel," conjured up a funny picture of me with wings, but I knew that to help these wonderful women required that I keep both feet on the ground. I had always been a responsible person, so I gladly accepted an opportunity that God had given me to help others.

Our original plan to visit ten-fifteen babushkas a day fell apart after the first three visits because we hardly managed to do just three the first day. It became obvious to us that each of our hostesses was so intent on offering us her finest that not to stay longer would have been terribly unkind. These women, who had practically no means for existence, possessed an incredible ability to share whatever little they had with their honored guests. Each of them, separately from one another, did the same thing that they all thought was appropriate—cleaned their little nests, cooked something special—sometimes it was just boiled potatoes and tea—and wore the best they had; often those clothes were pure rags but immaculately clean and their head scarves were crisply starched.

There was one woman who especially conquered our hearts. We found her place easily. It was right across from the beautiful Nicolski Cathedral—the church named after a popular Russian Saint Nicolai, the patron of all sailors. The church was built in the Russian Baroque style of the 18th century and painted in that gorgeous turquoise-blue and white, which matched the romantic image of the city. The location of the cathedral was cleverly chosen so that its five elegant onion shaped golden domes could be seen from many different points of the city.

The house in which Tatyana Fyodorovna lived looked well maintained from the outside, but when we entered the stairway hall to walk upstairs to the third floor, we had to fight with two unpleasant obstacles: first, we had to climb up incredibly steep stairs in dungeon darkness, and second, we could hardly breathe as the musty urine smell punched our noses.

Once we made our way to the third floor, we finally found the door with number six on it and rang the bell; the door opened immediately, and a short, anorexic elderly woman greeted us warmly. She used a lot of tender words calling us *'moi dorogiye bozhyii poslanniki, nezabvennyie angely-hraniteli'* (my dear God's messengers, eternal angels-saviors) and lots of other unusual word combinations. We followed her along a dark corridor that seemed infinite with bicycles hanging on the walls and boxes standing here and there covered with all sorts of fabric and tarp. I assumed it was a communal apartment shared by at least three or four families.

Just about the time our eyes had become accustomed to the darkness of the hall, she unexpectedly opened a door into her room. A bright, beautiful light momentarily blinded us. We stumbled into her world and once our vision was restored, we were astonished to see a large square shaped room with a vaulted ceiling and tall, rounded at the top windows. There were lace curtains over those windows so transparent that we could see the glamorous golden domes of the Nicolski Cathedral as if they were painted and inserted in the window frames.

The furniture was old but in perfect condition: a red mahogany bookcase with a collection of world classics, a matching cupboard with blue and gold china, rare Kuznetsov porcelain, and elegant crystal glasses and vases on the shelves—these were probably the family treasures of the old lady. A big oval table covered with a snow white starched table cloth and six soft chairs with hand carved backs in the shape of fruit and leaves were in the middle of this immaculately clean room.

The most impressive decoration of this room was a white fluffy cat with sky-blue eyes lying on the cushions of the sofa in the pose of a Turkish princess.

It was hard to believe that the harmony of this dwelling had been created by this small fragile woman. There was no way we could guess her age.

Suddenly she started touching each of us: she touched Stan's hands and the camera first, then she quickly moved towards me and touched my shoulder and hair, and then she came up to Father John, took his hand in hers and kissed it softly. We finally realized that this woman was blind.

We introduced ourselves and she invited us to sit down. Stan turned on his video camera. Father John said, "Bless you and your wonderful home, Tatyana Fyodorovna. Tell me how you've been. And please tell me if it's okay if Stan films our talk." I translated quickly. Tatyana Fyodorovna was silent for a moment, and then she said, "It would be a sin to complain. I'm a happy person, and your visit today is one of God's many blessings. I don't know why God is so kind to me. You, my dear pastor, have always been a miracle in my life, and now—you are making me a movie star." We all laughed, and she added, "You tell me, Father John, how you and your congregation are doing. You must have been very busy."

Father John started to tell this little babushka about what had happened lately in his church back in Florida. They had a conversation as if they had known each other for a long time. Then he said, "Dear Tatyana Fyodorovna, my church knew I was going to visit you and asked me to bring a few little gifts for you. Please accept this package. It's not much, but you might use all these things in your household."

Tatyana Fyodorovna seemed a little at a loss, "Oh, God Almighty, why did you trouble yourself so much? I really don't need anything; God is so generous to me. There are a lot of kind people around. But I don't want to be ungrateful. Please give all those people who sent the gifts to me my sincere thank you." Big drops of tears streamed from her blind eyes and sparkled in the sunlight as they fell on her cheeks.

"Absolutely, not only will I tell them 'thank you' for you but also show the movie that Stan is filming right now. The people of my church will be able to see your beautiful room and all these interesting things you have here." He touched the porcelain statue of a horse standing in the center of the table and said, "This horse, for example, it's such a fine work of art."

"Do you like it?" Tatyana Fyodorovna's fingers ran quickly over Father John's hands and the horse that he held. She said, "Please take it as a gift if you like it so much."

"Oh, no. Thank you, but I did not mean that. This horse looks very nice here on your table."

"Please take it, dear pastor. This is the least I can do for you, and I want to do something pleasant for you. I want you to be happy while you are here doing so much for us. Please take it and let it be a reminder of my city and my church," she turned her face towards the window. We all looked at the church that now looked dark blue in the background of the raging crimson sunset.

Father John hesitated, but I nodded at him showing that it was important to take the gift. He gave in, "All right, I'll decorate my desk in the church office so that everybody who comes to talk to me might see it, and each time I'll tell those people where this horse comes from and we'll pray for you."

"You see, I told you God is kind to me. What more could I ever desire but to be in my dear pastor's thoughts and prayers?" The face of this woman lit up with gratitude and satisfaction of having accomplished something important.

Our amazing conversation continued and was made ever sweeter by tea and ginger cookies.

Once we left the apartment and got back into our car, we all fell silent for a while in spite of the fact that we should have been planning for the next day. My silence gave me time to do a personal inventory. I am married and have a wonderful son. My father is alive, I have a brother and several cousins, lots of school and work friends. My upper class background has given me many privileges not the least of which is a good education. And yet am I any better off than Tatyana Fyodorovna?

This little *babushka* lives all alone; she is blind, and all she does every morning is to go across the street to her beloved church and spend the day praying, cleaning and tidying up. After she takes her evening meal there, she comes home to sleep. Tatyana Fyodorovna's life is as measured and predictable as the movement of the sun and moon; she does it over and over and over again.

The woman who cannot even see, who has no family, who has a small pension hardly enough to pay the rent and utilities—and yet her faith allows her to see so much that she radiates happiness and kindness; she actually considers herself a lucky person.

Why was that woman so happy, and I, who had everything—eyes, family, its love and support, friends, a well paid job, young age, and talents—I always complained about this or that and at times felt so miserable. That blind *babushka* 'saw' in life more than I could distinguish with my seeing eyes.

Finally, Father John said, "I really don't know what to do with this horse. I'll probably break it on the way home in the suitcase. It looks quite brittle."

"May I hold it?" I asked. When I took it in my hands, I was surprised how light it was for its size. I turned it upside down and was shocked when I read: *The work of Peter Carl Faberge, St. Petersburg, 1880.*

I exclaimed, "It's Faberge—a rare antique work of art! You'd better try your very best not to break it, and actually I'm not sure you'll be able to take it outside this country without a special permission of the Art Committee at the Hermitage."

"Didn't that Faberge make also fantastic Easter eggs?" Stan commented, and Father John mumbled, "I don't think it's good to take it if it's that valuable. We'll have to take it back tomorrow."

"I don't think it's a good idea. Did you see how happy she was when she gave it to you? Keep it and do what you promised—pray for her. And remember that in Russia you should never return or regift gifts; it's very offensive," I said.

"It's offensive in America, too," Stan added.

"Okay, you've convinced me, I give up. I'll 'ride' this horse back to Florida."

"Or you'd rather 'fly this horse'," Stan said and we laughed for the first time that strange day.

CHAPTER TWENTY NINE

God—It's That Simple!
1992-1993, St. Petersburg, Russia

The 'babushka mission' was over, and Father John went back to Florida. Now Stan needed my help in Moscow where he wanted to establish all the necessary contacts for his son, Michael, to come to study drama. So I went to the dacha for the weekend while Stan stayed in town to rest and visit some friends. On Monday we met a few minutes before midnight at the Railway Station where we boarded the *Red Arrow* headed for Moscow.

Stan and I were still 'camels' or had we finally reached a different phase in our relationship and become 'friends'? I still could not make up my mind whether to feel disappointed or relieved that Stan did not touch my hand or try to give me even a light kiss on my check. Maybe he did not want to put me in an awkward situation assuming that in my native city we could bump into many people who knew me. So when we finally found ourselves alone in the compartment, I thought Stan would immediately turn into a passionate man hungry for love. However, even behind the closed door of the compartment we were still acting like we were just acquaintances.

When we sat down on the berths, Stan took out of his suitcase a strange square flat wooden box and a long velvet case. He unfolded the box, and it turned into a checkerboard. Then he opened the case and started to arrange the chess pieces on the board. I was watching him with interest. I did not know why he was doing it.

When the pieces were all in their places, he moved a pawn forward, looked at me with his smiley eyes and said, "Well, my dear, it's your move now."

"Are we going to play chess?" I exclaimed in awe. I had not played chess for ages, and I did not really like it. To play chess on the train with Stan after midnight was the least I had expected. I was about to protest when somebody knocked on the door. Stan opened it immediately. It was a conductor. He was collecting the tickets and offering tea. When he saw the chess on the table, he exclaimed in surprise, "Are you playing chess at midnight? You must be really sleepless. Tea for two?"

"What else do you think two colleagues could do after a tiresome business trip?" I sighed. Stan was just smiling. He pretended he was Russian and tried not to give himself away by speaking. The conductor smiled back at Stan and was about to ask him something, but I quickly interjected, "Thank you for offering the tea, but we just had tea before we came here. I think we'll go to bed right after we finish the game. But in the morning we'll definitely have tea and the famous *Red Arrow* muffins." I looked at Stan, "Right?"

Stan nodded his head. The conductor said, *"Spokoinoi nochi"* (good night) and disappeared. I locked the door.

We played chess.

As soon as we arrived in Moscow, I called Stan's good friend, Boris. Stan and Boris became friends on the Peace Walk when Boris worked as a guard protecting the peaceniks from, as he put it, 'criminal elements.' He was an interesting person, a little loud and rough but with a kind heart. When I talked to him on the phone, I explained that I was Stan's interpreter and the reason why Stan was in Moscow. Boris was genuinely happy and excited to see Stan and to host him. We went to Boris's place right from the railway station. Boris and his wife, Tamara, were still on vacation at home after their two weeks on the Black Sea. They looked sun tanned and rested.

We had a nice day in the company of these hospitable people, ate great food, drank vodka and wine and told a lot of jokes. It was decided that Michael would stay with Boris and his family and that he would pay for room and board. The price was quite reasonable. Late in the evening I went to my cousin's place to stay overnight, and Stan spent that night at Boris's.

My dear cousin, Valya, stayed up late so we could have a chat. We had not seen each other for several years, and I wanted to catch up with all the events in her life. We had a long talk about our children, relatives, and jobs. Then suddenly Valya said, "Okay, now tell me what it's all about. Who is this guy and why are you so excited about him?"

"What do you mean?" I was completely taken aback. I had only mentioned that I was in Moscow as an interpreter accompanying a foreigner. I could not understand why Valya asked me that question.

"Do you think you can hide your feelings about this person? Just look in the mirror. You are glowing. When you came in, I thought a thunder bolt struck; I knew there was something extraordinary happening to you. So please stop denying the truth. I want to know all about you and him."

"To tell you the truth there isn't much to tell. Actually, I don't know what I can tell you because I don't know anything about us myself," I said sadly.

"But you are saying 'us'. That means there's something between you and him. Are you having an affair?"

"An affair? You know I've never thought of our relationship as 'an affair', but you are probably right. It's an affair because it doesn't lead any-where. I thought that both he and I were in love, but I'm not sure anymore. My friends at work tell me he's just playing with me as if I were his toy. Maybe they are right, but deep in my heart I know that he's not that type of a man. I know he loves me."

"Elena," Valya asked slowly, "But what about Vadim? Don't you love him anymore?"

"It's complicated. I don't want to leave him, but the truth is we've lost our love. It's gone forever; it's irretrievable…deleted, erased…" I kept us-ing computer terms that matched the context of our conversation so well, "You know, I feel empty there."

"Is it because of your American lover?" For the first time I heard the word that exactly characterized who Stan had been for me until this time we've been together.

"Believe it or not, but Stan is not my lover; at least not anymore. And as to Vadim? We started to drift apart and become more and more distant long before the American guy appeared on the horizon."

"Then why don't you get a divorce? It would be easier for you to have a relationship with Stan," Valya kept brainstorming trying to help me as if my life was a simple math problem with one 'x'.

"I don't want to divorce Vadim because of Alexei. I think he needs a father. It's bad if a boy has no father. I'll suffer until my son grows up. We'll see what will happen after that."

"Does your American…friend know that you don't want to divorce your husband?"

"You know, we've never spoken about it. We simply love to be with each other whenever we can, but when we are separated, we have our lives full of our own problems and questions. I know Stan is not happy in his marriage, but he did not ever mention a divorce. I know he won't change anything in his life until his children graduate from high school. So this whole love story is a sad business."

Tears started flowing down my cheeks. I could not stop them; they were filling my eyes up and when there was no space for them anymore, they flowed onto my cheeks and dropped on my hands.

Valya gave me a tissue and whispered, "Oh, my dear, I'm so sorry. You're going through a tough time. But everything will be fine. Just follow your heart; it never lies."

"My heart? I don't know if I even have one anymore. I'm so tired of this constant hope to see Stan, to be with him, to hear his voice, to feel his touch. Just hope and hope. I have known him for over five years and in those five years we have actually been together only thirty four days. Thirty-four days! And yet I feel like he's the dearest person in my life. How can it be?"

There was a long silence.

"I'm not surprised now why you don't see it as an affair. It's pretty unusual that two people living so far away from each other and being separated most of the time to still love and hope. You're a lucky woman. Not everyone is blessed with a love like this. Treasure it and nurture it, don't let it go. You'll regret for the rest of your life if you lose it," said my Angel.

I cried and cried that night. I did not want to lose my love, but I did not know how to keep it.

The next day Stan and I went to one of the most fashionable theaters of that time in Moscow—U *Nikitskih Vorot*—to see its director and the chief producer, Mark Rozovski. Mark had a drama school at his theater, and he accepted a few foreign students every year. Michael, who was dreaming of becoming an actor, read about this school in a magazine, applied and was accepted. So Stan decided to get acquainted with Mark and find out what he needed to do to help Michael before he came to Russia.

We had a nice visit with Mark and his young, beautiful wife. They gave us a tour of the theater and introduced us to the manager and music director. We had lunch together and after a long talk it was decided that Michael would take lessons in Russian and stage movement. Later when he mastered Russian, he would be able to play parts in the theater productions. Stan was quite content with the results of the negotiations.

We were finally alone that evening. We went to a restaurant on *Staryi Arbat* to have dinner. I was going back to St. Petersburg at midnight.

Stan asked me, "Do we still have to pretend we are camels or can I hold your hand?"

"I don't know. I think maybe it's better if we remain camels forever."

"Why? What's wrong?" Stan looked worried, "What are you saying? Has anything changed between us?"

"And what is 'between us'?" I knew it was a bad idea to start this talk especially when I was leaving soon, and we would be separated again—separated for an unknown period of time or forever—that was always a threatening option. We lived in an unstable world and to lose each other would have been easy. And yet I could not stop; I had to be honest and real; I had to express what I thought.

I added, "Last night, my cousin asked me if you and I were having an affair. Is our relationship 'an affair'? Am I really your toy as my friends keep telling me? You didn't really come to Russia to see *me* this time. It's been for some kind of mission. I'm an "addition" to the mission." I stopped and thought of the silly rhyme: *mission-addition*. It struck me that all my words were useless; they only made me sound ridiculous.

But Stan looked serious. He sighed deeply, "You are not an addition. Everybody knows that you are a very special and important person in my life. My wife knows it."

"What do you mean?"

"I told my wife I was in love with you. I did it back in 1989 when I returned from Washington D.C. To tell you the truth I hoped she would kick me out, and then everything would be easy. But she refused to admit the truth. She's been trying to change, to be a perfect wife and from time to time she would ask me if I had forgotten you. Each time I honestly tell her that I love you. I think she's hoping she will eventually win. She must believe that you and I will give up on us. But I'm not going to give up. No, I don't consider our love to be an affair. If this were an affair, I would not get up in the middle of the night and cry looking at the moon thinking how far you are away. If it were an affair, I would not try to find every possible opportunity to come to Russia or any other part of the world where I can see you for at least a day or two. If it were an affair, I would not have told my children about you and my love for you. Do you believe me?"

I did not know what to reply. I felt bad that his wife was living through such turmoil. On the other hand, I could not understand why she was still with him. If my husband had confessed that he had been in love with another woman, I would have left him—there would have been no reason for us to be together. And if I loved my husband, I would have let him go. If I couldn't make Vadim happy, I would be happy if another woman could. I stopped and considered what I had just thought and realized that to say such a thing about another woman making my husband happy was easy but to actually do it might be impossible. I suddenly found myself feeling sorry for Stan and Carol. How miserable their life as a couple apparently was.

I said, "I am sorry I started this unpleasant conversation. I didn't mean to spoil our evening. You've convinced me we have more than an affair and that our feelings are real and strong and much more significant than just being friends. I guess we will have to wait patiently to see if destiny will bring us any more gifts."

Stan touched my fingers gently, "I know, my love; it's hard on you, but believe me, it's no less hard on me. But I'm confident there will come the day when we'll be together forever."

I believed him at that moment.

I left that evening determined not to doubt Stan's love for me anymore. He had convinced me that we would do what must be done for us to be together in the future.

On October 22nd, I defended my dissertation and received a Ph.D. in English linguistics. The defense went smoothly without a single flaw. My dad was in the audience sitting proudly in the center of the big hall. After the defense some members of the committee as well as my colleagues, close friends and relatives gathered at my house for a party. Three of my friends had been cooking all morning so that by the time we arrived, everything was ready and looked beautiful. I had bouquets of flowers everywhere. There were lots of wonderful thank you toasts, encouragement toasts, funny toasts, and simply toasts—the usual Russian celebration. During the party, Nadya came up to me and told me that Stan had called and asked to tell me he was thinking of me on that day. I actually did feel some strong emotional support all day—that could be Stan's vibes.

Several weeks later I got a card from Stan:

Dear Elena,

Great news to hear you passed your final defense and received superior marks. I must confess that I was very anxious and on that day had to do something to let you know of my support for you. I thought calling Nadya would be the safest thing I could do. I am glad to know that she delivered my message. It surely sounds like you will have many parties to celebrate your victory over academia. I am only sorry I could not be there to celebrate with you. I will, however, give you a 'rain check' or promise of a party wherever we meet again. Whether that will be in Russia, the U.S., Paris, or the moon. It will be a grander party than the one we had in Washington D.C. or in California. The entertainment will be even more spectacular—I am feeling much better!

I do have one serious concern, however. You said that you were feeling and looking like an 'old rock'. Consequently, I am sending to you "a rock restorer." I hope all the products in the cosmetic kit will allow for ample restoration or revitalization. It would be a terrible shame that should we meet, I would not recognize you. I have, however, concluded that in spite of this new 'old rock' appearance your spirit will give you away, especially if I were to tickle the "rock".

As for my world, my wife and I have agreed to table, put off, any discussion about our situation until after school is out. In the meantime we are kind to each other and supportive. We each have very hard jobs and do not need any additional problems right now.

Michael is coming in December. He will visit you in St. Petersburg and bring this gift for you.

Love,

Stan

When Michael arrived, I was happy to spend some time with him. We had never met before, but I heard a lot about him from Stan, who adored his boy.

Michael turned out to be a nice young man. He was genuinely curious about Russia, its people and life. He became a good friend with Alexei and even with my husband using the world tongue—body language. We took him to different museums and theaters, to parties and restaurants. We had fun.

On his last day in St. Petersburg when I was taking him to the railway station to go to Moscow, he suddenly looked at me very seriously and said, "My father loves you."

It was so unexpected that I did not react at all. I simply ignored it, and he did not repeat it. But when he was on the train looking at me through the window of his compartment and waving goodbye, once the train started to move, his lips said very clearly again, "My father loves you." I whispered back, "I love him too."

Michael smiled happily; his blue eyes sparkled.

After Michael's departure and the final celebration of my Ph.D., life became normal. Now I had more free time. The feeling of an accomplishment was a good solid emotion, but the notion of freedom was the most valuable result of the long and hard work. Finally, I could think of doing a lot of things that I could not allow myself when I was working on the dissertation—I could spend more time with my son; I could play the piano whenever I wanted, and I could travel more. I wanted Alexei to go to study in the U.S. at high school. It was fashionable in Russia in those days to send children for a semester or two to study abroad. I was also dreaming of going to England or the U.S. as a visiting professor for a postgraduate work. I had some inspiring ideas about writing my own English grammar book.

Once talking on the phone with Stan, I mentioned those dreams to him, and in March I received a letter in which Stan wrote that he had exciting news for me. He talked to the principal of his high school about a possibility for Alexei to come for a semester to study there, and the principal gave his consent. Stan also found a family that was interested in hosting Alexei. He knew that family well, and they were reliable people with two sons of approximately Alexei's age. I told Alexei and my husband about this option. When Vadim asked me who the person offering this opportunity was, I said simply it was a friend from the Peace Walk. He never asked any other questions. Alexei wanted to go, but I felt he was a little scared to go to America all by himself. One evening he asked me if I could go with him. I did not think I could at that point, but that very night all of a sudden my dear New York Angel, Katherine, called. She said, "Hi, Elena. I haven't heard from you for such a long time. How have you been?"

"Oh, Katherine, what a surprise. I'm fine, thank you. What about you?"

"Everything's terrific. I'm working now for a different company. There are a lot of business trips to Europe, but I love it. You know how I love France and Italy. The business is going very well. I was wondering if you were planning to come to the States any time soon?"

"Theoretically, I'd love to come, but I haven't made any specific plans. I'm a much freer person now after I've defended my dissertation."

"You have? How wonderful! Congratulations! Definitely, you deserve some bonus. Come and visit me. We can have a great time. By the way, how is your Stan?"

I was not sure what to say. Katherine was my friend and I did not want to be dishonest with her. After a pause I said, "Well, Stan is fine. He is in his Idaho teaching as usual."

"So is there any change in your relationship?"

"No, we're still in love," I simply said.

"You mean he's still married and tells you he loves you..."

I was silent. She added, "Sorry, let's talk about something else. So how about coming to New York this summer?"

"You know what? It's amazing how life finds the mysterious ways out of difficult situations. My son's planning on going to Idaho to study for a semester at Moscow High School. He wasn't very happy about going all by himself. He's only fourteen, you know. I guess, your invitation is just on time. If I take him to New York, we can also go to visit my brother in Pennsylvania. Then I can put Alexei on the plane to go to Idaho and after that spend a few days with you. How does this sound?"

"Sounds great. When will that be?"

"Some time in the middle of August. Will that be good for you?"

"It'll be very good. The middle of August is still a very slow season in business. Lots of people are away on vacation and are not active in investing. I can usually take a few days off in August. So do you need an invitation to get a visa?"

"That'll be terrific. Katherine you can't imagine what an Angel you are. It's as if you've been reading my mind from thousands of miles away. There's definitely something special in this world," I said.

"It's name is God, my dear. It's that simple."

CHAPTER THIRTY

Not a Daughter Anymore
1993/1994, The United States of America

Alexei and I arrived in New York City on August 15th, 1993 at 8 P.M. and something unexpected happened at the passport control. The officer asked me for how long Alexei and I were planning on staying in the U.S. I said that my son was staying for six months to study in high school and I was going back home in four weeks. The officer asked if Alexei had a separate passport. He did not. He was only fourteen, and at that time in Russia an individual passport could be issued only to people after they turned sixteen. We had one passport and one entrance visa for both of us. The officer said politely, "Sorry, m'am, but if you enter this country together, you will have to leave together. Your son cannot stay here without a passport."

I was shocked with the news but did not show it. Alexei had been so excited about studying in America that I hated to disappoint him.

I said, "Thank you. We'll think how to change our plans."

The officer added politely, "You're welcome to stay for six months with your son while he goes to school. Do you have relatives here?"

"Yes, I do. My brother lives in State College in Pennsylvania. There'll be no problem."

"Okay. Enjoy your stay in the United States of America."

"Thank you, we will," I smiled trying not to show how terribly worried I was.

As soon as we found ourselves alone, my smart son asked me, "Mom, does it mean I can't study in America?"

"No, my dear, everything will be fine, don't worry. Of course you will study in America. That's why we came here."

I tried to be calm, but I did not know what to do. I had to go back to Russia in four weeks; I had to be at work by the end of September; my husband was expecting me back before the dacha season was over to help with gardening; my dad did not feel very well, and I wanted to be closer to him. There was no way I could stay in the States for six months.

I was delighted to see my brother, who came to meet us at the airport. After the first embraces and kisses (we had not seen each other for four years), I told Vlad about my problem with the visa. My brother thought for a while, "Well, I think it's great. You'll stay here for six months. We have enough space in our house."

"What are you talking about? I have to be back in September."

"Why?" he asked calmly.

"To go to work, to take care of our father, to be with my husband— don't you understand? I live there."

"My dear little sister, please calm down. Everything will be fine. Call your boss and ask for a sabbatical. As I remember, you wanted to do your postdoctoral program somewhere in the West. Here's a great opportunity for you. Your department chair won't be against a great specialist coming back in six months. As for Dad, he's going to come to visit us soon. He just called today and said he finally got the American visa. So you'll be able to take care of him here. And Vadim will be fine; he's not a little boy; he doesn't need a pacifier. I'll talk to him on the phone, and he'll understand. You can't disappoint your son."

"I know. Let me call my boss right now. If I don't do it, I won't calm down. It's about 9 A.M. in St. Petersburg now; he's definitely at work."

The secretary connected me with Yuri Petrovich. After I explained to him my situation, he said, "I have no problem with your staying there for several months. I have two TAs from the university assigned to work at the department this fall, and I guess they're lucky to work with your groups. But be sure to learn as much as possible and when you come back, you can give a series of workshops."

"It's a deal," I could not believe it had worked out.

One problem was fixed, and it seemed like the second one was solved, too. I knew that Dad had applied for the visa, but I did not know if he had gotten it. How wonderful that he was coming. We could all be together in Vlad's house.

The last and most worrisome problem was to talk with my husband. I knew he would be extremely displeased and even mad, and I was not ready to handle it at that moment. I decided to call him later.

On our way to the car my brother looked at me mysteriously, "Now if you're calm, I have something else to tell you, but please don't freak out."

I could not believe I had something else to deal with, after only twenty minutes in America. Will it be like that for six months?

Vlad whispered, "You're not going to State College with us today." He gave me a cunning smile.

"Why? Where am I going?" I was exhausted, tired and hungry; I did not want to play any silly games.

"You are not going anywhere. You are staying in New York City."

"What's going on?" I asked.

"Katherine's arranged everything. I'm going to take you to the hotel where you'll have a room, but as soon as she's back, you'll move to her apartment. Alexei's going with me and you'll come later."

"This is strange because Katherine and I planned to spend a week together after I visited you and Alexei goes to Idaho. Why has it changed?" I was puzzled.

"I really don't know the details, but let's move it. I still have to drive for five hours; that means Alexei and I will be home only after 2 A.M."

We finally got in the car. It was unbearably hot outside, and my poor boy immediately fell asleep in the air-conditioned Pontiac. In about thirty minutes we got to Manhattan and found the Barbizon Hotel on 63rd Street. To my amazement, as soon as I pronounced my name, the receptionist smiled widely and gave me a little form to fill out. He said that my room was prepaid for five days ahead, gave me a map of Manhattan, and wished me a wonderful stay in New York. A porter was ready to take my luggage upstairs. Everything was like in a fairy tale.

My brother went upstairs with me. He gave the porter a tip, and when we were alone, he started speaking in Russian, "Well, now I can be sure you are in a nice place. Lock your room and rest. Here's some money for you; order something to eat. Katherine will call you as soon as she can. Here's our phone number in State College, but don't call us from the hotel; it's very expensive. We'll call you in the morning."

"No, please call me as soon as you arrive home. I won't sleep until I know you are back home safe. Is it a difficult drive?" I was worried.

"It's a freeway, very easy, but it's getting late, and I might get sleepy, so I'd better get going. I'm happy you're finally here and can come and stay with us for a long time. We missed you, guys."

"We missed you, too. But how will I get to your place in five days?"

"Let's not talk about it now. We'll decide it later. Just relax and rest, and don't open the door to anyone. It's New York, you know." My brother gave me a kiss on the cheek and left.

I lay down, but I could not fall asleep. The jet lag was strong. It was about noon in my poor head, and I stayed wide-awake. I turned on the TV and watched the Late Show with David Letterman. It was funny and made me even more awake. Then suddenly I heard a light tap on the door. My brother told me not to open it. I looked at the watch; it was past midnight. The tap repeated more insistently. I froze. I did not know what to do when all of a sudden I heard a familiar velvet baritone, "My dear? It's me, your Bunnie."

I did not believe my ears. Could it be Stan? Was it Katherine's surprise? I rushed to the door and swung it open. He was standing there.

"It can't be true. God, I am thrilled to see you."

"Are you really? I thought I would spend all night by the door. Were you asleep? I kept knocking and knocking. What happened?" Stan was laughing.

"Nothing, let's not talk about it. You're here, and it's the most wonderful surprise I could have imagined. Now tell me everything about it. How did you manage to come? How long are you going to stay? It's incredible—on my first night in New York City, and here you are."

Stan looked definitely pleased with another successful surprise. He said he was hungry and we decided to go out and have a nightlife fun. There was a little Italian restaurant open till 2 in the morning, and we went there and had red wine and pasta. We giggled and talked; we were absolutely happy.

Stan had learned that Alexei and I were coming two weeks before school started. He had called Katherine and had a long talk with her. She openly asked him one question, "Do you really love Elena?" He said "yes". Then she asked why it had been six long years and there was nothing different in our relationship. Stan tried to explain to her how we both wanted to be together but that we both appreciated how painful such a change might be for our children. He told her that he had told his wife about me shortly after our meeting in Washington D.C. but rather than divorce him, she chose to save the marriage. Stan also told her that I was not able to divorce my husband, "Our situation is like the famed Gordian Knot that no one could untie until Alexander the Great came along and hacked it to pieces with his sword. Unfortunately a sword won't work in our case."

Then Katherine asked him, "Will you come to see Elena in New York?"

Stan was honest, "Unfortunately, I have no means to do so. Even if I could find an affordable ticket, I won't be able to stay in any of the hotels there without my wife knowing about it. But I can't do it to her. I have hurt her enough."

"And if I help you?" asked Katherine, "What if I pay for you and Elena to stay in a hotel in Manhattan? Will you come then?"

"It's very generous of you, but I'm afraid I won't be able to pay you back. My finances haven't been in the best shape lately; I had a lot of expenses—a drama school in Russia for my son, the mortgage, a vacation in Hawaii."

"Stan, I don't ask you to pay me back. All I want is to make a nice surprise for Elena. It'll be my gift for her successful Ph.D. defense. So will you come?"

Stan did not promise then, but incredibly enough, as it had happened before, the invisible door opened again. That August of 1993 Stan's wife and her two daughters suddenly decided to go on a 'girls' trip to California, just the three of them. Stan seized the opportunity to go backpacking alone as he used to do years ago. Only this time he went 'backpacking' in Manhattan.

Late the next morning the phone rang in our room. I picked up the phone. It was Katherine, "Hello, how are you?"

"Katherine, dear, thank you so much for this wonderful surprise and gift. You are our Angel. We love you." I wished I could hug her here and now.

"You're saying 'we'. Does it mean *he* is there?"

"Sure he is. He arrived last night. We had so much fun. I'm absolutely happy. And all this is thanks to you. I don't know how to express my gratitude."

"Don't be silly. You don't have to express anything. Just enjoy. I hope it'll be an important encounter. Push your Bunnie to make vital decisions. It's time."

"I'm not sure about that, but we'll see," I knew what she was talking about.

"Are you comfortable in this hotel? Do you need anything?"

"I've got more than I expected. We're very comfortable. We're going to do sightseeing today. When are you going to be in town? We'd like to do something together. I want you to meet Stan."

"When's he leaving?"

"He'll be here for five days."

"Great. I'm inviting you both out for dinner in two days, on Friday. I'll let you know where to come. Enjoy New York City."

"We will. Thank you. Have a good week and see you soon."

Everything was going well. Alexei had a great time at my brother's place. He quickly made friends with a neighbors' daughter, and they spent all days biking, playing all kinds of games and eating the famous State College ice cream. My father was coming in two weeks. And Stan was with me for the whole five days.

Those were unforgettable five days in New York City.

We went on a two-hour *The Big Apple* bus tour.

We spent three hours in the Metropolitan and fell in love with the Frick Collection.

We toured the Ellis Island and climbed all the way up to the top of the Statue of Liberty.

We walked in the Central Park and enjoyed exotic animals in the Zoo.

We took pictures from the top of the World Trade Center and at the Rockefeller Center.

We hiked Manhattan up and down.

We prayed in St. Patrick's Cathedral.

We loved it all, but most of all we cherished our quiet morning coffee hours in a small café on the second floor not far from our hotel on Lexington Avenue. We enjoyed sitting there by the wall-to-wall-ceiling-to-floor window in the light of the rising sun, observing early pedestrians going to work. We talked about our love.

On our last morning we told the friendly waitress how we liked it there and how sorry we were to leave. She smiled, "I'll miss you, guys, too. It was such a delight to watch you two being so much in love." She shook her bronze curls and sighed.

Then she continued, "I have to tell you something. I had been dating this one guy for two years and we broke up last week. But I've been so inspired by the two of you this week that I got in touch with Fred. When I told him I wanted to give our relationship another chance, he proposed to me right then and there. We're getting married in September. I'm so incredibly happy. You are two Angels sent from heaven. So I want to thank you and I wish you all the best."

"Thank you," Stan was delighted to be called an Angel.

I only smiled and did not say anything. Of course it was pleasant to be somebody's Angel, but at that moment I could use an angel myself. I was in a bad mood. It was our last day together. I always was in a terribly sad mood before Stan was leaving. There was this unknown blur of a future hanging over our heads again—where nothing was certain, absolutely nothing...

Finally, the magic five days passed and Stan and I went to La Guardia Airport to meet Vlad and Alexei. We turned into 'camels' when we saw my brother and son entering the airport. Alexei was a little scared to leave without his mama to some unknown Idaho, but Stan teased him lightly and my boy's mood improved. When it was time to say good-bye, I hugged my dear son and promised to call him often. My eyes filled up with tears. Now the two most important men in my life were leaving me. It was hard.

Right after their plane took off, Vlad and I drove to State College.

I spent two and a half wonderful months in that small university town. I rested, enjoyed time with my little niece and sister-in-law. In the end of August, my dad arrived and I helped him to communicate with Vlad's friends who did not speak Russian. We went camping and hiking, on picnics and explored the wonders of American yard sales; we had parties and went on little trips. I loved our family gatherings in the evenings when we could listen to Dad's stories about his and Mom's life in the past. Those were sweet days.

Overall my dad enjoyed his stay in Pennsylvania and a trip to Washington D.C.—he always wanted to see this great city. I was surprised that my father was taking blood pressure medicine for the first time in his life. He took naps in the middle of the afternoon; he was definitely not feeling well. Maybe the combination of jet lag, a change in diet and lifestyle were robbing him of his normal energy. My dad was a person who cherished his little life routines, which were disrupted during his trip to America. But he never complained about anything and it was hard to know what his real feelings were.

Then my dad went back to St. Petersburg. I called Vadim and asked him to meet Dad at the airport. That was when I finally told him about our passport/visa problem and how stupid bureaucracy forced me to stay in the States till mid-January. I mentioned that I was trying to find a post-doctoral program.

Surprisingly, he didn't seem to be too upset by this news, but he could not help commenting, "What's new? You never make an effort to find out all the necessary information and then you get into trouble. Now you have to deal with more problems. You should blame yourself for that and not bureaucracy." At least he did not yell at me this time.

I lived with my brother's family for a few more days, but soon I was bored. I had nothing to do in State College, so I decided to go to New York. This was the beginning of my "American education."

The next several months were a nightmare.

I got in touch with my former classmate from the university. She and her husband had managed to immigrate in the early 1980s according to the agreement between Leonid Brezhnev and Jimmy Carter that allowed Russian Jews to leave the Soviet Union and reunite with their relatives abroad. Anna and Misha were happy to see me and invited me to stay with them as long as I wanted, especially because they could use some help with their new six-month-old baby. They lived in a beautiful expensive house and both had to work hard to pay the mortgage.

My friends were kind people, but their baby cried all night long, and I often got up in the middle of the night to rock him so that his parents could have some sleep. I considered this "baby rocking" my payment for their allowing me to live in their house and eat their food. I took care of the baby when they were at work. I also cooked and cleaned during the day since I had nothing else to do.

Apparently that heavy-baby-rocking was too much for me and after three weeks, my feet got swollen; I started to suffer from severe headaches and I was completely exhausted.

I was saved from this torture simply by chance. One day I was window-shopping on Fifth Avenue when I ran into my long-time friends, Charles and Ruth Putnam. I had met them in Leningrad in the House of Friendship in 1985. I had not been in touch with them for several years, and it was unbelievable to run into them in New York City.

They immediately invited me out to dinner, and I told them how much I was going through in order to give Alexei a chance to go to school in America. They were impressed with my devotion to my son. I, on the other hand, only considered it the normal expression of a mother's "unconditional love" for her child. However, Ruth thought I deserved not to suffer anymore and promised to help.

A week later I got a call from Ruth. She asked me if I was interested in helping out her friend's mother, an elderly lady who had bad fortune and broke both legs. She needed a companion. For that I could have free room and board. "At least I won't have to get up at night and rock this lady," I thought and after hugs and kisses with my good Anna and Misha, I moved to New Jersey.

Grace was seventy-eight years old, a kind woman with good sense of humor and a lot of courage. It was neither easy for her to stay in bed twenty four seven nor for me to spend all day long in the company of a sick old person. But at least I had a good night's sleep, and sometimes I could go out and walk in the little town of Ho-Ho-Kus. I also watched a lot of TV with my lady companion, who was addicted to soap operas. Our favorite was *"Days of Our Lives."* It was a great everyday listening practice for me.

But I found myself listening to much more than language. Now that I had nothing to do, I began to look for meaning in the day to day experiences of my life. I became much more reflective and thoughtful. I learned to be more compassionate, tolerant, and patient. I found that my "misfortune" had actually provided me with a chance to be a better person, but I was still lonely and depressed at times. It was impossible to get into any post doc program in the middle of the year. I had little money, no connections, and I did not want to impose myself on my brother or friends. I used to complain that I had to survive in Russia, and now I learned how to survive in America. During sleepless nights sometimes I would tell myself, "This is my destiny—not to live but "survive" no matter where I am—in Russia, in America or on a different planet."

At least Alexei was doing well. He had always been an excellent student and quickly accepted the challenge that reading, taking tests, writing papers, and giving oral presentations in English posed. He was enjoying school.

He liked his new teachers, classmates and the host family. But by his letters I could tell that he missed his Russian life and me. He did not complain, but I knew my son; I could read between the lines. We were counting the weeks and days when we would finally be back together. His semester was going to finish in the middle of January, so there was about two months left.

Stan called me in Ho-Ho-Kus once a week. We had long talks about Alexei, his progress in English, his adjustment to American culture; we talked about everything but one topic—we avoided talking about us. There was not a single word of love or our future together on the phone. But I knew that nothing had changed in our relationship; I still received letters from Stan full of passion and promises. I also received beautiful flowers first on Halloween, then on Thanksgiving and finally on Christmas—always red roses.

Right before Christmas I got an invitation to a conference in St. Petersburg, Florida. It was a social studies convention, and Stan was going there to give a presentation. He registered me as a participant.

I felt sorry to leave my little lady, but I longed to see Stan before Alexei and I were scheduled to leave for home, so on the first of January, 1994 I flew to Tampa. Stan's flight arrived thirty minutes after my plane landed. We did not try to be camels and had a kiss of desire at the airport. I'll never forget that kiss.

We spent four interesting days at the conference and five beautiful nights walking along the shore of the Gulf of Mexico. One evening we watched the sun spin bands of color across the ocean from the top of the Hilton Hotel. Sipping his favorite Diet Coke, Stan suddenly said, "You know, my dear, you're invited to be a visiting professor at the American Language Institute in Clarkston, Washington. I talked with the director of the program, and he's excited about your visit. He has already sent a letter to the INS, and I hope your visa will be extended."

"This is a great surprise, Stan. Thank you. But why do I need an extension? When am I supposed to be in Clarkston and for how long?"

"They want you to come on the first of April and stay for two months."

"What?" I exclaimed, "I can't do that. Alexei's school is over on the 10th of January, and we are leaving on the 15th."

"But didn't you promise your boss to do some professional development while here? I doubt he'll be interested in your experience in taking care of old ladies with broken legs." Stan smiled.

"I know I didn't manage to do what I had planned. Instead of what you call professional development in American English, I got solid training in companionship, cooking kosher meals, and overcoming loneliness, which was all good for me, but I doubt Yuri Petrovich will appreciate it.

To tell you the truth, I don't know how in the world I will come back and look him in the eye."

"You see," said Stan, "I was thinking about you and accomplished a difficult project. It wasn't easy to find an English center where they would want a foreign teacher as an observer."

"Stan, but you understand that I can't do it, don't you? What will Alexei do while I'm in Washington State?" I felt desperate.

"I have thought of it, too. I called the Palmers. Remember them? The family with four kids on the Peace Walk? They live here in St. Petersburg, and they're eager to host Alexei. He'll go to school here for the next semester."

"Isn't it ironic? Alexei came from St. Petersburg, Russia to study in America, and where—Moscow and St. Petersburg. What a paradox."

"It's not a paradox, my dear. It's destiny."

Stan had again arranged everything, but this time I could not do it. I had to go home. I knew my dad was sick. He had high blood pressure and a heart condition. I was determined to go to Russia. I told Stan about my dad. He said, "Why don't you call him and find out how he is; maybe he's better by now."

When I was dialing his phone number, I had a strange feeling; I was trembling inside. The phone was ringing for a long time; then all of a sudden my husband picked up the receiver. I asked, "Vadim? Why are you at Dad's? Is he all right?"

There was a long pause. It took an eternity. Then he said, "I don't know how to tell you...Your Dad...he died today. I was trying to find you."

I felt dizzy and started shaking. It could not be true. No, not my dad, not my dearest papa...I just talked with him on the phone three days ago...

I heard my husband's voice, "He had a severe stroke. He did not suffer. It was quick. I took him to the hospital and the doctors did their best, but they were helpless. They lost him."

"They lost him?" I screamed, "How could they lose him? He's not a needle. How could they lose him? My dad is strong. They did something wrong. They killed him!" I was talking about my dad in the present tense; I could not accept the fact he was not in this world anymore.

Stan was stroking my hand gently. He did not understand what we were talking about, but he saw how pale I turned and knew that something bad had happened. I uttered, "I'll contact Alexei, and we'll be back as soon as possible."

"I've already started to make funeral arrangements. Your dad's will says he wanted to be cremated, so it has been scheduled for Saturday. It gives you three days. Do you think you'll be able to get back by that time?"

"Of course, I'll call you as soon as I find out the time of our flight. Thank you for everything."

"I am sorry. I am very sorry," he said.

"I know."

I hung up. Stan was looking at me intensely. I burst into tears. I cried and cried, and nothing could stop me. Stan was patiently holding me in his arms gently stroking my back. Finally I whispered, "My dad...." I sobbed and sobbed and sobbed.

"I know, dear."

When I finally calmed down, Stan whispered, "Your dad is now in a better, more beautiful place without the burdens of this earth." Stan was talking about my dad in the present tense, too, and I liked that. He continued, "I know it's hard to feel that you are not a daughter anymore. But you should think about your dad's love for you, and how his spirit is still among us, and how desperately he wants you to be happy—now more than at any time before—because he can't protect you directly. But his spirit is still here with you. So listen to your soul, and it will tell you what your dad wants for you in this life."

"I am not a daughter anymore...I am not a daughter anymore..." was ringing in my heart.

CHAPTER THIRTY ONE

Please Go Home
1994, The United States of America

I never made it to my father's funeral.

When I called Alexei's host family to ask them to make arrangements for my son to fly to New York immediately, I only heard a message on the answering machine; they had left for Oregon to go camping for four days. The weather was unusually warm for January, and they wanted to take advantage of the sunny days and show Alexei the coast before his departure from Idaho. Stan called a few mutual friends who might be aware of the family's destination, but nobody knew where they would be on the coast. He called numerous motels and hotels along the coast, but it was all in vain. We found out later that they had rented a cabin several miles south of Coos Bay, had a fantastic time and had come home on Sunday evening.

It was too late.

That day, when I received the tragic news, Stan went back to Idaho, and I arrived at my friends' waterfront home in St. Petersburg, Florida.

I was a wreck, crying constantly, dialing Alexei's phone hundreds of times, desperate and destroyed by guilt. I felt guilty for everything: that I went to America; that I was so far from Alexei; that I did not take Dad's illness seriously; that I was in love with Stan—absolutely everything in my life was a failure. I hated myself. I was disgusted with myself. I could not stand myself.

On Saturday night, when it was clear that I was not going to be even present at my beloved daddy's funeral, I was sitting on the edge of the fishing pier by the Palmers' house looking at the stars in the deep black sky. The night was silent with only a few splashes made by flying fish. The stars were twinkling beautifully and the huge silver disc of the full moon reflected on the surface of the black water.

I was wondering, "Where are my Angels?" Why have they abandoned me? Why did they save my life on July 14th, 1985 so that I could say "good-bye" to my mother? And why couldn't they help me one more time, just this last time, so that I could be with my father before his departure for eternity?"

Suddenly I started to experience a strong feeling of unity with the sky as if some invisible force was absorbing my entity slowly, devouring my consciousness. It was almost soothing; for the first time in those sleepless nights I felt serenity and peace. I knew it was my daddy calling me to be with him. I could feel his smiling eyes looking at me and I could hear his soft whisper, "I love you, my little daughter. I love you.…. I love you.…"

All I had to do to be with my daddy forever was to step down into the black quiet water. He was so close. I leaned forward still balancing on the edge of the pier when suddenly I heard the patio door open and then quick steps approaching me. I turned to look but was momentarily blinded by the bright patio light. I heard Audrey's voice, "Elena? Are you here? There is a phone call for you, dear."

I got angry. How dared she interrupt my wonderful connection with my father; I was so close to him, but now I had lost that magic link. "How will I find him now?" I thought.

Audrey saw me. She handed me the phone and gave me a quick hug, "Here, honey, it's for you."

She walked me slowly toward the patio holding my hand. Audrey's warm hands and tender heart helped me understand that the "magic" of that moment was actually "madness, insanity" because more than anything, I knew, my dad would want me to live, to be his daughter, Alexei's mom.

I finally whispered into the phone, "Hello?"

"My dear, I've been thinking of you. You know I could almost feel your heart beating very fast a minute ago. I had to call and tell you how dear you are to me."

"Stan? I can't talk now. I've just lost my daddy. He was calling out for me and I was about to go to see him, but your call spoiled it all."

"No, my call is only making it easier for you to be closer to your dad. Believe me, my love, he is in your heart, and you will be with him always no matter where he is in the universe. You are together forever. Please understand that."

I was silent.

"There is something else important you need to understand. Alexei needs you. I need you. We all love you. Please stay with us."

I cried, and he kept telling me how he loved me.

He saved my life that night.

Audrey stayed up talking with me for a long time. By morning I fell asleep exhausted from grief and despair. When I woke up, the sun was shining brightly; the new day was happily alive. Right in front of my bed there was a vase with an elegant bouquet of hyacinths—the flowers of sorrow—and a note:

"Dearest Elena,

I am searching for words of comfort but send these bright messages, which may in fact speak more eloquently of my love and regard for you. Stan"

There was also an envelope with a short letter in it:

"I am only sorry that I cannot be with you at this dark time, but I'm consoled by the fact that you are in the company of a loving, good family. I know that they love and care for you as I do and will do what is humanly possible to help you in this time of grief. I have said nothing to Alexei about his grandfather but will be happy to do so and to check on his condition once he learns about your father. I am sure that this man you loved so, would have wanted to be liberated from his prison of ill health.

Love,

Stan"

I got up and started writing a letter to Alexei. He deserved to know what had happened. I didn't want to disturb my boy with the terrifying news right before his final exams, but life is merciless and never gives us special time to get prepared for unexpected blows. My son had to learn how to survive the cruelty of life. I spent most of my morning composing a difficult letter, but each new version ended up in a trash can and eventually I gave up on it. I simply called my son, and we had a long talk about poor grandpa.

Soon Alexei came to Florida and started his new experiences in St. Petersburg High. We did not talk much about 'dedushka', but I knew that my boy felt very sad about the loss of his grandpa. He would write in his little diary for a long time in the evenings, but I was afraid to ask what he was writing about.

I was trying to do as much as possible around the house so that I had no time to think about the tragedy of my heart. Thinking was my worst enemy. I cleaned, cooked Russian food, did the laundry, and bless Audrey's heart—she had a collection of five hundred silver tea spoons that took me three days to polish. But all that was not enough to occupy my days. I started looking for something else I could do, so I went to the local church and volunteered to help with any cleaning projects they had. I washed fifty-two windows in two days. And then I had nothing to do again.

Sometimes I accompanied Audrey to her small shop—a business sewing holiday flags. I liked to sit by the four women-workers and listen to their enchanting stories about their lives while they were measuring, cutting and putting together intricate patterns for flags and home decorations.

Audrey's small, cozy shop was located downtown in St Petersburg right across from the Art Museum. I became its frequent guest and soon memorized the titles of many paintings and the names of their creators-artists. It was pleasant to walk along the beach, sit in the shade of the palm trees and look at the sea after my museum visits.

I finally trained myself to simply admire nature without torturing myself with the thoughts about my worthless life. At that time of loneliness and grief I was convinced that my life was nothing but a nuisance, without any specific purpose. I was a burden to a busy family, a professor without a chance to use my knowledge, a mother who separated her son from his father, and not even anybody's daughter. I was a 'nobody'.

The only bright moments were when I saw my son in the evenings. We did a lot together—we discussed his school, homework, plans and ideas; we went for long walks every night, or we went shopping on our bicycles. Alexei told me fun stories about his new school. He was fascinated by the variety of hairstyles of African-American girls in his classes. He said his school was the center of great hair design art, and that if he only had time and talent, he would have published a book of pictures of all those girls' heads.

In March something unusual happened. The mayor of St. Petersburg, Russia paid a visit to St. Petersburg, Florida. Audrey, a member of the Rotary Club, was invited to the luncheon in Mr. Sobchak's honor, and she invited me to that gathering. I was excited to meet Mr. Sobchak as he had been a famous professor at my university, and he was also a brave politician of the new post-communist era in Russia.

When I was introduced to him, he was surprised to meet a compatriot, and we had a little talk. It turned out that he did not have a professional interpreter in his delegation, and he asked me to translate his speech at the meeting the next day. I happily agreed to do it.

The next day I dressed up and looked good for the first time in several months. I was nervous but willing to demonstrate my professional abilities—finally I was of use, somebody needed my help. The speech was difficult to translate because of jokes and lots of metaphors, but I did well. The local newspaper even mentioned "the brave interpreter" in the article describing this event.

During those three months I always felt the support and love of my dear friends, Audrey and John. They were patient, gentle and understanding. They definitely had hearts made of pure gold. They were two of the most compassionate people I have ever known. They were my saviors, my Angels.

Finally, it was time for me to go to Washington State for my eight-week 'sabbatical'. I was excited to fly across America to the 'Wild West', the world of rodeos, cowboys, and Indians. After dealing with the hustle and bustle of New York City and the hubbub of Florida, I was looking forward to the "casual rural lifestyle" of the West.

It was a long and tiring trip to "the wild west." I flew from Tampa to Las Vegas and finally to Spokane on the Red Eye special. A bus took me to Clarkston. The Language Institute had rented a small apartment with a view of the Clearwater River for me. My "American education" continued, but this time it was wonderful.

The experience at the American Language Institute was precious. I got acquainted with a lot of wonderful instructors who were truly passionate about their work with students from Japan, Korea, the Congo, Taiwan and Costa Rica. I observed classes every day, and I took a computer-typing course. I gave a slide presentation about St. Petersburg and a workshop on the differences between Russian and American customs. I went to the recreation center to do step aerobics and weight lifting. I made new friends. Gradually I began to feel that I was becoming a worthy human being again—the healing process had started.

Stan lived only a thirty-five-minute drive from Clarkston. He came to see me once or twice a week for an hour or two. We could never go out because he was terribly afraid to run into somebody who knew his wife. When we saw each other, all we talked about was how guilty we both felt. For the first time in seven years we lived so close to each other, but I felt as if we were further apart than ever. Perhaps this was the end of our "affair." The spring was coming, but a chilling cold had penetrated our relationship.

Then once in April, during spring break, Stan arrived in an unusually good mood with happy news. He wanted to take me on a trip around Idaho. His car had been checked and was in good shape for a long journey; the trunk was full of emergency items such as blankets, pillows, flashlights, warm sweaters and gloves. And off we went.

That was an unforgettable trip.

From flourishing spring in Clarkston, we drove into the bright snowy winter of McCall and then Sun Valley. We stopped many times at scenic spots to admire the majestic beauty of Idaho. We took pictures of the Sawtooth Mountains, the white waters of the Salmon River, and the Easter bunnies in the antique and gift stores everywhere we went.

We finally arrived in Boise, the capital of Idaho, where we planned to stay for three days. I thought we were going to find a hotel, but suddenly Stan stopped the car and said he had to make a phone call. He left me in the car and did not come back for a long time. When he finally appeared, I asked, "Is everything okay?"

"Yes, everything's fine, dear. I know where we are going to stay. We'll be with my folks," he said.

"What do you mean by 'my folks'?" I did not know what that meant.

"Oh, 'my folks' means my parents. They'll be delighted to meet you."

"What?" I was horrified, "Stan, we can't do this. Do you understand in what situation you're putting your parents? What will they tell your wife?"

"There'll be no problem, please don't worry. I just said to my mom that you're a friend from Russia and that you had been very kind to Michael when he was there. We are not going to sleep together if that's what you are afraid of. You'll have your separate bedroom, and I'll sleep at my middle brother's house next door. Please relax, everything's fine."

"So are we supposed to be 'camels'?"

"Of course, isn't it fun?"

It wasn't fun for me. The trip that had started and gone so well so far had now turned into a nightmare.

Even though Stan's parents were polite and hospitable people, I knew they didn't feel comfortable to have me in their house, but they tried not to show it. They didn't ask a lot of questions, and I was silent most of the time praying that the third day of the visit would come to an end, and we could finally go back to Clarkston.

When we were driving home, I asked Stan, "Can you tell me the real reason why you introduced me to your parents?"

"Of course," he said simply, "because I wanted them to meet the woman I love."

"Did you tell them that?"

"I did."

"Honestly?"

"Yes, honestly," Stan said distinctly, "A child cannot easily hide anything from his parents. Although my parents did not know about you, they have known I was not happy in my marriage for a long time. Even though they love Carol, I know that like any parents they want me to be happy. You have always been that mysterious "something" or "someone" they felt existed but just couldn't figure out," he smiled.

We didn't talk about it anymore, but deep in my heart I felt happy that Stan had taken me to his parents' home and I had a chance to meet them. I thought that the fact of us being introduced to each other proved that he really meant everything he had promised me. I didn't know how and when we would be together, but I happily adopted a new attitude about a future we would share one day.

In May I returned to Florida, and in June Alexei's school was over. As our visas allowed us to be in the U.S. till August, I decided to do some traveling and to show Alexei Washington D.C.

We did not have a lot of money, so we went to the capital by a Greyhound bus. The trip was tiresome but interesting. We met several eccentric individuals on the bus, and if I were a writer I could have written a separate book about each person.

We spent two weeks in Washington D.C. living in the basement of the Palmers' town-house for free. We drank tap water and ate pizza—the only food we could afford—every day. But we had a great time because all the city's major museums are free to the public—real communism in action! Alexei loved all the adventures, especially the National Geographic Museum where he was given a souvenir—the front page of their magazine with his picture on it.

The Vietnam War Memorial impressed us both; we spent several hours reading name after name carved on the black marble that was icy cold even on a hot July day.

The Holocaust Museum shocked us. We had read books and seen movies about the horrors of the war with Nazis and especially about the tragedy of the Jewish people, but this museum was a real eye opener. I cried in every hall, and Alexei didn't ask a single question; he was speechless.

The Smithsonian was an expedition that took several days. Our favorite became the Museum of Modern Art.

Then my Angel, Katherine, invited us to spend ten days in her summer house (her American 'dacha') in East Hampton, Long Island. She told me where to find the key to the house and promised to come on the weekend. Her friend gave us a ride there.

Those ten days were a real vacation. We didn't have to do anything but walk on the beach, ride bicycles, swim in the pool, watch TV and play cards in the evenings.

The weekdays had their special schedule.

On Monday morning, a man in a small van arrived with a huge box full of all kinds of food and left it on our doorstep.

On Tuesdays, another man came to clean the swimming pool and weed the garden.

On Wednesdays, a hairdresser came to do my hair and nails—I loved that!

On Thursdays, a cleaning lady did the laundry and the cleaning.

One Friday morning, two guys planted fresh flowers along the driveway and the steps to the house.

Late on Friday, Katherine arrived in her new dark green *BMW*, and three of us went out for dinner. Then we got a video for Alexei and while he was enjoying the movie, Katherine and I went out for a drink or two. In a noisy and happy bar, I was telling Katherine about our adventures in D.C. and how we loved the museums there. Then Katherine asked me, "So, what have you decided? Are you staying in America?"

"How can we stay here? No, there's no reason for us to be here any longer," I said sadly, "I don't think Stan wants me to stay. We are going home."

"Have you asked him?"

"No, I'm afraid to ask him questions that will force him to make a final decision."

"I think you should. Don't you think it's better if you finally know the truth about his plans?"

"Maybe you are right. I'll talk to him."

I was thinking about Stan and our relationship all night. I knew he loved me, but when I was in Idaho, so close to him, he changed nothing. And now, he knew we were leaving in three days, and yet he never called to stop me from going back to Russia. I wanted to ask him a lot of questions, but I asked none. I was afraid that his answer wouldn't be the response I wanted to hear.

He had not called for several days. Those three last days in America were filled with a strange sadness and foreboding about our future.

We were leaving on Tuesday morning. On Monday at about 10 P.M. Stan finally called. He asked, "Have you finished packing?"

"Yes, I have," I was surprised that we were talking about such trivial things.

"Are you excited to go home?"

"Stan, do you want to know the truth? No, I'm not excited. I'm actually not sure I should go home. I'm scared to go to the place that is not my home anymore. Now that Dad is not there I don't feel any strong connection to the life I had before. A whole year in America has made me a different person. I'm not sure I'll fit with the Russian reality anymore. My husband has become a stranger to me. But the most devastating thought is that you and I might never see each other again. Can you live with this fear in your heart?"

"You know that I'm an optimist. Everything will be fine, believe me."

I didn't feel either love or worry in his voice. I was talking to a 'camel'. He was probably afraid that some member of his family could hear him talking with me. I was tired of his 'camelism'. Maybe he finally told Carol that our relationship was over.

I made my last effort, "Stan?" I said softly, "If you only tell me one word right now, just one word—'stay', I will."

There was a long silence.

"Please go home." I heard the same dull voice in the phone.

Tears rolled down my cheeks. I felt rejected, thrown away like a piece of trash. I was worthless all over again.

Suddenly I heard, "I want you to know that you should never doubt my love for you. You are the love of my life."

I didn't answer. I couldn't speak. I didn't trust his words. At that moment they were empty sounds vibrating in the air, "The time will come, my love, and you and I will have a happy life together. Please trust me."

I was listening, but I didn't respond. Then I heard him repeat those dreadful words again, "Please go home."

I slowly put the receiver down.

"What a trivial end of our love story," I thought. "And how it hurts to lose a friend."

CHAPTER THIRTY TWO

Because You Love Me
1994, St. Petersburg, Russia

We had a safe flight home. My husband was waiting for us at the airport. He seemed happy to see us back.

Everything around looked strange and different. People did not smile; cars did not stop to let pedestrians cross the streets; buses and subway trains were overcrowded, and shopping was time-consuming and boring. Life was in many ways inconvenient and irrational, and I realized that only after I had lived for a year in America. But thanks to the survival instinct genetically implanted into the consciousness of human beings, people get used to all kinds of circumstances and conditions of life, and soon I was back to my normal 'post-capitalist' routine.

After Stan had told me to return home, it became clear that he was not going to change anything in his life. The game was over; I did not want to be *a toy* anymore. How right my friends were who had told me all along that he would never marry me. And how blind and naïve I was to believe in everything Stan had told me about our future together. There was no *future*, and there was no *together*. Yet the seven years of my life that I had given Stan were important years. They had helped me become a stronger person—a survivor.

Now that my dreams to be with the man I loved were shattered, I was determined to start a new stage in my life—new in all its aspects. I wanted to mend my marriage, to establish a stable and solid relationship with my teenager-son, to adjust to life without my parents' support, and to change my career. All those tasks were hard to accomplish, but I started working on each of them.

First of all, in the relationship with my husband, I was trying to go back to our early years of passionate love and admiration. I focused on all positive recollections of our life together, and during the first month it worked. We were gentle and understanding, supportive and encouraging.

But deep in my heart I had this gnawing guilt about the many things I had failed to accomplish in our marriage. I did not have energy to mend it.

The more I thought about what I had done the more I tried to find explanations to defend myself. I knew that had Vadim behaved himself differently on so many occasions I would have not stopped loving him. And then I would remember the darkest moment in our life as husband and wife, the day my mother died. My rage and hatred were rekindled and I knew tragically I could never forgive him.

The easiest way to cope with my faults was to blame my husband for all the problems we had. He was the villain who had ruined my relationship with my parents and destroyed our marriage. I even blamed him for my affair with Stan. I was thinking that if he had been a perfect husband, I would have never looked at another man, not to mention fallen in love with one. Although in my more rational moments, I knew I had to share the blame, I also recognized no matter whose fault it was there was no way back.

Then one day I came across a small notebook among old newspapers at home. Before throwing it away, I opened it and read on the first page a woman's name, *Lubochka,* and a phone number written in my husband's hand. This phone number was not local; it had the area code of a different city. I decided not to throw it away in case it was of some importance and left it on my husband's desk.

The next day, this notebook had disappeared from the desk. I was curious, but I did not want to let my husband feel that I was suspicious. Deep down I was actually excited to be able to accuse him of unfaithfulness. It could be a business relationship or a simple acquaintance, but I secretly hoped that he was having an affair. I hoped that I wasn't the only one suffering from guilt, but what really thrilled me was the notion that I might have a chance for a divorce, and that I might have finally found a way to be free. I was tired of pretending to be in love with a man I had stopped loving long ago. I was tired of feeling guilty.

It seemed to be ridiculous, but I was praying that *Lubochka* was my husband's lover.

I checked with the phone operator to find out the city of her phone code, and it turned out to be a town in the Caucasus, where my husband had gone several times to treat the veins in his legs. *Lubochka* could be simply a nurse or a friend, but she could be his girl friend as well.

I did not feel bitter or angry. First, I did not know for sure what their relationship was, and second, if she had been his lover, I deserved it. I was also thinking that he had the right to find someone who would care about him since I could not. I was actually happy for him. I really was. But even more I was happy for myself—I had a chance to finally free myself from my guilt. It was selfish, but I was trying to survive.

I knew if I could get a divorce, I would need to be able to support my son and myself. My "Stanley Survival Lessons" of the past seven years helped me believe that I would find a better-paying job. As it turned out, a few angels were still surrounding me with their care. In August, right before the end of the summer vacation, I received a phone call from my friend Alena. She used to be an English teacher, but she had changed her profession and become a translator in a joint Russian-Cyprus venture. That firm was doing market research for a large British-Dutch company that was starting joint venture business with a famous cosmetics factory in St. Petersburg. They were looking for a person who spoke English and Russian fluently and would be interested in being trained to become a market research manager. I made an appointment for the interview, got the job, and started my new career.

It was different from what I had known before. It was interesting, but it was not *me*. I could not express my individual character as a teacher anymore; instead, I was now a stupid over aged student with absolutely no business background. I was sent to Poland and the Netherlands for training practically every other week, and each time when I was back, I had to organize and conduct a particular kind of market research no matter whether I knew how to do it or not. There was a lot of stress, worries and failures, but there was also a large paycheck at the end of each month. At that time the inflation in Russia reached its peak, and lots of people could hardly make both ends meet; I was definitely in the black. I was literally a millionaire: my salary reached three million rubles—about $800 a month—big money in Russia at that time. Now I had enough cash, but I had to figure out how to live with a new profession that I hated—I had to survive.

Once I was walking along the Fontanka Embankment thinking about my misfortunes. Life is such a funny trickster, promising so much but then snatching it away. I was abandoned by both, my husband and my lover. I recalled the grins on the faces of the cupids above the entrance to the

Friendship House that I had seen in the spring of 1987. I looked above the entrance at the moldings hoping to see those cupids and confront them with a question, "Why did you smile at me?" The cupids were not there. I even examined the balcony and the molding around the widows on the second floor. I had mistakenly thought they were "playful" when it fact now I understood they were mocking me. Seven years of my life were an illusion.

With the new job, I lost all my old collegial friends, and my previous boss publicly called me a traitor. He could not forgive me that after everything he had done for me I had left his department 'for the sake of money.'

Finally, I reached the point in my life when all my angels ignored me; even my parents had not given me a single sign of support or understanding from heaven. I often went to the cemetery and spent hours there looking at the smiling pictures of my mother and father that decorated their tombstone. Their remains were resting in one grave, and their souls, I hoped, were sharing eternity together. Although they were no longer in this world, I hoped my prayers to my parents would be answered. I hoped my Angels—Mom and Dad—would somehow help me find a way to survive all the changes that I had planned for my new life.

As the days and weeks passed, I found no new inspiration from my parents-Angels or anyone else. I had done so much to change my life since I had come home, but the last goal to be free of Vadim seemed more impossible than ever. I had never felt more alone in my whole life. In that dark void I began to lose the last resource of my soul—hope.

I was in this state of mind when Stan called me at work. It was a depressing gray September day. The rain's relentless drumming on the windows drowned out his tired, dull voice. I could barely hear him. We were strangers. We had little to talk about. This call was like the final chord of a classic symphony.

The next day I wrote Stan a letter:

"Dear Stan,

I've never felt so much difficulty in writing a letter to you. I want to write about good things, but I can't pretend that all is okay. I'm sure you know it's not all right. You shouldn't think I have stopped loving you. No, I'll never do it because there has been too much between us, and you are the Bunnie I love no matter what. But you surely feel that there has formed a crack between us. It's getting wider and wider, and eventually it will destroy our relationship.

Sometimes when there is a crack on a crystal vase, it can be glued carefully so that the vase may look ugly but it becomes even dearer. I don't know what will become with 'our crack'; I wish we had never had it.

Your voice on the phone sounded sad and unhappy. I was sorry to hear that.

Even though you don't love Carol 'as a wife' as you put it, you might love her as somebody else, for example, as the mother of the children she and you have been raising together, and she should be the very person to share grief and joy with you. I know now for sure I won't be able to be that person. You told me I was a survivor and you are right—I will survive. But I don't want to be a survivor. I want a simple life of a simple woman. I can't live only supported by hope and expectations. Should I live my life or should I pretend that I live? Is it my destiny to survive? To be just a survivor?

I've been thinking about all this for hours and days. I sacrificed a lot, and I was ready to stay in the U.S. only for you. But you told me not to do so. You weren't ready to sacrifice anything, and I didn't want to be a burden. You made your choice. Now I am making mine. I choose living instead of surviving. I hope I sound clear. Maybe it won't be the kind of living I was dreaming of, but at least it will be real. Elena"

The letter was a hodge-podge, and I was a mess when I was writing it. I did not reread it; I was afraid I wouldn't mail it.

I sent it off.

Strange as it was, I felt energized and free. I had my entire life ahead of me with a chance to start over. I was determined to live and not to survive.

In October, my friend Alena and I decided to go on a boat trip north of St. Petersburg to one of the most fascinating places—Valaam Island. It is a secluded island with an ancient monastery built in a picturesque forest. This place was also famous for the Northern Lights—the Aurora that could be seen from that island—it is that far north.

Alena and I were ready to have a good time away from our daily routine and worries. We planned to lock ourselves up in the cabin on board the ship, drink cranberry liqueur and chat all night. But this plan was not realized as after dinner all sorts of entertainment were announced on the radio, and we decided to go to the show of a famous comedian. Two young men sat next to us. They were friendly; we got acquainted and after the show all four of us decided to go to the dance party on the upper deck of the ship. We danced till four in the morning. I finally lived and enjoyed it.

The next day we slept till noon but managed to go on the afternoon tour of the island. It was fascinating but sad. Most of the buildings looked abandoned. Nevertheless these ruins set against the background of a virgin forest on a bright cold day made a beautiful picture that I will always remember.

In the evening, after dinner, the four of us went outside on deck to admire the Aurora. After a while, I realized that Alena and her new friend had disappeared. I was alone with this attractive, strong and very young man; he was probably in his late twenties. We talked. Then he touched me by my shoulders and turned my face towards his. He whispered, "You are beautiful. Your gold hair is gorgeous with the shining Aurora in it."

I was shaking. My heart was about to jump out of my weak body, but I did not move. After being rejected by everybody whom I had loved I desperately needed attention and appreciation. I wanted to be cherished; I longed for even a cheap meaningless compliment. I couldn't survive the loneliness anymore. I did not move, and he slowly reached for my lips and kissed me lightly. I liked it, and he felt encouraged. He kissed me again; this time it was a passionate kiss. Suddenly I felt as if I was struck by lightning. That kiss was so incongruous with what I expected or wished for. I almost felt as if a snake had stung me. I pushed him away, ran downstairs to my cabin and locked the door. I wept.

When Alena came to the cabin, I was still awake. I had been crying ever since I locked the door. I realized that it would be even more difficult to begin a new stage in my 'Just Do It' life style than to continue with my 'good old survival routine.' I felt trapped. I did not blame anybody; I knew I was the person who had created and built that trap, and I had to be the one to find my way out.

After my letter to Stan, he was silent. I thought that "our book was finally closed." However, to my surprise, he called at the beginning of November and asked me just one question, "Are you going to be in town next week? I am planning on coming to St. Petersburg for Thanksgiving, and I'd like to see you."

"I'll be in town, but I don't think I'll be able to celebrate your holiday with you. I'll be busy," I replied and quickly asked, "Have you received my letter?"

"I have. It is sealed and put away. I've been saving all of your letters, and this one is not an exception, but I don't want to read it ever again, so I've sealed it."

"You can throw it away as well as the rest of them. What's the purpose of keeping them?" My heart sank with the painful thought that I had actually kept all of Stan's letters, too.

"They are mine, so I'll decide what to do with them."

That conversation was so unlike those Stan and I had usually had. Where did this coldness and desire to hurt each other come from? Why did we fail to preserve our love?

For the first time in seven years I was not excited about Stan's plan to come to St. Petersburg. Instead, I was irritated and annoyed. What if he really came? What would I do then? I wouldn't change my mind—the affair was over. I would simply tell him, "Please go home."

"My dear, don't worry, everything will be fine," I heard and then the line was disconnected.

But then destiny became the master of my life again and a strange chain of events followed Stan's call.

First, when I came home that very day, my husband said, "You know, today my boss announced that all those who haven't yet used all of their vacation days for this year should do it before the end of November, otherwise they'll lose them. When I checked my record, I found out that I still have ten days of vacation left. I called the resort where I usually go in the Caucasus, and guess what; they have a free space, so I'm leaving on November the 19th around noon. Is it okay with you?"

I was stunned. It couldn't be true. Was it okay with me? Again it was as it had been before so many times—the invisible door was opening. I felt dizzy and sat down on the sofa, "Of course, you should go. It'll be good for you."

What happened next did not even surprise me; it was a simple confirmation of the role fate plays in our lives. Every conceivable thing that could happen to bring Stan and me together for Thanksgiving happened.

When I came to work on the next day, I received a memo: "All the employees of the company should use all their leave days before November 30th. Please plan to spend the first twenty days of December to finish up the annual reports. December 23rd will be the last working day before the Christmas recess." I checked with the registrar's office and found out that I had five days to be used for a vacation. I could take them at any time in November. Our invisible door had opened even wider.

And finally, the same day at home, Alexei announced he was going skiing with his friends on November 19th for four-five days.

The coincidence of all these events had to be surreal so that the encounter between Stan and me could be a reality.

Stan called for the second time on November 17th. He said, "I know you aren't excited about my coming, but it's important for both of us. Please try to find at least one hour for me. That's all I'm asking for—one hour. We need to talk. I'm arriving on November 19th at 2 P.M. Will you meet me at the airport?"

"I will," I replied simply. I had no energy to explain all the incredible coincidences that had occurred since our last conversation. I was simply amazed that even all the dates in our schedules lined up perfectly.

On November 19th at 10:30 A.M. I was driving my husband to the airport. When we left home it started snowing lightly. I got nervous thinking that probably my 'invisible door' was not that magical and that everything would be crashed by a simple flight cancellation. Amazingly, the soft snowflakes melted while they were still in the air, and the runways were clear. No flight delays were announced. My husband gave me a hug and a light formal kiss on the cheek. "He is mentally preparing for his *Lubochka*," I thought.

Soon his airplane was high up in the air.

I went slowly outside the airport towards my car with an emptiness that tore my heart apart. I felt painfully sad as if a close friend had died. Hot tears were streaming down my cheeks. It was my grief for my unfulfilled hopes about our marriage. Oddly enough I was even angry that some far away *Lubochka* would get a passionate kiss from my husband.

The snow turned into huge chunks of white 'flying yogurt'. The cold wet splashes on my nose, forehead, cheeks and eyelids mixed with the salt of the tears acted as a soothing compress. As I began to calm down I realized that I had to go to one more place today.

I got in the car and drove to the International Airport, which was only a ten-minute drive away. I did not know why I was going there. Seeing Stan one more time would only add to the pain I had already endured. I had stopped hoping for any future with him.

I was not looking forward to this meeting, but I kept driving through the snowstorm secretly hoping that his flight would be delayed forever. I hoped that Mother Nature would intervene to keep us apart.

I parked the car and went reluctantly into the airport. I passed by the flower stand and did not even think about buying a carnation this time. The long slow escalator took me upstairs to the waiting hall with huge windows through which people could see the departing and arriving airplanes. I stood in front of one of the windows admiring the beauty and mystery of the swirling snowflakes thinking that only the Snow Queen from Anderson's fairy tale could land safely in her magic golden flying sled in this weather. I sat down in a soft armchair and closed my eyes. I dreamed that the snow would never stop and Stan's airplane would turn around and head back to America.

After a while I felt a strange warmth on my face. I opened my eyes but had to close them immediately because of the blinding sun shining in the wide pale-blue winter sky. I looked at the clock; it was 2:00 P.M. and at the same moment I heard the announcement of the arrival of flight 2124 from New York. It was Stan's airplane landing on time. I walked to the arrival gate and leaned over the window glass—almost all the snow had melted.

A young man was sitting nearby with a tape recorder playing softly a pleasant tune. I listened carefully and heard Jo Dee Messina singing...

I don't know how I could survive
In the cold and empty world all this time
I only know that I am alive
Because you love me...

Stan was coming up to me slowly. The melody was filling up the space:

Because you love me...